VEXING THE VISCOUNT

Books by Christie Kelley

Every Night I'm Yours

Every Time We Kiss

Something Scandalous

Scandal of the Season

One Night Scandal

Bewitching the Duke

Enticing the Earl

Vexing the Viscount

Published by Kensington Publishing Corp.

VEXING THE VISCOUNT

CHRISTIE KELLEY

KENSINGTON BOOKS
KENSINGTON PUBLISHING CORP.
www.kensingtonbooks.com

KENSINGTON BOOKS are published by

Kensington Publishing Corp.
119 West 40th Street
New York, NY 10018

All Kensington titles, imprints, and distributed lines are available at special quantity discounts for bulk purchases for sales promotion, premiums, fund-raising, educational, or institutional use.

Special book excerpts or customized printings can also be created to fit specific needs. For details, write or phone the office of the Kensington Special Sales Manager: Kensington Publishing Corp., 119 West 40th Street, New York, NY 10018. Attn. Special Sales Department. Phone: 1-800-221-2647.

Kensington and the K logo Reg. U.S. Pat. & TM Off.

First Electronic Edition: August 2014
eISBN-13: 978-1-60183-168-2
eISBN-10: 1-60183-168-4

First Print Edition: August 2014
ISBN-13: 978-1-60183-230-6
ISBN-10: 1-60183-230-3

Printed in the United States of America

VEXING THE VISCOUNT

CHRISTIE KELLEY

KENSINGTON BOOKS
KENSINGTON PUBLISHING CORP.
www.kensingtonbooks.com

KENSINGTON BOOKS are published by

Kensington Publishing Corp.
119 West 40th Street
New York, NY 10018

All Kensington titles, imprints, and distributed lines are available at special quantity discounts for bulk purchases for sales promotion, premiums, fund-raising, educational, or institutional use.

Special book excerpts or customized printings can also be created to fit specific needs. For details, write or phone the office of the Kensington Special Sales Manager: Kensington Publishing Corp., 119 West 40th Street, New York, NY 10018. Attn. Special Sales Department. Phone: 1-800-221-2647.

Kensington and the K logo Reg. U.S. Pat. & TM Off.

First Electronic Edition: August 2014
eISBN-13: 978-1-60183-168-2
eISBN-10: 1-60183-168-4

First Print Edition: August 2014
ISBN-13: 978-1-60183-230-6
ISBN-10: 1-60183-230-3

Printed in the United States of America

Chapter 1

Staffordshire, England, 1814

The door to Braden Tavers's study hurled open and crashed against the wall. Glancing up from his papers, he cringed to see Mrs. Featherstone standing in the threshold with a look of fury upon her face. He'd never met a woman who could terrify him as she did. The cold stare she could give a person would scare the devil.

Mrs. Featherstone had been a wise woman for his friend, the Earl of Hartsfield, for years, but Braden had only met her a few times. Hart had forewarned him about her disposition and bluster. Braden wondered what brought her here to his estate. Her daughter, Tia, tended the ills and birthed the babies here. If there were something wrong with Miss Featherstone, one of the tenants would have informed him. And yet, based on the look upon her face, this was not a social call.

He rose slowly from his seat and bowed toward her. "Good afternoon, Mrs. Featherstone," he said, as if her sudden appearance was a normal part of his day. "Is there something I can assist you with today?"

"Where is he?" she demanded before blustering into the room like a gale.

"Which *he* are you speaking of?"

She tilted her head and pursed her lips. "Mr. Jonathon Tavers."

"My brother had some business to attend to in London." If gambling and whoring could be called *business*. He prayed Jonathon's exploits would be limited to only gaming and prostitutes. He had done so well spending a few weeks away from town. His brother's abrupt return to town had Braden on edge.

She crossed her arms over her chest and stared down at him with her intense blue eyes. "And what are *you* going to do about this?"

What had Jonathon done now? Braden had rescued his younger brother from more scrapes than he could remember. Since Jonathon had run off again, Braden had hired two Bow Street runners to find him before he succumbed to his craving. After a fortnight of searching, they had no idea where he'd gone. "I have no idea to what you are referring, Mrs. Featherstone."

"You don't know?" She heaved a sigh before taking a seat in the chair across from him. "I must apologize, my lord. I thought you must have heard by now."

He waited for her to continue, but she stared at her hands for a long minute. With her graying hair pulled back from her face, she appeared far younger than he knew her to be.

"She left, my lord."

"Who?"

"Tia," she whispered in a shaky voice.

He'd never seen Mrs. Featherstone look so vulnerable. And where the bloody hell had his wise woman gone? "Where did she go?" he asked gently.

"She sent a letter over a week ago stating that she was leaving for London. Chasing after your brother." She sighed. "I assumed you would have departed to bring them back, but only this morning, I discovered you were still in residence."

"Why would I try to return them?"

Mrs. Featherstone stared at her hands. "She doesn't even know what happened to her sister."

"What happened to her sister?" Miss Mia Featherstone assisted her mother at the Earl of Hartsfield's estate. Surely, he would have heard if something had happened to her.

"Yesterday she was beaten by a man who was her lover."

Braden closed his eyes. "Does Hart know?"

"Yes, he's keeping her at the house to ensure her safety."

He actually felt a twinge of pity for the man who had the gall to hurt the woman Hart loved. Braden doubted it would end well for the fellow. "Is she going to be all right?"

"She will be once she heals in a few weeks. But I couldn't bear anything happening to my other daughter, my lord."

Oh, hell. Braden clenched his fists. He might have a reputation as a rake, but Jonathon was far worse. Jonathon seemed to enjoy ruining every woman he could seduce. And if the rumors Braden had heard were anywhere near the truth, Miss Tia Featherstone would be in serious trouble if she found his brother.

"So, exactly what are you going to do to about this mess?" Mrs. Featherstone demanded again.

Nothing. He was done saving his brother from trouble. Braden had done everything in his power to help his brother, but Jonathon was six and twenty, and it was far past time for him to grow up. And Miss Featherstone was no better, running off after him.

"What do you expect me to do?"

She had the audacity to laugh at him. "I expect you to go find your wise woman and bring her back to your estate, my lord. I can help out here but Tia is your healer. Bring her back home."

Braden blinked. "You want me to drop everything and run after *your* daughter because she had the foolishness to chase after a man?"

"Not just any man," she replied coldly. "*Your* brother. And don't think I haven't heard what he does to innocent women."

He clenched his hands into tight fists to keep from throwing something. The last thing he'd expected was for Mrs. Featherstone to know how his brother liked nothing more than to defile innocent women and leave their reputations in ruins. While Miss Featherstone might not care about her reputation, her mother certainly did. Still, that didn't mean *he* had to chase after her.

"I'll hire another runner to find her and return her safely to you."

Steely blue eyes pinned him to his seat. Slowly, she rose and leaned over the desk. "No, my lord. You will go to London yourself and bring her home. I don't trust a runner for this business. Only you."

"I have no authority over her."

"She works on your estate. She is your responsibility."

His jaw tightened. There had to be some reason he couldn't do this. And yet, the more she stared at him, the more he realized he had no choice in the matter. But he wasn't about to let this woman one-up him. He rose slowly until he towered over her. "I will do this, but if Jonathon has already defiled her, there is nothing I can do."

Instead of backing down like every other woman he knew would have done, she straightened herself and crossed her arms over her chest. Glaring up at him, she said, "Then you will make certain she returns a married woman."

He laughed coarsely and shook his head. "I will do no such thing. I would never force my brother to marry—"

"Be very careful what your next words are, my lord."

"Any woman," he continued as if he hadn't heard her. "Neither would I force your daughter into marriage with my disreputable brother. She deserves far better than Jonathon."

Mrs. Featherstone relaxed slightly. "At least on that we can agree."

Braden released a sigh. It wasn't as if he had anything better to do right now. He'd only come out to the Midlands to get away from the constant barrage of gossip regarding his sudden ascension to viscount. Rumors of his involvement in both his uncle's and cousin's deaths were driving him mad. Becoming Viscount Middleton was the last thing he'd ever wanted or expected.

He had earned enough money on his own that becoming a viscount held no interest for him. But now that the choice had been taken out of his hands, he'd decided to do what his mother would have wanted and become a respectable lord.

"Well?" she said impatiently.

"Do you have any idea where she might be?" he asked, feeling defeated by a cantankerous middle-aged woman.

She tossed a letter on his desk and then walked toward the door. "That's all the information I have."

"Mrs. Featherstone, wait." Braden waited for her to stop and look back at him. "Why Jonathon?"

"She thinks she is in love with him," she replied with a shake of her head. "Foolish girl."

Foolish indeed. And now he'd be on a fool's errand, trying to rescue a woman who would not want to be rescued. Well, this should be an interesting trip. As Mrs. Featherstone departed, Braden sat down and scanned the letter. Thankfully, Tia had left an address where she would be staying with friends. He folded the letter and put it in his jacket pocket. At least finding her wouldn't be terribly difficult. Only convincing her to return would be a chore. If he could find Jonathon, then his brother could tell Tia the truth about his feelings for her. Once she heard his brother didn't love her, she would run back to the estate and perform her job there. Braden knew if he tried to tell her himself, she would never believe him.

Knowing it would take a few days to reach London, he ordered a horse saddled and a small bag packed. In less than a week, he would be on his way back with his wise woman in tow.

Tia Featherstone hurried her step as dusk fell. The area around Whitechapel became particularly unsafe as darkness swept over the dirty streets. She needed to be back in her tiny room at the Goat's Horn Inn as quickly as possible. Her walk to Mayfair had taken much longer than expected today. After investigating more places that Jonathon should have been, she had no idea where to look next.

"Come on over and let me take a look at ye," an older man said from a step outside a decrepit house. He sipped from a gin bottle. "I got enough coin for the likes of you."

Tia choked back a sob. "I am not for sale."

She hurried to get farther away from the drunken man. Hearing footsteps fall into the same rhythm as hers, she peeked back and noticed a man in black stalking her. Her heart pounded in her chest as she broke into a run. It wasn't the drunken man who'd propositioned her, but in this part of London, it could be anyone chasing after her. The rumors of women being sold into prostitution and white slavery had reached even as far into the country as the Midlands. Before she'd thought those stories were to keep women from running to London, but after seeing the crime here, she wasn't so certain. Glancing back, she realized the man was starting to gain on her position. She rounded the corner and raced inside the inn.

"Good evening, Miss Featherstone," Mrs. Turner's disapproving voice sounded from the salon as Tia slammed the door behind her.

"Good evening, Mrs. Turner." Tia leaned against the door to catch her breath. At least now, she was safe.

"Tomorrow you shall have to pay if you wish to stay any more days here."

"Of course, that won't be any trouble at all." Tia climbed the stairs slowly, wondering where she would come up with another week's rent. After opening the door to her room, she pulled out her small reticule and dumped the few coins on the bed. She barely had enough for the post carriage back to the Midlands.

Problems had riddled this trip from the start. Her plan had been to stay with her friend Amy and her husband, but when she arrived at their flat, she'd discovered they had been evicted the week prior and left no forwarding address, forcing Tia to find more expensive accommodations. Mrs. Turner's establishment was one of the few that would accept an unmarried woman traveling alone, but the weekly rent was not cheap, even for Whitechapel. With breakfast provided, it came to be her only meal most days. Even now, her stomach grumbled for a bite of something.

She cursed softly and pushed the coins back in her reticule. For almost a fortnight, she'd spent every day walking back to Mayfair in search of Jonathon. He wasn't at any of the places he'd told her about during their talks at the estate. She'd been certain he would stay at either the viscount's town home or perhaps the Albany. But the servants at Middleton's home hadn't seen or even heard that Jonathon was in town. The man at the Albany had told her bluntly that Jonathon was not staying there. She had to locate him before he dove back into his old habits. He'd done so well while at the estate, finally breaking from the control the opium had over him.

The idea of not finding him before he succumbed to the drug was driving her mad. She couldn't face losing another patient after little Amelia. The guilt she felt over that child's death a year ago haunted her even today. She should have known what was wrong with her. The symptoms were obvious.

"Where are you, Jonathon?" she asked the ceiling as she collapsed on the hard bed. Even though Tia had walked the estate every day while she was the wise woman for Middleton, trudging through the streets of London was far harder as she dodged carts, horses, and people the entire time. And so far it was all for naught.

With a long sigh, she pulled out her small map and stared at the streets in Mayfair. Tomorrow might be her last day here. Mrs. Turner would evict her when she didn't pay for another week. Then what would she do?

Slowly, she sat up and pulled off her short boots. She rubbed her aching feet and wished for a moment that she could sit by the pond at the estate and dip her feet into the cold water. Reaching for her hair, she pulled out the pins holding it in place. She ran her fingers through the mass of curls.

What she needed was a plan.

But what?

She could tuck her tail between her legs and go back home. Middleton would let her resume her duties caring for his tenants and servants. She barely knew the man, but he didn't seem to be the type who would care if she lived on his land as long as his tenants and servants were happy.

But she didn't want that. London called to her. And Jonathon too. With his blond hair and amber eyes, he was beyond handsome, almost bordering on beautiful. His skin was fashionably pale and he wore only the finest of garments. She had to devise a plan that would help her find him. She stared at the map. Tomorrow, she would rise early and walk to Hyde Park. All the gentlemen took their morning rides through the park and she would be there waiting for him.

With a satisfied smile, she placed the map on her nightstand and worked at the buttons on her dress. Just as she reached the second button, loud voices sounded from the hall.

"You can't just force your way in there, my lord," Mrs. Turner said loudly.

"She's my wife and I can do damn well whatever I want to get her back."

Tia wondered who was hiding from a husband. There were two other women staying at the inn but Tia hadn't socialized with them.

She had heard the woman in the room across from her say she was a widow. Perhaps she truly wasn't. It wasn't that uncommon for women to leave their husbands, especially if abuse was involved. Unfortunately, the husband had every legal right to drag her back to his home. Heavy footsteps drew near but she went back to the buttons on her dress.

"Unlock it," the man demanded.

"Yes, my lord," Mrs. Turner replied. "Shouldn't you at least knock?"

"Now."

With a slight shrug, Tia slipped the last button through its hole and started to remove her gray muslin dress. As she bared one shoulder, the door to her room swung open. Tia gasped and she clutched the gaping dress at her breast. Shocked, she could only stare at the man in the doorway. His black attire was dirty as if he'd been riding for days. From the look of the growth of hair on his jaw, she realized he probably *had* ridden for days.

"You may leave us now, Mrs. Turner."

"No, Mrs. Turner, you need to stay," Tia replied as she stared at him. His icy blue eyes narrowed on her.

Mrs. Turner glanced between the two of them. She hesitated before saying, "Miss Featherstone, he swears you are his wife."

"I am most certainly not his wife!"

"But it is your word to his," she said. "The man is—"

"A bloody viscount. I know that," Tia replied as she turned her gaze to him. "And do I look like a bloody viscountess?"

Mrs. Turner shrugged. "I—I—"

"Leave us," he demanded, staring coldly at Mrs. Turner.

"Mrs. Turner," Tia implored her. "He is lying."

"Perhaps," she whispered. "But I can't take the chance that he is speaking the truth. I could lose everything." She eased out of the room, closing the door behind her.

Tia turned her fury on the smirking man leaning against the closed door. "What are you doing here, Middleton?"

He crossed his arms over his chest as his sneer turned into a frown. "Bringing my wise woman home."

How dare this man attempt to bring her back to the estate as if he owned her! "I am done with that position."

He tilted his head. "Indeed? I do not remember receiving a letter of resignation."

"So you came all the way to London to get one?" She started to reach for a piece of paper before remembering her state of undress. She grabbed her bodice to keep it from falling.

"Is there a problem?" he asked with a slight grin.

His stare burned her skin as if he'd touched her. Ridiculous thought, she told herself. The man was only angry because she left without notifying him. Still, that wicked grin reminded her of his reputation with the ladies in London.

"If you want a letter of resignation, just give me a minute. Turn around."

His gaze never wavered from hers. She'd never noticed just how light blue his eyes were until now, but they also held a coldness that she'd couldn't abide.

"Please turn around, my lord."

"I didn't come all this way for a letter of resignation," he remarked.

"Then why are you here?"

"As I said, for you."

Chapter 2

Braden watched Tia's eyes widen. Good. He wanted her off-balance. He didn't want her to think about what he was doing until he had her in the carriage and on the road back to Middleton Hall.

"And I already told you I wasn't returning with you."

There was a slight change in her demeanor that he couldn't comprehend. He had the strangest sensation that she was up to something. "Mrs. Turner already believes you are my wife. As such, it is within my right to put you over my shoulder and carry you out of this godforsaken place."

"I wouldn't try that if I were you, my lord. I am a wise woman and therefore know all the delicate places on a man's body." She raised a brow as her gaze slid down his body until reaching the junction of his legs.

Damn his body for reacting to such a practiced act. "Then you should also know that men are inherently stronger than women. So it's doubtful that you would succeed."

She bit down on her lower lip, drawing his attention to her full lips. Slowly, she rose off the bed and let her hand drop from its job of keeping her dress closed. Her fiery hair curled down to the middle of her back. Braden waited for the seductress to come closer to him. He had no doubt that she was an accomplished flirt. No woman looked as she did without learning such alluring behavior.

But with each step closer, she buttoned her gown. Her brown eyes narrowed as she stared at him. "I am not returning to Middleton Hall," she said deliberately. "Now, you can either accept that and leave or I will make your life miserable."

"You are coming home, Miss Featherstone." This had gone on long enough. As much as he didn't wish to embarrass her by dragging her over his shoulder, she'd given him no choice. He reached for her but she must have anticipated his lunge. She slipped around him and ran out the door. "Dammit, Tia, get back here."

Did that slip of a girl think she could outrun him? He strode out the door to the corridor and stared. Hearing the front door slam, he raced down the stairs after her. Darkness had already fallen making it harder to spot her. That ugly gray dress didn't help matters. He walked up the street, glancing down each side street as he went. It only made sense that she would have turned as quickly as she could to get out of sight.

He shook his head when he reached the corner and saw her sitting on a step, examining her foot. Foolish girl had run off barefoot. When she noticed his approach, she quickly rose and hobbled down the street. He only had to walk fast to catch her.

He reached out and grabbed her waist, then heaved her over his shoulder. "You should have put on your boots before trying to outrun me."

"Put me down or I'll scream!" She punched his lower back.

"Have you not realized where you are living, Miss Featherstone? Do you honestly think anyone is going to help you here?" He cursed as she punched him again, this time harder. "Stop."

"You have to let me go."

"Why?" he asked, but truly didn't care to hear her reason.

"I need to find Jonathon," she whispered tearfully.

He hailed a hackney and dumped her inside before clamoring into the carriage. "Why?"

She scrambled into a seat and crossed her arms over her chest. "I need to see Jonathon."

"I believe you said that," he said impatiently. "But what you haven't said is why."

"I cannot speak of such things to you," she replied, staring out the window.

Braden tried to remain calm, but his patience had worn thin. "I am his brother and know more about him than most. You can confide in me."

She shook her head. "It is most private, indeed, my lord. I am afraid I cannot confide in you."

"Miss Featherstone," he bit out. "Tell me."

She turned her blazing brown eyes on him. "Have you always been this arrogant? Or was this a consequence of gaining the title?"

He smirked. "My attitude has nothing to do with my title. Now tell me what you need to say to Jonathon."

Instead, she pressed her lips together and returned her gaze to the dark night.

Braden clenched his fists as anger fired deep within him. He was certain that he knew what she wanted to say to his brother, but he wanted to hear her say it. Instead, she crossed her arms over her chest and remained silent. Rather than continuing a fruitless conversation, he would wait until she was in a vulnerable position to get her to talk.

The silence stretched as the carriage rumbled toward his town home. A few times, he caught her slide a glance to him, but instead of acknowledging her, he remained quiet. It was far better to let her wonder what he was thinking. Keeping a woman off-guard was a time-honored secret of his.

Slowly, the carriage rolled to a stop in front of his home. He jumped down, paid the driver, and waited for Tia to disembark the carriage. "Are you coming?" he finally asked.

"No. I am returning to the inn. All my things are there."

What had his mother always told him? Count to ten. *One. Ten.* "Out now!" He pulled her legs toward him until she fell off the seat. "I would have let you walk inside with your dignity intact, but now you'll suffer the embarrassment."

"I can barely walk on my right foot anyway," she retorted. "I need to get this piece of glass out."

Braden blew out a breath. He'd completely forgotten that she'd hurt her foot. "I will carry you inside and to a guest room. Then I'll send Mrs. Abbott up to assist you with your foot."

"I don't need assistance. I need my things from the inn and some water and brandy for my foot."

"As you wish," he said and then strode to the front door. Mr. Nelson opened the door for him. "Evening, Nelson. Please make up the blue room for Miss Featherstone. She will be staying with us tonight."

Mr. Nelson glanced down to the step and then said, "I believe she needs some assistance, my lord."

"Yes, but she doesn't want my help. Settle her in the blue room and ask Mrs. Abbott to see me."

"Of course, my lord."

Braden glanced back to verify she wasn't trying to run away again. Nelson rushed to assist Tia as she hopped up the steps. Stubborn girl. He wasn't about to throw her over his shoulder again. He paused after taking a step. He supposed he should have let her know that.

Tia grabbed the wrought-iron rail and pushed her weight on it to climb up the first stair. A man came running down the steps.

"Miss Featherstone, please let me assist you. My name is Mr. Nelson and I am the viscount's butler." He held out his arm for her to put her weight on. "I have heard so many wonderful things about you and your mother."

Tia looked at the man and realized he wasn't the one who had answered the door the two times she'd called on Jonathon. It must have been one of the footmen who had sent her away. "Thank you, Mr. Nelson."

"Do you need a footman to carry you to your room?"

As much as she wanted that, she shook her head. "No, thank you, Mr. Nelson. I can walk." Barely. But she would never let Middleton see her appear weak by needing help up the stairs.

Together they hobbled up the steps until they reached the entryway. She hadn't gotten this far when she'd knocked on the door. The cold white marble chilled her bare feet and up her body. Her right foot throbbed, which meant she most likely hadn't removed whatever she'd stepped on in her rush to get away from Middleton.

Taking a step forward, she realized her foot was still oozing blood. "Oh, drat! I've bled on this beautiful floor."

"Not to worry, miss," Nelson said with a kind smile. "Let us get you upstairs so someone can take care of that for you."

"Thank you, Mr. Nelson. I can manage binding my foot."

"We shall put you in the blue room," Mr. Nelson said as they hobbled up the marble staircase.

Tia had been in Middleton Hall before, but rarely had she walked through the elegant house. Most of the times, she was called only to help a servant below stairs. But the beauty of the town home astounded her. Large paintings hung on the walls. They must be relatives but she had to admit none of the images looked like Middleton. The people in the portraits were fairer in complexion, more like Jonathon.

They entered the room and Tia stopped. This was not a room, but a suite of rooms. The salon was larger than her bedroom in the cottage of his estate. A large sofa and two light blue velvet-covered chairs were situated near the commanding fireplace. A small cherry desk faced the windows that overlooked the street. Mr. Nelson opened the door to the bedroom and Tia followed behind him.

"This is such a beautiful bedroom," she said with a wistful sigh.

Mr. Nelson smiled. "Yes, it is."

Spying another door, she asked, "What does that lead to?"

Mr. Nelson's smile faded. "Just another bedchamber. But not to worry, the door locks from in here."

"Very well, then." Tia eased herself down on the bed. "Would it be possible to have a bath? I wouldn't wish to put someone out, but I need to soak my foot and then get the last piece of glass out."

"Of course. Mrs. Abbott will be up presently to assist you. I shall send the footmen up with the tub and hot water."

"Thank you, Mr. Nelson."

"If you need anything, just ring."

Tia sat down on the bed as the butler left the room. She had wanted nothing more than to lie back against the bed and fall asleep. But her dratted foot throbbed. Soaking it would help get the last few shards of glass out.

Drat Middleton for catching her. But at least now, she had an advantage. Hopefully, his brother would come to call on him and then she could make sure Jonathon was all right and tell him how she felt about him. Surely, the man had to feel the same after all the compliments he'd paid her over the summer. It wasn't everyday she was told how beautiful she was or how her amber eyes were like a fire, flaming his desire. That was the day she'd fallen in love with him.

The door to her room opened and an older woman with a scowl entered. "What are you doing on that bed? Get off those clean bedcovers this instant!"

Tia jumped off the bed as if it was on fire. "Are you Mrs. Abbott?"

"Of course I am." She shook her gray head as she walked into the room and stared at her. "I don't know why you aren't downstairs where you belong," she muttered.

"What do you mean?"

Mrs. Abbott glared at her. "You're nothing more than a servant, Miss Featherstone. I have no idea why the viscount would want you upstairs . . . unless you are here for another reason."

Another reason? What did that old witch mean? Tia wasn't about to ask. "Have you brought my bathwater?" she asked in her haughtiest tone.

Mrs. Abbott's lip curled. "Yes, the footmen are coming up presently. Do not worry, princess, you shall have your bath."

Oh, she didn't like this woman one bit. "Thank you."

After the footmen brought up the tub and water, Tia worked on the front buttons of her dress. Mrs. Abbott didn't even offer to assist her, but that suited Tia just fine. She preferred undressing herself anyway. She was used to taking care of herself at the cottage. Although, she did wonder why Mrs. Abbott remained in the room if she wasn't going to help her.

"There is no need to stay, Mrs. Abbott. I can bathe myself."

"I am only waiting for your clothing."

Ah, that explained it. Middleton must have told Mrs. Abbott to clean her dress. Tia climbed into the tub and sighed as the hot water soothed her tired muscles. It had been a week since she'd been able to have a proper bath and that only lasted long enough for her to wash quickly. Tonight, she would savor this bath.

Mrs. Abbott picked up her clothing and walked toward the door. Tia glanced around.

"Mrs. Abbott, if you take all of my clothes, what shall I wear?"

"The viscount said he would give you a dressing gown to wear for tonight," the older woman said with a smirk.

A dressing gown! "I need more than that."

Mrs. Abbott shrugged her shoulders. "You will need to take that up with his lordship. He may care what you wear, but I certainly do not." The door slammed as Mrs. Abbott left the room.

Tia sank into the tub to wet her hair. As she resurfaced, she heard the door open again. "Have you brought me a dressing gown?"

"Yes," a husky voice replied.

Chapter 3

Braden leaned back against the door and ignored the spark of passion scurrying through his body. He was only here to drop off the dressing gown so she had something to cover her naked body. Her lush, naked, wet body. *Stop thinking about that*, he commanded himself. *You are not that man any longer.*

"Middleton?"

She had yet to turn and look behind her. He briefly wondered why. None of the wise women he'd met seemed to have a care about their modesty. Tia's own sister had made no attempt to hide her relationship with a man.

"Middleton, is that you?" She craned her neck to glance back. Spying him, her brown eyes widened and her full mouth gaped. "What are you doing in here?"

He shook his head to clear his lecherous thoughts. Remembering his true reason for being here, he held out a dressing gown. "I brought this for you to wear until I can get a dressmaker here tomorrow."

"A dressmaker? There is no need for that. If one of the maids could just clean my clothes, I can make do with that until I return to the inn and pick up my other belongings."

Braden laughed coarsely. "I'm afraid there has been a slight problem with your dress."

"What do you mean?"

"I believe it fell into the fire."

"What fire?" Her voice rose higher.

"The one in the kitchen."

"You, sir, must have the most incompetent servants ever. How could a person 'accidentally' drop a dress into the fire? I knew that Mrs. Abbott didn't like me, but this is uncalled for. I demand you do something about it."

He moved away from the door and walked past the tub. As he did, he couldn't help but smile when she attempted to cover herself with her hands. He sank into a chair near the window, but just far enough away that he couldn't quite see her naked body. "I don't believe I said it was an accident."

"So she did it on purpose and you knew that?" she sputtered. "That woman needs to be sacked."

"No, *I* told her to burn your clothing." The poor girl slipped deeper into the water until it lapped against her chin.

"Why would you do such a thing?" she whispered.

"Lice and fleas. I will not tolerate them in my house." While he had no reason to believe her clothing might have carried the vermin, he'd still ordered it burned. That mousey gray dress was the most hideous gown he'd ever seen on a woman.

"I do not have lice or fleas!"

He shrugged. "I wasn't about to take the chance after seeing the conditions you were living in. I thought you were supposed to be staying with a friend."

She looked down at the water and shook her head. "They were evicted for not paying their rent a week before I arrived. The landlord had no idea where they went."

Braden crossed his arms over his chest. "So instead of returning to the safety of Middleton Hall, you decided to stay at that disgusting inn. And in one of the most undesirable areas in London to live."

He attempted to keep his anger under control, but her utter lack of sense only frustrated him more. How could an intelligent woman make such a foolish choice? Love, of course, he reasoned. There was no other reasonable explanation.

"I couldn't return to the estate until I had finished what I had come here for." She lifted her head and stared at him.

"And what was that?"

"I am done speaking of this matter. My bathwater is cooling and I would like to finish bathing before my teeth start chattering. Please leave this room."

He rose slowly, but not before admiring her body in the tub for a brief second. "Your towel and dressing gown are on the table next to you. I will have a tray sent up to your room. Tomorrow after the dressmaker brings something she can make work for you, we shall depart for Middleton Hall."

"I am not leaving London yet."

"Yes, you are. I will make sure of it." He opened the door before she could retort and walked to his room. His valet Wilson was already there, getting Braden's evening clothes ready. The last thing he wanted to do was attend a party, but as long as he was in town, he had to try to find Jonathon. His brother loved to be around the *ton*.

Between Tia and Jonathon, Braden felt as if he was the only person with any sense. He understood Tia's motivations far better than Jonathon. She thought she was in love with his brother. If she only knew him for what he truly was, she might think differently. The two months Jonathon spent at Middleton Hall this summer, he'd been a man anyone could love. But his brother couldn't maintain that façade for long. He always returned to the habits that were ruining his life.

After dressing, Braden headed for Berkeley Square and the crush of people that even the late summer couldn't keep away. Most of the landowners headed out to their estates to escape the heat and foul odors of London in the summer. Those who remained tended to run in a fast set, something Braden had finally outgrown.

Walking up the steps of Lady Hargrove's town home, he wondered who the young widow had taken to replace him in her bed. Not that he cared. It was strictly a morbid curiosity.

"Well, this is quite a surprise," she drawled as he strolled into her salon.

"Lizzie," he said with a nod, before seizing a snifter of brandy from a passing footman. "How have you been?"

The elegant blonde strolled closer. "I have been wonderful." She leaned in closer. "But no one can ever truly replace you in my bed. I would be more than happy to kick a young pup to the street if you wish to return."

"I believe I will pass on that offer," he said with a hint of disdain.

Lizzie's face hardened. "Why?"

"Because we both know that young pup, as you call him, entered your bed before I had even left it."

She forced her chin upward, turned, and walked away.

Braden smiled. He had wanted to do that for the past six months. Lizzie had only wanted him because he'd just inherited the title.

"Look who has returned from moldering in the country."

Braden turned to see Jack Cranborne grinning at him. "Jack, thank God there is one friendly face at this damned party."

Jack smiled and nodded. "I didn't expect to see you *here*."

"I'm looking for Jonathon. Have you seen him?"

"He's not here. In fact, I didn't know he was in town. The last I'd heard he was spending the summer at Middleton Hall . . . with you."

"He left."

Jack's smile disappeared. "How has he fared?"

"He was quite well out in the middle of nowhere. But if he has truly returned, I fear he shall fall back into his old habits."

Jack's lips turned downward. "I'd be happy to help you find him. Especially if it means getting out of here tonight."

Braden laughed. "No one worth seducing?"

"Not a one."

"Who is Lizzie with these days?"

"Stephenson."

"Ned Stephenson? Isn't he only twenty-two?" Braden could not believe Lizzie would have an interest in such a young man. There had to be an ulterior motive. "Why?"

"He was just named heir presumptive to an earldom of his uncle's. Since his uncle is seventy and in poor health, it seems apparent that Stephenson will inherit before too long."

"Makes sense that Lizzie wants to get her claws into that one. She'd much rather be a countess than a dowager baroness."

"Exactly. And he's young enough to control." Jack shook his head.

"I heard there is some action at Handler's tonight. Perhaps Jonathon is there."

"Give me a minute to just look around here."

Braden scoured the rooms for Jonathon, but found no sign of him. He and Jack tried Handler's gaming hell to no avail. While Jack played some faro, Braden made a few inquires but no one had seen Jonathon since spring. Braden walked back through the smoke-filled room, choking back a cough. He hadn't missed this.

His friend sat at the faro table with a smile and a good amount of coins in front of him. One man left the table, so Braden slid into his seat. Immediately, one of the many whores sat down on his lap and whispered in his ear.

"I have an empty bed upstairs just waiting for you."

"Not tonight, darling. Go try another man," he choked out. Good God, the woman must have soaked in perfume. The disappointed woman slipped off his lap and walked toward another more willing victim.

"Anything?" Jack asked.

"No one has seen him," Braden said, then checked his cards and frowned. The scowl on his face had nothing to do with his cards. If his brother hadn't been at the most popular party of the night, nor at one of the most popular gaming hells, where the bloody hell could he be?

Unable to concentrate on his cards, he folded and scraped back his chair. "I'm going home," he said to Jack.

"Now?" Jack replied, staring at his cards. With a groan, he tossed his cards down, picked up his winnings, and followed Braden out the door.

"You didn't need to leave."

"Safety in numbers, my friend. I wasn't about to leave alone with this much coin in my pocket. You never know what might happen."

"True," Braden replied. Handler's wasn't in the best location.

They walked the quiet streets in silence but the hairs on the back of his neck stood straight. Braden had the oddest feeling that someone was watching them. The sound of pistol fire filled the air. Both Jack and Braden fell to the street. A burning sensation spread from Braden's upper arm. "Dammit."

They both slowly rose and glanced around but noticed no one.

"You're bleeding," Jack said, staring at Braden's arm.

"All over my favorite jacket." He gritted his teeth against the pain. "Come on, my carriage is just up the street."

They rushed to the safety of his carriage and collapsed onto the velvet squabs. Braden pulled a handkerchief from his pocket and held it to his wound. It really was no more than a scrape, but it hurt like hell.

"Was the shooter after you or me?" Jack asked with a worried look.

"You won the money." But even as Braden said those words, he wondered if he spoke the truth. He was the viscount now. Both his uncle and cousin had died in questionable situations. His uncle was killed in a carriage accident in Scotland and his cousin Randolph drowned at a hunting lodge in Suffolk. It couldn't be proven that either death was not accidental, but for Randolph to die only two weeks after inheriting had put the suspicion on Braden.

And no one had approached Jack after the shooting in an attempt to steal his money. *Dammit!*

"Bloody hell," Jack muttered. "One of us might have been killed. Should I take you to the surgeon?"

"No, take me home."

"You need to have that looked at."

"I will." Miss Featherstone was about to earn her keep.

After her bath, Tia finally drew the last piece of glass from her foot. She bound the wound and lay back against the soft pillows. Her hands still shook from her interaction with Middleton. She'd only seen him a few times at the estate this summer. Their conversations had been brief and concerned the well-being of one of his servants who'd had an attack of gout.

Those short talks had never left her feeling as shocked as tonight when he walked into the bedroom while she bathed. She couldn't help but notice the way he slid a glance at her naked body. His blue eyes had darkened to the color of sapphires. But it was her reaction that frightened her. With her hands covering her breasts, she felt her nipples grow taut under his heated gaze.

What was wrong with her?

She didn't want Middleton. She didn't even like the man. He was cold, dark, and the type of man who used women purely for his own benefit. Nothing like his brother. Oh, where could Jonathon be? And how was she supposed to find him if Middleton insisted on leaving tomorrow? She couldn't run off from the house in his dressing gown.

Somehow, she had to figure out a way of leaving before they departed for Middleton Hall.

A knock disturbed her musing. "Yes?"

"I have a tray for you, miss."

Tia forced herself off the comfortable bed. Padding across the thick carpet, she loved the way the fibers caressed her feet, unlike the threadbare carpets in her cottage at the estate. "Come in," she called.

A tall footman entered the room with a tray in one hand. "Evening, miss. His lordship said you might be hungry."

As much as she didn't want to take his charity, her stomach growled in protest. "Thank you. Will you ask Lord Middleton to come to my room? I need to speak with him."

The younger man frowned. "He left, miss."

Tia glanced at the clock. It was nearly eleven. Where would a man go at this hour? "Where was he going?"

"I believe he meant to attend a party."

"Oh," she said, slightly disappointed. She'd only wanted to confirm their departure time so she could plan her escape. "Thank you."

Once the footman had left, she ate her small meal and decided there was nothing else to do but go to sleep. If only it had been that easy. The minute she closed her eyes, his face flashed in her mind. She wondered why he wore mostly black. Perhaps he was vain enough to realize that it accentuated his blue eyes, which it did. Still, she didn't like the man or his aggressive demeanor with her. She forced herself to think about Jonathon.

She fell asleep, dreaming of the man she loved, until shouting from the entryway awakened her.

"Wake her up," a deep voice demanded as footsteps faded down the hall. "Now!"

Tia sat up in her bed and looked around in confusion. A knock hammered her door a minute later.

"Miss Featherstone, you must wake up."

She glanced over at the clock on her nightstand. It was barely three in the morning. They couldn't be leaving for Middleton Hall at this hour. "What is wrong?"

"You must come quickly. His lordship wants you."

Tia blinked in confusion. Middleton wanted her? "Where is he?"

"In his bedchamber," the footman replied from behind the closed door. "You mustn't keep him waiting."

She had no idea why she couldn't keep him waiting. Instead of arguing with the servant, Tia grabbed the dressing gown and wrapped it around her. She wished he'd given her a shift to wear under it or she'd had the sense to ask for one.

Tia followed the young man down the hall. There had to be a good reason Middleton would demand her presence at this hour. As she walked into the room, she noticed him lying on his bed with only his trousers on. The footman quietly closed the door as he left.

"Absolutely not," she exclaimed and turned toward the door.

"Miss Featherstone, get yourself back here this instant."

Tia stopped. Turning slowly, she faced him. She stepped into his bedroom with her hands on her hips. A tremor of fear slid down her back.

"Where do you think you're going?" he drawled.

"I am returning to my bedroom. If you think for one moment . . ." her voice trailed off as he crooked a finger.

"Come here."

What was it about the sound of his voice that made her do things she had no desire to do? "I am leaving." But even as she said that, she moved closer to the bed.

"I did not ask you here to warm my bed." A slow smile drew his full lips upward. "At least, not right now."

Tia seemed unable to look away from his mouth. "Th—then why am I here?"

He cocked his head toward his right arm. Seeing the handkerchief with bloodstains, she gasped.

"Why didn't you just tell me you were injured?" Years of her mother's training came back to her. "Where is your brandy?"

"You're going to drink before you stitch me?"

She rolled her eyes. "No. Now, where is it?"

He nodded toward the salon. "Corner table. Your bag is in there too."

Tia strode to the salon, picked up her bag, and then the brandy decanter. She walked back into the room and set to work on him. As she neared him, the smell of cheap perfume, cheap liquor, and cheap cigars overwhelmed her, making her gag. "You are disgusting. Let me guess . . . you were cheating at cards and someone called you out."

"No."

"Whoring and cheated her out of her money, so she took a shot at you?"

He chuckled in his low, husky voice. "Hardly."

"Then how?"

One black brow lifted. "No idea. I was leaving a gaming hell with a friend and someone took a shot. My friend had won a substantial amount so we assume the shot was meant for him."

"Disgusting," she muttered again. She searched her bag for her needle and thread. After pouring the brandy into a glass, she dropped the needle into the glass. Then she poured another one, added a few drops of laudanum, and then handed it to him. "Drink."

He reached for the snifter and drank it down in one gulp. "I doubt one more glass will have much of a numbing effect."

"We shall see." Tia brushed his hand away from the bloody handkerchief and stared down at the wound. The long cut wasn't terribly deep, but she could see some fabric from his clothing in there. Without a thought, she poured a large amount of brandy over the gash.

A violent string of curses erupted from Middleton. "Bloody hell, woman. Are you trying to get revenge for earlier tonight?"

"No," she said, as she wiped as the wound and then picked a few more strands of fabric out. "I am trying to make sure you don't die from blood poisoning. Now just be quiet and let me work."

Middleton clenched his jaw as she started to stitch him back together.

Knowing it sometimes helped to keep a patient's mind off the task she performed, she said, "So why were you at a gaming hell tonight?"

"The usual reasons."

"And the perfume?"

"Not the usual reason."

She waited for him to continue but when he didn't, she asked. "Oh?"

"Some poor woman thought I might be interested, so she came and sat on my lap." He stared up at her with his penetrating blue eyes. "But I wasn't interested in her."

"I see," she replied, moving her gaze back to the task at hand. "Unfortunately, this will leave a rather long scar."

He looked over as she finished the last stitch. "You are a fine seamstress. Your stitches are straight and neat. I doubt the scar will be all that bad."

Tia glanced over at the large, jagged scar on his lower ribs. "Compared to that one, anything would be better. Who did that to you?"

"A local surgeon. Probably the same man who I would have called tonight had you not been here."

Tia shook her head. "I meant, what happened?"

Middleton leaned back against the pillows and scowled. "That was a long time ago. Just a slight duel over a woman."

She knew when not to press a man for more and there was obviously a lot more to that story. She covered his wound with some strips of cotton to keep the dirt out. "As long as you don't get an infection, you should heal well."

"Thank you." He reached for her hand and pressed a quick kiss to her palm.

She yanked her hand back and jumped off the bed. He still hadn't shaved and the sensation of his bristly beard and soft lips against her hand sent shivers through her. She walked to the window and stared down at the dark, empty street.

"Why would you want to give up doing something you are so good at?" he asked quietly.

Leaning her head against the window, she glanced back at him. She couldn't tell him the truth. He would, like her mother, tell her to forget what happened and learn from it. "It's all I've ever known. From the time I was two, I was following my mother to tenants' houses and watching what she did. How many people do you know who by age ten could stitch a person's wounds or set a bone?"

He closed his eyes for a long moment. "Not many at all."

"I wanted to see another part of life," she whispered the lie. "See London and all the fancy people here. Do something other than heal people all day long."

"Why else?"

"I need to find your brother."

His scowl returned. "Why?"

"Because he needs me."

Braden stared at his wise woman as she gazed at the street below her. Her reasons for going to London to get away from a life where she'd done nothing but help other people made some sense, but he felt she was hiding something from him. Perhaps she truly needed a little holiday to refresh herself. But why would she think Jonathon needed her? She couldn't possibly know of all his problems.

Could she?

"Why?" he finally asked.

"Why what?"

He sighed and felt his head start to spin a little. Damn her. She must have sneaked some laudanum into his brandy. She should have asked him first. "Why does Jonathon need *you*?"

"I promised him I would not speak of it to anyone."

He scowled. Perhaps Jonathon had admitted his past transgressions to her. Braden doubted that his brother would have confessed his sins to someone he barely knew, but it was possible. Had their relationship progressed farther than Braden had thought? And why did that bother him? It certainly should not. They were both adults and could live their lives any way they wanted . . . as long as Jonathon had stopped the opium.

"Miss Featherstone, this is my brother we are discussing. I am worried that something might have happened to him. Now, what do you think you know?"

She shook her head. "He told this in confidence and I will not break that confidence." Tia moved to the table to gather her things as if to leave the room.

Ignoring the biting pain in his arm, he reached over and grabbed her arm. Tugging her back to the bed, he forced her to sit down. He sat up and leaned closer until their noses were almost touching. He stared into her amber eyes. "Tell me."

"I don't have to tell you anything. And even if I do, chances are you will never remember it come morning."

The spinning in his mind was driving him mad. Or was it her nearness? Either way, he needed some control. He forced himself to lie back against the pillows. "Why?"

"Because in about a minute, you will be fast asleep."

Braden fought for control but that damned drug was making him sleepy. "You did this on purpose, didn't you?"

Her light laugh filled the room. "No, but now I am quite happy I did."

He closed his eyes, but when he tried to reopen them he found his lids too heavy to lift. The bed squeaked as she rose. There was nothing he could do to stop her.

"Good night, my lord."

And then darkness overcame him.

Chapter 4

Tia awoke early the next morning and rang for assistance. Her encounter with the viscount last night had emboldened her. Mrs. Abbott arrived a few minutes later with a sour look upon her face.

"Back in your bed, I see." The woman folded her arms over her measly bosom.

"Mrs. Abbott, I would like a suitable dress to wear immediately." She tilted her head and gave the housekeeper smug grin. That old biddy could believe whatever she wanted. Tia Featherstone could take care of herself.

"Lord Middleton has not ordered me to give you any clothing."

"Why?"

Mrs. Abbott stared at her. "He didn't want you to run off."

Tia laughed. "Where would I go? I have no money and have no friends in town."

Mrs. Abbott shrugged.

"Besides, Lord Middleton is in no condition to give orders."

Mrs. Abbott's face drew pallid. "I heard he was hurt but nothing more. I assumed he was perfectly well since the surgeon was not called for."

"I cared for his lordship, as is my duty as wise woman. Now, I would like to dress so I might get some air."

The housekeeper nodded sharply. "Very well. I suppose you deserve a little air since you saved his lordship's life. I shall have something brought up to you immediately, Miss Featherstone." She turned to leave and then stopped. "He is all right, then?"

"Yes, Mrs. Abbott. Lord Middleton should be fine, but he needs rest right now."

"Thank you, miss. He is a fine master."

Tia wondered about that as the housekeeper left the room. The former lordship had been a hard man. She'd only met him a few times and then he'd been curt with her. Perhaps Middleton, even with his rakish demeanor, treated the staff better than the previous viscount. She was glad that the tenants had a more compassionate landholder.

Her only priority was finding Jonathon before it was too late. Every day he was gone increased her concern for his well-being. The things he'd told her frightened and worried her. She needed to get him back under the physician's care until he had completely recovered from his issue.

Mrs. Abbott entered the room without even a knock and then handed her a dress. "This will have to do. Mr. Nelson informed me that the dressmaker was set to arrive at noon. Make certain you are back to the house before then."

"I will do just that," Tia said softly. Unless she found Jonathon.

She dressed quickly and then ate breakfast. She needed to leave the house before Middleton awoke and wondered where she was this morning. Hopefully, the laudanum would make him sleep longer and deeper so she could escape. She pushed away the tray and stood, only to discover yet another issue. While Mrs. Abbott had brought her clothing to wear, Tia's boots were still at the inn.

"Drat it." Now she would have to beg for Mrs. Abbott's help again. She doubted the cantankerous housekeeper would allow her too many favors. She rang the bell and waited fretfully. Footsteps sounded closer to her door. *Please let it be Mrs. Abbott and not Middleton.*

"Come in," Tia responded after a light knock. After last night, it was unlikely that Middleton would rap on the door.

"What do you need now?" Mrs. Abbott said as she crossed her arms over her chest. "I have a house to run."

"I need shoes," Tia replied, staring at her feet.

"Your boots are in the linen press."

"They are?" She walked to the linen press and found her short boots on the bottom. "How did they get here?" She hadn't thought to question how her bag of herbs ended up in Middleton's room last night.

"A footman returned last night to the inn and gathered the rest of your things."

Tia frowned. "Then where are the rest of my dresses?" she asked, but knew the answer—burned.

Mrs. Abbott nodded as if she understood what Tia was thinking. "I saw no reason to waste a perfectly acceptable pair of boots. No matter what his lordship said."

"Thank you, Mrs. Abbott."

Mrs. Abbott frowned and then nodded sharply. "Is that all?"

"Is his lordship awake yet?"

"No, why?"

"I wished to walk to the park for some air. If the viscount were awake, I would need to check on his condition before I departed. That is all," Tia said in an innocent tone. The housekeeper didn't need to know Tia would prefer to check his wound while he slept, so as to avoid another confrontation with him.

"You are free to walk. Do you need a maid with you?"

"I am fine. You need the maids helping you out around the house, not following behind me."

"You are quite right, miss," Mrs. Abbott replied.

"Once I check in on him, I am off to Hyde Park then." Tia found an old bonnet in the linen press and then tied it under her chin.

Tia walked the short distance between the rooms and knocked softly. Hearing no reply, she opened the door and peeked into the room. It appeared he still slept. Quietly, she crept inside toward the bedroom. She peered into the bedroom and smiled as she noticed his eyes were still shut and his breathing even. Not wanting to wake him, she tiptoed to the bed and looked at the bandage. No blood was seeping through and there was no sign of redness around it. He would be fine until she returned.

She left the room and rushed down the stairs, bid Mrs. Abbott a good morning, and walked out of the house determined to find

Jonathon at the park. She wandered the streets of Mayfair until the park opened before her. As Tia walked the path toward the Serpentine, the noisy world of London melted away. She strolled by the water and sat down to watch the passersby.

After an hour of watching people and seeing no sign of Jonathon, she decided to walk around the park. That proved even more mundane than gawking at the finely dressed people. While she'd nodded to a few women, not a single one had taken the time to acknowledge her. With a sigh, she sat down on a bench, feeling completely defeated.

"I shall be all right. Just let me rest a moment."

Tia glanced over at a petite woman as she sat to fan herself. After receiving cuts from the other ladies she'd passed, Tia saw no reason to greet the finely dressed woman. Although, the more she spied her, the more she realized the woman did not look well. Her face was pale and drawn as if fighting something. "Are you all right?" she finally asked.

"It's dreadfully warm, that is all," the woman murmured.

"Is this woman bothering you?" a footman asked, drawing nearer.

"No, Arthur. She is only being kind." The woman pressed her hands to her stomach.

"Miss—"

"That would be Lady Eldridge to you, miss," the footman said.

"Arthur, be a dear and go sit over there," Lady Eldridge said, pointing to a bench out of earshot. Once the footman had stomped over to the other bench like a petulant child, she said, "He is a very nice man, but takes his responsibility to watch over me far too seriously. We are only in Hyde Park. I scarcely think anything will happen to me while I talk with you."

Tia laughed softly. "I rather doubt it too. Now, what is really the matter? I have some expertise in this area. I already have an idea of what is troubling you."

"You could not possibly know. And we have not been properly introduced. I am Lady Emily Eldridge."

"I am Miss Hestia Featherstone, but most people call me Tia."

Lady Eldridge frowned. "Are you a servant with a family nearby?"

"No," Tia said with a laugh and then went quiet. Mrs. Abbott had said she was nothing more than a servant and deserved to sleep downstairs with the others. But out at the estate, no one had treated her as such. They all respected and admired her for helping them with their ails.

"Indeed?" Lady Eldridge pursed her bow lips and scanned Tia's attire. "You certainly dress like a servant."

"I am a wise woman, my lady." She glanced at her dress. "And my gown is a very long story."

Lady Eldridge gave a little shrug. "A gown doesn't make a woman," she muttered. "Now, what is a wise woman?"

"I am a healer and midwife for Lord Middleton at his estate in the Midlands."

"Lord Middleton?" Her eyes shuttered for a long moment. "How is he? Is he in town? I hadn't heard he had returned."

"Yes, my lady, he is in town, but not for long." Tia wondered how this woman was acquainted with Middleton.

"And his brother?" she whispered in an uneven tone.

Tia realized Middleton might be an acquaintance, but it was Jonathon this woman was most interested in. "I have not seen him for a few weeks, since he left the estate."

Lady Eldridge's shoulders sagged as a crestfallen look swept across her face. "I see."

"My lady, you look dreadfully pale. Perhaps you should return to your home now."

"I would prefer speaking with you." Lady Eldridge picked up her silk fan and resumed fanning herself. She stopped for a moment and held her stomach.

"My lady, please let me help you home. I can make up some peppermint tea that will help with the nausea."

The woman's hazel eyes widened. "To what are you referring? I am having no such ills."

Tia's lips twitched. So, the lady didn't want anyone to know she was with child yet. She rose from her seat, knowing that Lady Eldridge was about to stop her. "If you say so, then I should return to Lord Middleton's home now. Good day."

Lady Eldridge moaned softly. "Can you really help me?"

"Yes, I can but only if you are truthful with me about all your symptoms." Tia held out her hand to assist the young woman. "Shall we return to your home?"

"Oh, please." Lady Eldridge tightly clasped her hand around Tia's.

The footman immediately rose and strode toward them. "My lady, might I be of assistance?"

"Bring the carriage around to us."

"B—but I mustn't leave you alone," he stammered. "Lord Eldridge will have my head if something befalls you."

"Miss Featherstone will be my companion while you summon the carriage. She will also accompany me back to the house."

The footman scowled at Tia and then nodded. "Of course, ma'am."

"Ma'am?" Tia swore softly. "I am most likely older than you and he would never deem it necessary to call me *ma'am*."

Lady Eldridge laughed. "In Society, it's all about who you are and with whom you associate. Now that I have decided you and I shall be fast friends, he will have no choice but to treat you with the respect you deserve."

Tia almost laughed. *Respect?* Did she deserve respect from anyone after leaving her position as the wise woman for Middleton's estate and then running off to London to save his brother? Most people would assume she was a strumpet for chasing after Jonathon. No one knew the truth of the matter of why she felt the need to follow him. It was purely for his safety. Not that she'd managed to find one sign of him yet.

"Tia?"

"I'm sorry, my lady—"

"Emily."

Tia blinked. "Pardon me?"

"You will call me Emily," she said as they ambled across the park.

Tia had no idea what to say. From what she'd heard, Lady Eldridge's request was most uncommon. Ladies in Society wanted to look down on the lower classes and the use of their titles was the easiest way to do so. "I couldn't possibly call you by your Christian name."

"Of course you can. I decide who calls me Lady Eldridge and who calls me Emily." Emily glanced to the ground. "I could use a friend in London. Like you, I'm from the country. I don't have that many true friends and none in town. But I believe you and I shall be wonderful companions."

"I shan't be here long enough for that to happen, my lady." Tia bit down on her lower lip. She actually liked Emily and had felt an instant connection that warmed her heart. Back in the Midlands, her only real friends were her twin sister Mia and their mutual friend Selina.

"And why not? I know it's not the Season, but there are still many people in London who prefer to stay in town."

"Lord Middleton has decided that we should return to the estate posthaste."

Emily laughed as they reached the street. "Middleton? He is one of the worst of the group."

"Perhaps, but now that he is the viscount I believe he feels a need to be more responsible and that includes taking care of his estate." Tia had no idea if that were true or not. She also had no idea why she was defending him to someone who most likely knew him better than she did.

"He's a rake, through and through," Emily added with a hint of scorn.

Tia only shrugged as she clamored into the carriage. She sat back against the velvet squabs with a long sigh. Beautiful red satin lined the enclosed carriage. She had never been privileged to sit in such luxury. The post carriage was far from plush.

"What is wrong?" Emily asked as the carriage rolled down Brooke Street.

"Nothing," she replied softly.

Emily cocked a blond brow at her. "Indeed? As much as you can tell I am feeling unwell, I can tell you are bothered by something. Now, what is wrong?"

Tia stared down at her ugly brown dress. "I do not belong in such a beautiful carriage. Perhaps I should return to Middleton's home now." The last thing she wanted to do was face the irate man who only wanted her to return to the Midlands, but starting a friendship with a lady like Emily seemed improper. They were from very different stations in life. And once Tia left London, she doubted she would get the opportunity to visit for a very long time.

"No, you said you would help me feel better." Her face scrunched. "And you will do that."

"I shall help you and then return."

"Perhaps," Emily mumbled.

The carriage ride was over so quickly, Tia realized she could have walked to the Eldridge home quicker. Arthur assisted Emily down and then looked at Tia.

"Shall I escort Miss Featherstone home?" he asked in a hopeful tone.

"No, Arthur. She is paying a call on me. Help her down."

Tia smothered a laugh as Arthur held out his hand to assist her down from the carriage. "Thank you, Arthur."

He only shook his head in reply.

Tia still found it odd that Arthur immediately recognized her for what she was—no one—while Emily insisted Tia return to her home and befriend her. Could Lady Eldridge be that lacking in female companionship?

Once they reached the entrance, Emily turned to her. "Would you mind if we talked in my bedchamber? I find myself very tired and unwell."

"Of course, Lady Eldridge."

Emily stared at her without moving. "Emily."

"Of course, Emily," Tia said, feeling as if she'd been reprimanded. She followed behind her new friend as they ascended the steps. Almost as soon as she entered the room, Emily's lady maid blustered into the room.

"Did you have a fine day out at the park, my lady?" the woman asked as she removed Emily's beautiful ivory spencer.

"Lovely, but I am a bit tired. Could you bring some tea up for Miss Featherstone and me."

It was as if Tia hadn't existed until the countess proclaimed her presence in the room. The maid bobbed a quick curtsy. "Good afternoon, Miss Featherstone."

Tia had no idea the maid's name, so only nodded at her. "Could you find some peppermint to brew some tea?"

"Peppermint tea?" The maid slid a glance to the countess.

"Yes, Mallory. Some peppermint tea for Miss Featherstone. Thank you."

Tia watched as Miss Mallory backed out of the room looking dreadful confused by what she'd just encountered in her mistress's bedchamber. Once the door shut behind her, Tia's skill took over. "To bed with you, my lady."

"I cannot retire at this hour. Everyone will be suspicious."

"Not another word," Tia said before setting to work at removing the woman's dress and stays. "Bed, now."

Emily scampered under the covers and then lay back against the pillows with a sigh. "You mustn't tell a soul."

Tia nodded. "Is there some specific reason you are not ready to tell your husband about his impending fatherhood?"

"No," she answered quickly.

"Surely, he will be pleased with the idea of you carrying his heir?" Tia said.

The countess stared at her long fingers splayed against the coverlet. Tears fell like rain from her eyes. "I cannot be certain it is his child," she whispered so quietly Tia barely heard her.

"Why not?"

"I was with another man not long before my marriage. My family did not consider him husband material. Once Eldridge expressed an interest in me, my mother paraded me before him at every opportunity until he proposed only a fortnight later. We were married a week later by special license. I didn't wish to marry him and when the other man returned a few days before the wedding. . . ."

"When did you discover your condition?" Tia asked as she felt Emily's belly.

"In all the upheaval of the marriage, it wasn't until a week ago that I realized I had missed two monthlies."

"I'm surprised you haven't been nauseated until now."

"Every now and then but today was the worst." Emily smiled up at her. "Which is why I am so glad I discovered you at the park."

"Good fortune indeed." Tia took a seat near the bed as Mallory returned with the tea tray.

"My lady, are you unwell?"

"Just tired. That is why we are having tea upstairs." As Mallory placed the tea on the bedside table, Emily asked, "Did you find the peppermint for tea?"

"Yes, my lady. I brought both the peppermint and the black."

"Thank you, Mallory. I shall ring if I need anything more."

Mallory nodded and then departed.

Emily looked over at Tia. "Would you mind pouring today?"

"Of course not." Tia prepared the peppermint tea and then handed it to Emily. "This should calm your stomach." Then she made some black tea for herself. Sitting back against the chair, an odd sense of discomfort overcame her. She needed to drink her tea and return to Middleton's before the dressmaker arrived at noon. It was already eleven, so she must make her excuse rather quickly.

"Where did you learn so much about pregnancy?"

Tia explained how her mother had taught her and her sister from the time they were old enough to follow her around the estate. They would watch her heal people and treat them for sicknesses with herbs.

"It seems so odd to me that your mother would allow you to see people's bare limbs, especially a man's," Emily commented and then sipped her tea.

"Perhaps, but seeing it at a young age takes the fascination out of it. Once you've seen one bare leg, the others are all the same." If only the same could be said of a man's chest. She had never seen a chest like Middleton's, finely muscled down to his belly. And that line of black hair that crossed his chest, down his belly, and disappeared beneath his trousers had fascinated her.

"I suppose that would be true."

Tia placed her teacup down and rose. "I must return to Middleton's home before he becomes concerned." Or irate. But still, she hoped his arm was all right. She needed to check his bandage for signs of infection.

"Are you certain?" Emily asked softly. "I would love to have you stay with me. My darling husband is usually too busy with his mistress to escort me to many of the parties. With you along with me, we could both go. I could introduce you to all the handsome young men and then perhaps you wouldn't need to return to the Midlands ever again."

Tia bit down on her lip in thought. If she stayed with Emily, Middleton wouldn't be able to force her to return. But she couldn't take charity from a woman she'd only just met. "While I would enjoy that, I must decline."

"Why?"

"I shouldn't wish Middleton to worry."

Emily's brows rose. "Indeed? Is he worried about ruining your reputation by having you stay in his home with no proper chaperone?"

Tia laughed. "Emily, no one cares if I am at his home whether I am his mistress or not."

"Are you?"

"No."

"But everyone will assume you are."

Tia shrugged. "I know no one in town. They will just believe he has installed a mistress to his home. Since I will be leaving possibly tomorrow, very few people will even realize I was there."

"Why will you not stay with me?" Emily asked quietly with a slight pout. "Have I offended you in some manner?"

"Of course not! But, Emily, we have only just met this very day. Why would you want a complete stranger in your home? Besides, what would your husband say?"

"Yes, Emily, what would your husband say?" A deep voice sounded from the threshold.

Emily's face brightened. "Eldridge, come meet my new friend," she said, extending her hand outward.

Emily's husband was older than Tia had expected. Gray hairs peppered his dark brown locks, and wrinkle lines around his eyes foretold his age to be much closer to forty than Emily's youthful twenty.

The earl approached the bed and gently kissed his wife's cheek. "Baines said you were not feeling well, so I came up to check on you."

"My new friend has helped me feel much better." Emily quickly introduced them. "I was just trying to convince Miss Featherstone that her reputation might be in jeopardy by staying alone with Viscount Middleton. Wouldn't it be wonderful if she stayed with us? She could accompany me to the parties you are unable to attend. And she could give me someone to talk to while you attend to your duties."

"You are more than welcome to stay with us, Miss Featherstone. For my wife's sake, I hope you will." He gave a quick bow and then left them alone again.

"See," Emily said with a tight smile. "Eldridge would give me anything I desire as long as I don't make a fuss about his mistress."

Tia cringed. This was no marriage.

"Say you will stay with me," Emily implored.

"Middleton will be furious." That alone should make her want to stay with her new friend. After what he did to her last night, he deserved a little retribution. But staying with Emily also would give her access to her friends in Society. This might help her find Jonathon.

"He doesn't have to know you're here," Emily said with a smile.

"I suppose he doesn't."

And if he could not find her, he couldn't force her to return to a position she no longer wished to do. Even as a tingle of worry crept over her, Tia said, "I'll stay."

Chapter 5

Braden woke slowly with a muddled feeling in his mind. He blinked a few times before lifting his hands to rub his eyes. A searing pain tore through his right arm. "Damnation."

Looking over at this arm, he noticed the bandaging and then closed his eyes in an attempt to remember what took place the previous evening. He remembered attending a party and finding Jack. They went to a gaming hell . . . but what happened after that? Dammit, why was his brain so fuzzy this morning? Had he imbibed a bit too much?

He wondered about that for a minute. There was no sign of nausea, no headache, but his arm was aching like the devil and bandaged too. He slowly reached over and rang the bell for a footman. Not more than two minutes had passed before a knock sounded at the door.

"Come in," he said gruffly.

"Good morning, my lord," Nelson said in an unusually soft tone. "Can I get you anything?"

"My memory." Braden eased into a sitting position. "What the bloody hell happened last night?"

"You don't remember, sir?"

"No. I went to a party and then a gaming hell. That is the extent of my memory."

Nelson cleared his throat. "You were shot outside the gaming hell, my lord. Miss Featherstone patched you up. She did a fine job too."

That was not what he wanted to hear. Now he would be indebted to the little hoyden. Nelson's words helped clear some of the cobwebs from his mind. "Thank you, Nelson. Ask Miss Featherstone to come in here. I need to thank her. And bring up some tea and toast."

Nelson stared at his feet.

"What is wrong?"

"Miss Featherstone went for a walk in the park this morning. She told Mrs. Abbott that she would return before noon when the dressmaker is scheduled."

Braden closed his eyes as fury rose from deep within. "You let her go for a walk. How did she even get a gown to wear?"

"Mrs. Abbott felt that since she saved your life, Miss Featherstone should be rewarded with a dress and the ability to get some air," Nelson said softly.

"And since when is Mrs. Abbott in charge of this house?"

Nelson continued to stare at the floor, unable to meet his gaze. "I am terribly sorry, my lord. I should have stopped Miss Featherstone from leaving."

Braden raked his fingers through his hair. "Please tell me she took a maid or footman with her."

"I am sorry, sir. She did not."

"What time is it?"

"Half past eleven. Miss Featherstone should return at any moment."

Braden breathed in deeply to calm his anger. Somehow, he doubted Miss Featherstone would return in a few minutes. "Pull out my clothes, Nelson."

"Yes, my lord." Nelson started to the linen press and stopped. "Did you still want your tea and toast?"

"No, I am going to find Miss Featherstone." And she would rue the mad idea she had to leave his house without his permission.

"What am I to tell her when she returns?"

"To wait for me in my study. And not to leave this house again."

Nelson nodded and quickly assisted him in dressing.

To Braden, the few minutes it took to dress felt like hours passing by. The possibility that she was still in the park was miniscule. The little hoyden was long gone. But perhaps someone had noticed her, if she'd even gone into the park. If he'd seen her walking, he would have noticed her.

What was it about Miss Featherstone that heated his blood and passion? He wanted to put her over his knee for all the bother she'd caused him. And the idea of her over his knee with her bare buttocks in front of him made him think of all the lovely things he could do to her in that position. None of which involved scolding.

Banishing those sordid thoughts, he adjusted his jacket and waited for Nelson to find a hat. Nelson returned quickly with a black hat. He handed it to Braden with a nod.

"I spoke with Michael to get your horse saddled, my lord. I assumed you would prefer that over the carriage."

"Thank you. If Miss Featherstone does return, send Michael to the park to let me know," Braden said curtly.

"Yes, my lord."

"I will also speak with Mrs. Abbott when I get back."

"I will let her know."

Braden nodded and then left the house, ignoring the ache in his arm. Riding might not have been the best idea after all. Entering the park, he scanned the area in front of him. Several people greeted him and a few tried to start a conversation, but Braden wanted no part of that. He'd thought about asking if anyone had seen her, but then realized how odd it would seem to his acquaintances. He made his excuses and returned to searching.

After two hours, he realized his first assumption was correct, Miss Featherstone was not at the park. And he doubted she even visited it today.

He returned to his town home in Berkley Square, all the while wondering where she could have gone. Based on where she'd been staying, she couldn't have much money left. Her friends had deserted her. She had no one here. Guilt assuaged him. Perhaps if he hadn't treated her so poorly last night she might have stayed willingly, but he'd been a complete ass with her.

Still, she should have told him where she was going!

The door opened as he approached. The black mood that had surrounded him earlier returned.

"Did you find her, my lord?" Nelson asked in a cautious tone.

"Do you see her with me?" he replied acerbically.

"No, sir."

"Send Mrs. Abbott to me immediately." He walked the long corridor to his study. "And bring some tea and food."

"Yes, my lord."

Braden wanted to pour a large glass of brandy but knew doing so on an empty stomach would not help him find Miss Featherstone. Instead, he sat down behind his large walnut desk and tapped his fingers on the wood. He was perplexed by her actions. Staying here ensured her safety. After his meal, he would return to the Goat's Horn Inn and if she wasn't there, he'd do as he had before and systematically call on every inn until he found her.

"My lord, you wished to see me?" Mrs. Abbott stood at the threshold, nervously playing with her apron.

"Yes, Mrs. Abbott, please come in and close the door."

The poor woman's face went whiter than the first snow of winter. He supposed he should put her mind at ease, but after the day he'd had due to her poor judgment, he figured she deserved a little worry. "Sit down."

She nodded and then sat in the chair across the desk from him. "My lord, I am dreadfully sorry. She promised me she would just walk to the park and return before noon. If I had ever thought she would run off, I never would have let her go alone."

"Alone? My instructions were she was to have breakfast in her room and wait for the seamstress to bring her some proper clothing."

"Yes, my lord," she mumbled, staring at her feet. "I shall pack my things."

"I don't remember asking you to leave, Mrs. Abbott."

She looked up slowly, her brown eyes as large as saucers. "Thank you, my lord."

"However," he said sternly, "I do expect you to follow my orders."

"Of course, my lord." She nodded her head vigorously. "It will never happen again."

"See that it doesn't."

Mrs. Abbott left quickly, as if afraid he might change his mind. After the footman brought his tea and some food, Braden contemplated the situation at hand. He now had to find two people since the Bow Street runner he hired had discovered no signs of Jonathon in London. It was as if both Jonathon and now Miss Featherstone had just disappeared into the air. But Braden knew they had to be somewhere and London was the most likely place for both of them.

He was determined to find them both. And when he found her, she would regret the day she thought to thwart him.

The next fortnight flew by even as Tia was beginning to feel like a prisoner in this beautiful house. Emily had decided she would introduce Tia to the limited Society still left in London in September. Every day Tia endured fittings for dresses, dance instruction, and etiquette lessons. She had never imagined the life of a lady could be so tiring.

They started at eight in the morning and continued nonstop until luncheon. If Tia were lucky, Emily would tire and need a nap, giving Tia her only break. Once Emily would wake from her nap, they were at it again. Emily explained to her that since most of the ladies of the *ton* would have learned all this over the span of a few years, they had to learn this all in a fortnight.

"Come along, Tia," Emily said, leading her to the ballroom for dancing instruction. "The party is tomorrow night and you must be able to dance every dance."

Tia sighed. For the past few days, she'd tried to no avail to make Emily understand that no one would believe Tia was her cousin from the Midlands. "Emily, this is fruitless. No one is going to dance with me."

Emily only laughed. "Everyone is going to want to dance with you." She dragged Tia into the room.

Mr. Blackwell waited impatiently, tapping his foot. "You should never leave a man waiting for so long," he reprimanded them both.

"I do apologize, Mr. Blackwell. My cousin was detained with an important letter from her mother."

Tia shook her head and gave Emily a curious look. She supposed she should go along with the lie. "Yes, my mother had some news of my sister." If only that were true. She might not miss the Midlands, but she did miss Mia dreadfully. Lately, she'd felt as if something could be wrong with her twin. But that was impossible. Nothing ever happened out there.

"Very well, our last dance to learn is the waltz," Mr. Blackwell stated.

"My cousin has not been given permission to dance the waltz," Emily said quietly.

"That does not matter. She still must learn it."

Tia still did not understand how she must gain permission from some ladies she'd never met in order to dance a simple dance. Emily told her the dance was scandalous because a man held onto her while prancing across the dance floor. Tia doubted it was as bad as Emily stated.

As Mr. Blackwell taught her the dance steps, Tia confirmed her suspicions. The waltz was hardly as scandalous as she'd been told. It was quite an enjoyable dance, but not as strenuous as some of the country dances. By the fourth time, she had mastered the steps and could enjoy the beautiful music that accompanied them.

As their hour of lessons concluded, Tia glanced over at Emily. For the past few minutes, she'd been rather quiet, just sitting on the sofa watching them. Her face had grown quite pale.

"Are you all right, Emily?"

"Just tired. I believe I shall take a nap."

"I will be up in a few minutes to check on you."

Emily nodded and slowly headed to her bedroom. Once Mr. Blackwell departed, Tia walked up to Emily's bedchamber and knocked on the door. "May I come in?"

"Of course."

Tia entered the room and then strolled to the bedroom where Emily lay resting on the bed. "What's wrong, Emily?"

"I'm tired."

"Very well then, why aren't you closing your eyes, trying to sleep?" Tia sat down at the bottom of the large bed.

"I have to tell my husband," Emily whispered.

"Yes, you do. Before long he will notice."

Emily laughed scornfully. "I doubt that. He barely notices anything about me. He rarely visits my bed, preferring the company of his mistress to me."

Tia nodded, not knowing what to say.

"And when he does visit my bed, he makes no effort to pleasure me. My mother confided in me that women can take pleasure from the act, but so far the only time it was pleasurable was the time with . . ." Her voice trailed off, as if realizing she was about to say too much.

Again, Tia could only nod, not having the experience to offer much consolation.

"The act should be pleasurable, shouldn't it?"

This time, she would have to say something. Her mother had also told her that women could enjoy the act with the right man. "I suppose it should," Tia muttered. "Honestly, I wouldn't know."

"You've never been with a man?" Emily smiled sadly. "I am sorry. I shouldn't have assumed you had been with a man before now."

It wouldn't be the first time. Even Jonathon had made the same assumption. "I'm not offended."

"You should be."

"Does your husband know you weren't a virgin when you married him?"

Tears shimmered in her eyes as she nodded. "When he discovered the truth, I admitted what happened, but I lied and told him I knew I wasn't with child. He must have assumed that my incident occurred a few months before I had met him."

"He must have been angry."

Emily nodded quickly. "He was. I think that is why he returned to his mistress so quickly."

Tia now understood why Emily had befriended her so fast. If there was a hint of scandal to her name, she probably had no friends in town. With an insensitive lout of a husband, Emily had no one in which to confide. "Do you love him?"

Staring at the window, she shrugged. "No."

"You have to tell him about the baby, Emily."

"I will tonight," she whispered, then sat up on the bed. "And then tomorrow, we shall go to the party and all the men will fall at your feet."

"As you wish," Tia said. "Take your nap. You and the baby need some sleep."

"I know, but I enjoy your company. Aren't you glad that you decided to take my advice and leave Middleton's home?"

She wanted to agree, but every day she'd thought of him. Had his arm healed well? Had it become infected or poisoned his blood?

"You're not, are you?" Emily whispered.

Tia shrugged. "He was injured before I left, so I worry about him."

"There is more to that look than simple worry."

"I hardly think so. I barely know the man."

"Hmm," Emily said. "It doesn't take long to know if you're attracted to a man."

"Go to sleep, Emily. I am not interested in Middleton in any manner, except his well-being."

"If you say so."

Tia wandered the house for a while before slipping into a chair in the salon with a book. After a few hours, a footman came to announce dinner. She entered the dining room to see only one place set. "Where are the earl and countess?"

A footman smothered a grin. "They have elected to have dinner sent up to their bedchamber."

Bedchamber? This was an interesting turn of events. Perhaps Emily had decided to seduce her husband and then inform him of his impending fatherhood. Tia certainly hoped that was the case. After a lonely dinner, she returned to the salon and her book until the earl walked into the room and closed the door behind him.

"Miss Featherstone, I would like a word with you."

Hearing the commanding tone of his voice, she closed her book without bookmarking the page and then sat up straight. "How can I help you, my lord?"

"My wife informed me that she is with child. Is this true?"

"Yes, my lord."

"And that is one of the reasons she asked you to stay with her, is it not?"

"Yes, my lord. I am a healer and midwife," Tia replied.

The earl started to walk the length of the room. "How far along is she?"

Tia kept a sigh from escaping her lips. The man must suspect his wife of carrying another man's child. "I am not certain, my lord. I would say between two and three months."

"Is it two or three?" he asked roughly.

"It is hard to tell. She is not that far along. I will know more in a few months as the baby grows."

He turned to face her with his cold blue eyes. "She must have told you how many of her monthlies she'd missed."

"Yes, she did, my lord. She told me she'd missed two. However, since I don't know if it was unusual for her to miss a monthly as it is for some women, I can't say for certain exactly how far along she is right now."

He sent her a sardonic grin. "I believe you can, but you are being a good friend to my wife. You might not believe this, but I appreciate that, Miss Featherstone."

"Why did you allow me to stay with your wife?"

"Because she's had a difficult time adjusting to married life and Society. I thought a friend might help her acclimate. While I don't understand this need to show you off to all the unmarried men in London, if it makes her happy, then I shall allow it."

"I see."

"I only have one request, Miss Featherstone." The earl folded his arms over his chest. "Do not let her near Mr. Tavers."

"I beg your pardon?"

He laughed. "You mean she didn't tell you who her first lover was?"

Chapter 6

An entire fortnight had passed with no sign of either Jonathon or Miss Featherstone. It made no sense to Braden that he could not find either one. He hired another Bow Street runner to search for Miss Featherstone, but again it was as if she'd fallen off the earth. Every morning, he rode to a different section of town, hunting for any sign of her. In the evenings, he turned his attention to gaming hells and even a couple of opium dens in his pursuit of Jonathon.

"My lord, a missive has arrived for you."

Thank God, Braden thought as he retrieved the note from the outstretched arms of his footman. This must be a note about Jonathon. The runner said he was getting closer to finding him. "Is the man waiting for a reply?"

"No, my lord. He left the letter and departed."

"Thank you," he said as disappointment filled him. Just scanning his name on the note, he realized this was a woman's script.

You should attend Lady Whitfield's soiree tonight. I believe you might find who you are looking for there.

Braden scoured the note for a signature or even an initial, but there was nothing to indicate who'd sent the missive. A slow smile lifted his lips. Someone knew where Jonathon was and wanted Braden to find him. And by the handwriting, that someone was a woman. He would have to thank her properly, whoever she was.

He rifled through the papers on his desk until he found the invitation that had arrived earlier in the week. The party was to start at eight. That gave him just enough time to dress and check out a gambling hell before arriving. He strode upstairs to prepare.

One hour later, he had bathed and dressed for a party. He ate a quick bite of dinner to keep him satisfied until he arrived at Lady Whitfield's Grosvenor Square home. As he placed his fork back down on his plate, he heard a commotion at the entryway. Nelson's heavy footsteps quickly followed.

"My lord, the Duke of Northrop is in the salon."

North was here? He pushed back his chair and headed to the salon. "North? What are you doing here?" Braden shook his head. "Please excuse my manners. Would you like a sherry or brandy?"

"Brandy," North replied.

Braden poured two snifters and handed one to his friend. "Sit. What is new in the Midlands? Did you finally have enough of the estate and decide to return to town?"

North smiled. "Not quite. I thought my wife should see London."

Braden's mouth gaped. He'd been gone less than a month! "Your wife?"

"Selina."

"You married your wise woman?"

"Yes, I did."

"How? When? Why?"

"You're sputtering, Middleton. A few weeks ago and the *how* was the usual manner by special license. And the *why* is because I love her." North took a large mouthful of brandy and smiled. "Excellent stuff. I am actually here on a mission."

Braden shook his head to clear his mind of the bewilderment of his friend falling in love again. He tilted his head with a grin "Oh?"

"Mrs. Featherstone wanted me to inquire if you have found her daughter yet."

Should he even bother telling North that he let the girl slip away?

It would only make him look foolish. "No, not yet. The friend she was staying with had been evicted before Miss Featherstone arrived."

"And you have no other leads?" North asked with a frown.

"Unfortunately, no."

"You do know about Miss Featherstone—excuse me, Miss Mia Featherstone."

Braden nodded. "How is she?"

"Recovering quite well, according to Selina."

That bit of good news assuaged his guilt for not telling Tia about her sister the day he'd found her. Perhaps if he had, she would have returned to the estate without issue.

"Excellent," Braden finally remarked.

North finished his brandy and placed the glass on the table next to him. "I won't take up any more of your time. Good luck finding her."

"How long are you in town for?"

"We're leaving in the morning. Selina felt guilty for leaving Mrs. Featherstone with the work of three estates."

"I see. Tell Mrs. Featherstone that I haven't given up just yet. I will find her."

"Thank you."

As soon as the duke departed, Braden ordered his carriage to be readied. He left the house soon after, feeling frustrated at his inability to find either his brother or his wise woman. With North's arrival, he'd lost too much time to search a gaming hell, so instead he proceeded directly to the party. Hopefully, he would get some good news tonight.

The line to Lady Whitfield's party was far longer than usual for a late-summer fete. Finally able to disembark the carriage, he walked up the steps and a butler opened the door for him.

"Good evening, my lord," he said, as if recognizing Braden.

"Thank you," Braden said, removing his hat.

"Fitzworth, my lord. If you need anything while you're here, just let me know."

"Very well." How odd. The man was quite odd indeed. Perhaps he treated all the guests in the same manner, but somehow Braden doubted that.

With a shrug, he walked into the salon and searched the room for the woman who might have sent him the note. He had nothing to go on, not even an initial. As a footman paused by him, Braden snatched a glass of brandy and then sipped it slowly. Down the hall, the sounds of music told him the dancing had begun. But he had no interest in dancing. If Jonathon was in attendance, he would be in the gaming room.

Fighting the crush of people, he walked down the corridor and glanced into the ballroom. A flash of red hair caught his attention, but he lost it just as fast. Braden almost laughed at the idea of Miss Featherstone being here. It was absurd indeed.

The gaming room was set up in the library. He entered the room but once more Jonathon was not here. At least, not yet. Braden decided to sit and play a few games. Perhaps in time, Jonathon would arrive.

"Middleton, I'd heard you were back in London."

Braden stifled the urge to roll his eyes as his cousin Alistair sat down next to him. "Tavers," he said with a nod before turning his gaze back to his cards.

"What brings you back to town?"

"Just a little business to clean—I mean, clear up. How are my cousins?"

"Constance has been full of herself since marrying the baron a few weeks ago. Louisa is heading for the shelf. At two and twenty and four seasons out, she seems destined to spinsterhood."

"Well, that is a shame. Between the both of them Louisa was the kinder of the two."

"There is nothing wrong with marrying your cousin, you know. She would make a wonderful viscountess. Unless you have your sights on someone else?"

"Perhaps I do. After all, I must keep the family name intact, do I not?"

"Yes," Alistair said with a cough. "You must at that. If you need an extra footman or maid while in town, please let me know. I'm quite sure we could do without for however long you are in town. How long might that be?"

"I'm quite well suited with the servants, thank you. And I haven't decided how long I shall be in town. It depends on the business to which I must attend." Why was Alistair so curious about his affairs all of a sudden? He'd never taken an interest in anything he or Jonathon had done in the past. Most of the time, he'd been more interested in their uncle and his heir Randolph. Perhaps his cousin was just trying to get on his good side now that he was the viscount.

"Did Jonathon join you?" Alistair said, placing his cards down on the table in defeat.

"No."

"Oh." Alistair picked up his drink and leaned closer. "I've heard those rumors circulating about, but I have supported you completely. I know you had nothing to do with the untimely deaths of our uncle and cousin."

"I thank you for that, Tavers." So the rumor mill was still churning out the same rubbish. If he ever found out who started that rumor, he'd kill them.

Tia couldn't stop her hand from trembling even an hour after they arrived at the party. She had heard stories of how the balls of the upper crust were so stunningly beautiful, but nothing prepared her for this party. Every woman wore a silk gown in amazing colors and the men were terribly handsome in their finery. Glancing about the room, there had to be at least seven footmen serving people drinks and checking on the refreshment table.

"Just remember, you do not introduce yourself to anyone," Emily whispered as two women approached. "I will introduce you as my cousin from the Midlands."

Tia nodded.

"Lady Eldridge, how lovely to see you," the slightly older woman drawled. "And just who is this?" she asked with a direct look to Tia.

"Miss Hestia Featherstone," Emily replied in a confident tone. "She is my cousin from the Midlands." Emily turned to Tia. "Tia, this is Lady Bunworth and her sister, Miss Louisa Tavers."

Tavers? As in Middleton and Jonathon? Tia's mind fluttered with questions. She knew Jonathon had no sisters so there was no relationship in that manner, but could they be cousins? Perhaps they had some knowledge of Jonathon's whereabouts. She longed to ask them, but glancing over at Emily there was a slight shake to her head, as if she knew exactly what Tia was thinking.

"It is a pleasure to meet you both," Tia said in a demure tone. There was something about these two, especially Lady Bunworth, that she didn't like. While her mother had always told her not to make sweeping decisions based on a first impression, something told Tia that Lady Bunworth would never be friends with either her or Emily.

Lady Bunworth nodded in a condescending manner as if she was better than any of them. As Tia looked at her, she realized Lady Bunworth couldn't be more than twenty-three at most. And yet, she held herself up as far more superior in every way.

"It is a pleasure to meet you too," Miss Tavers murmured.

"I do not remember seeing you at any of the Seasons in the past"—Lady Bunworth paused, looking Tia over from head to toe—"well, shall we say, the last few years."

"I—"

"Unfortunately, my dear cousin hasn't had the opportunity," Emily interrupted quickly. She leaned in closer and whispered, "Poor dear, one death after another in her family. First her father and then her dear mother became sick, so she was caring for her. And then Mrs. Featherstone succumbed."

"Oh, my," Miss Tavers whispered in return. "I am dreadfully sorry for all the losses, Miss Featherstone."

Tia blinked as if holding back tears. "Thank you. It has been a difficult few years."

"But now, you're free to enjoy all that Society can bring," Miss Tavers said brightly.

"I suppose I am." Tia sipped her lemonade, wishing it were a glass of wine. Emily had insisted on no spirits to muddle the mind. How could Tia bring up Jonathon's name without admitting she knew him? That would only draw suspicion to her and possibly ruin the sham of a background Emily had created for her.

"You must dance with my brother, Alistair," Miss Tavers announced. "I shall find him at once."

"Louisa . . ." Lady Bunworth tried to intercede, but Miss Tavers had left just as quickly as she'd made her proclamation. "Good evening, Lady Eldridge, Miss Featherstone."

Emily giggled once Lady Bunworth left them in peace. "I truly have never liked that woman. Miss Tavers is a fine person."

"Are they related to Middleton?"

"Oh dear," Emily whispered. "They are cousins but I don't believe they are close. You shouldn't worry that they will speak of you to Middleton. Lady Bunworth would consider you unworthy of mention."

"And her brother?"

"Handsome enough." Emily frowned. "There have been some rumors about his fortune lately. He never had much to start and recently let go his valet."

Tia wanted to slam her hand against her forehead. "But is he close to Middleton?"

"Tia, you must stop worrying over Middleton. I am sure no one will speak of you being here to him."

Tia supposed Emily had a point. "Should I dance with Lady Bunworth's brother, then?"

"Of course. The more men who see you on the dance floor, the more attractive you will seem to them."

"Why?"

"Because the more you dance, the more other men will see something in you that makes you worthy to take to the floor."

Tia felt as if she'd stepped into another world. A world that made no sense to her. She watched in fascination as a man close to her in age strode toward them. He was, as Emily said, handsome with sandy brown hair, cut neatly short. He smiled as he approached.

"Lady Eldridge, my sister insisted I come over and greet you," he said in a warm tone.

"Mr. Tavers, it is lovely to see you again. This is my cousin, Miss Hestia Featherstone."

Mr. Tavers faced her and bowed over her hand. "It is a pleasure indeed, Miss Featherstone."

"Thank you, Mr. Tavers." Tia knew she had to pry a little about the family name to see if he knew anything about Jonathon. It was tricky business because she couldn't admit to knowing him. "Tavers? I feel I know that name from somewhere."

Emily shot her a glare. "A common enough name, Tia."

"Most of my family originates from the Midlands," Mr. Tavers said with a touch of pride to his voice. "Viscount Middleton is my cousin."

"That must be it, then. I am from the Midlands and have heard the name." Tia smiled at him.

"The musicians are starting the next set. Would you care to dance?"

Tia slid a glance to Emily, who nodded. "That would be lovely, thank you."

She linked arms with him and allowed him to guide her to the dance floor. Nervousness slid through her—not at the idea of dancing with Mr. Tavers—but it was the idea of dancing at all that had her apprehensive. How would it look if she forgot the steps? She would embarrass Emily in front of the people she wanted as friends, though Tia wasn't sure why Emily wanted any of these ladies as friends.

She took her place across from Mr. Tavers. He smiled at her as the country dance started. Tia concentrated on her steps while Mr. Tavers attempted to make conversation as they came together and then apart. She honestly had no idea what he was trying to say. The steps were complicated and it took all her mind to focus on that. Unable to determine his conversation over the music and concentration, she only smiled up at him and nodded occasionally.

Finally, the music ended and he escorted her back to Emily. "I shall wait impatiently for our next dance, Miss Featherstone."

As he walked away, Emily giggled and said, "You made quite the impression. Did you really promise him a second dance?"

"I have no idea. I couldn't hear a word he was saying."

Emily laughed. "Oh, Tia. Just remember no more than two dances."

"You have drummed that into my head all week." She looked across the room and noticed a man with dark hair paused at the door. For a quick moment, the figure in mostly black reminded her of Middleton.

"Come along, Tia," Emily said, pulling Tia out of her musing. "We should get some more refreshments.

They walked toward the dining room where the table and side-board was lined with food. "Emily, would Middleton attend a party such as this?"

Emily gave a nervous laugh. "I highly doubt it. This party is far too tame for a man like Middleton."

"Whatever do you mean?" Tia asked as she picked up a stuffed mushroom and added it to her plate.

"He always ran with a fast crowd."

"What do you mean?" She ignored Emily's look of disdain and grabbed a glass of wine from a passing footman. She sipped the wine slowly, savoring the fruity taste as it warmed its way down her belly.

"Middleton prefers the loose women and gambling hells to a se-date party like this. Besides, you must know that many people be-lieve he had something to do with the death of the former viscount and his heir."

"That cannot be true. I heard both deaths were accidental."

"I'm afraid that is what the gossips are saying about him. It has damaged his reputation—not that it was sterling before the rumors."

Tia had heard the rumors of his rakish ways from the servants at Middleton Hall, but she couldn't imagine him committing murder to become the viscount. She must have imagined seeing him in the hall. She took another sip of wine and strolled back to the ballroom. Not wanting to draw attention to herself, she slipped behind a large plant for a moment of peace.

"Did you see Miss Bingham?" a woman said to another woman on the other side of the plant.

"That gown is hideous on her," replied another. "What was she thinking wearing pink at her age?"

"She is almost three and twenty!"

"And firmly on the shelf."

One of the women laughed coarsely. "No man will have her now."

"I also heard she had been seen kissing Lord Ranston in the li-brary of Lady Somerfield's home."

"But Lord Ranston is a married man!"

"Exactly."

Tia strolled away, shaking her head. Staring at all the people danc-ing, she briefly wondered why anyone wanted to be a part of this. The people were gossipy wasps who only seemed to want to sting each other. A part of her missed her quiet life on Middleton's estate. The only time people gossiped was to let her know that they had heard someone might be ill and was not calling for her.

With a sigh, she took another sip of wine. Melancholy struck a chord deep inside her. She could return to the estate, but then she might never find Jonathon and try to help him. Then again, she'd been in London for over a month and hadn't caught even a glimpse of the man. During all the upheaval of the past week, she'd almost forgotten her true mission.

"There you are," Emily said with a smile and a short man behind her. "Lord Upton wanted to meet you."

Of course he did. And what would Lord Upton think if he knew he was dancing with a nobody from the Midlands with no name, no fortune, and nothing to offer him? "Good evening, my lord."

"We must hurry if we are to make the dance. The couples are lining up already."

It wasn't until she reached the dance floor that she realized he hadn't even asked her, he'd just assumed she would be eternally grateful to dance with him because he was a lord. As they clasped hands to circle around each other, Tia thanked God the man wore gloves. Even through the cotton cloth, she could feel the sweat from his palms. If this was what all the ladies of the Beau Monde put up with, no wonder so many decided to stay spinsters.

She danced the steps of the contra dance with ease, since it was the first and therefore the most practiced of the dances Mr. Blackwell had taught her.

"You look quite fetching tonight, my dear," Lord Upton commented.

"Thank you."

"I believe I should call on Lady Eldridge tomorrow. I do hope you shall be at home."

What was she supposed to say to that? *Don't bother? I have no interest?* She had no idea. "I believe I shall be at home," she said and then wanted to glue her lips shut for saying such an insipid thing. She should have been blunt with him.

"Excellent."

Until he mentioned it, she hadn't thought about the fact that men might attempt to call on her at Emily's home. Some might even suggest a ride through the park. There had to be a way to stop this.

As she circled around him, she had the strangest sensation of being watched. She scanned the room as she twirled around. One set of blue eyes fixed on her. Even from this distance she knew his eyes were blue. Icy cold blue.

Her heart raced in her chest as the dance ended. Lord Upton escorted her back to Emily, chattering on about seeing her tomorrow. She could only nod as she attempted to find an escape route away from Middleton. Glancing back, she realized she'd lost his position.

"Emily, I must leave," she said, trying to interrupt her friend from a conversation with another woman.

"Not now, Tia."

"Yes, now." Before it was too late. Unable to wait a second longer, she headed for the hall. If she could get out of the house before he noticed, she might make it. But make it where? If he'd seen her with Emily, then she couldn't return to her friend's home. Where would she go?

Only a few steps before the threshold, a strong hand clasped onto her arm. Without looking, she knew he'd caught her yet again.

"Going before we've even had a dance?"

Chapter 7

Braden turned Tia around to face him. Awareness shot through him with her close proximity. What the bloody hell was wrong with him that he could find his wise woman attractive? Scanning her, he noticed everything from her upswept red curls, down her long slender neck that begged for his lips, to the swell of her full breasts exposed from a pale blue silk gown, and further down her slender belly and curve of her hips. The real question was how had he *not* noticed her while at the estate.

"Well?"

"I—I was not feeling well and decided to leave," she said in a shaky tone.

"Tsk-tsk, Miss Featherstone. A viscount wishes to dance with you and so we shall."

Her mouth opened and closed slightly, as if getting ready to rebuke him, but no words managed to emanate forth. He had timed his appearance at her side perfectly as the musicians were to play a waltz next.

"I don't know how to dance this dance," she muttered as they walked through the crowd.

"Indeed, and what are the musicians about to play?"

The confused look on her face almost made him laugh. She didn't have any idea of what was coming up next.

"I just haven't learned that many dances, is all," she said.

"You did just fine with Lord Upton." He stopped and stared down at her. "And why in God's name did you dance with that man?"

"I didn't seem to have any choice in the matter. We were introduced and then he was escorting me to the dance floor." She glared up at him. "Not much different than you."

He leaned and inhaled the sweet, intoxicating scent of jasmine. "Oh, but we were already introduced." He turned and pulled her closer as the crowd tightened around them. Finally, space opened as they reached the dance floor.

"So what is the dance?" she asked.

He dragged her closer until their bodies almost touched. "The waltz."

Her eyes widened. "Emily told me I could not dance the waltz until I am given approval by Lady Jersey."

"We can't wait until next Season for approval." Because nothing was going to stop him from dancing a waltz with her tonight. The music started and he led her with ease. "I do believe you lied to me."

"Oh?"

"You most definitely know how to waltz." He stared down at her brown eyes and felt mesmerized by the amber flecks, reminding him of a fine sherry. "And would this Emily be Lady Eldridge?"

She nodded. "Yes."

Of all the women, she had to meet Emily. "Do tell me how a wise woman from the Midlands is suddenly befriended by a countess."

"We met at the park the day . . ."

He smirked. "The day you left me?"

She frowned. "You make it sound almost scandalous."

"Smile, my dear. We are the talk of the party."

Her brown eyes widened. "No." She quickly glanced around. "Why would one dance with you cause such talk?"

"Don't you know how notorious I am?"

"You're nothing more than a rake, like most of the men your age," she retorted.

"Perhaps Lady Eldridge should have given you more information about the man you slept with."

She stiffened. "I did not sleep with you."

"That is not what every man and woman would think if they discovered you had stayed overnight in my home."

"Servants stay in your home every night and no one accuses them of sleeping with you." She tilted her chin, as if in her mind she had won that argument. "Even if they do."

"I never sleep with the servants. Besides, servants don't comport themselves at parties and befriend countesses." He scanned her body again. "And no one would think you are a servant after tonight."

Her cheeks reddened slightly. "I'm not sure if I should thank you or slap you."

"Both are options," he said seductively. He leaned in and whispered, "But I get to tell you where you will slap me."

"You go too far, Middleton."

"Nowhere near far enough."

Her lips gaped slightly. "I believe our dance is over."

"Excellent," he said, clasping her upper arm. "Then we can leave now."

She stopped on the dance floor. "I am not leaving with you."

"Yes, you are."

"You cannot force me," Tia said in an overly confident tone.

The poor woman had no idea just what he could do. Without a second thought, he brought her up against his body and leaned down to kiss her. She struggled against him, but it was no use. Braden was stronger and that short kiss did exactly what he'd intended.

"How dare you!"

The pain in his cheek faded almost as quickly as her hand moved away. "You are coming home with me."

"I will be ruined."

"You already are," he said coldly. "The servants will talk with other servants as soon as they hear you attended this ball. Word of your stay at my house will be all over London in less than a week."

Her hand covered her mouth as tears filled her eyes.

"Tia, what is going on?" Lady Eldridge said, arriving far too late to help.

"Lady Eldridge, Miss Featherstone will be leaving your home tonight," he said softly so no one else would overhear them. "She belongs back in the Midlands."

"She has no place to go." Lady Eldridge turned to face him. "How dare you humiliate her like this!"

"I will do whatever I please. She is my wise woman and is returning home."

"No—"

"Emily, it's all right," Tia said in a resigned tone. "I don't belong here."

Lady Eldridge looked at Tia. "If you go with him you will be ruined."

"I already am," she said, glancing around the room. "Look at the disaster I made."

"He made it, not you."

"Come along, Miss Featherstone." Braden held out his arm for her. He should feel remorse for his actions tonight, and yet, he refused to allow those emotions in. Her own mother had sent him on this mission and he had finished the job tonight and would see her off in the morning.

She ignored his arm and marched out of the room before he could take a step. He started forward, only to be stopped by Lady Eldridge.

"This is not how I intended the night to go."

"Good evening, Lady Eldridge." What the bloody hell had she meant by that? He strolled out of the room, but suddenly looked back at her. People crowded around her asking her all sorts of questions. She smiled at them all and whatever she'd said seemed to quiet them down.

She had sent the note.

She had wanted him to find Tia here.

Why?

He continued out of the room to find Tia standing in the front hall as a footman handed her shawl to her. She walked outside before he had reached the entrance. "Miss Featherstone, it may take a few moments for my carriage to be brought around. You might wish to wait inside."

"No."

Braden took the shawl from her hands and wrapped it around her shoulders. "There. It's getting chilly tonight. You would be more comfortable inside."

"You ruined me. Deliberately. I could never set foot in a home like that again."

He laughed. "How little you know, Miss Featherstone. All it takes is marriage to the right man and they will beg you to come back. It would be as if nothing ever happened."

"It matters not. You will force me back to the Midlands where I will live a dull life of healing the sick and never finding . . ."

"Never finding what?" He was genuinely curious about what she wanted out of life.

"Love," she whispered, then brushed a tear aside.

Damn. Guilt spread over him like honey, sticking to him and making him unclean. He had set out to ruin her, knowing it was the only way to make her return. It was far from the worst thing he'd ever done, and yet, he did feel dreadful. "I am sorry."

She laughed in a coarse tone so unlike her. "I highly doubt that. You got what you wanted."

The carriage pulled up in front of the house. Braden escorted her to the coach. After assisting her, he jumped in and took the seat across from her. A part of him wanted to talk with her and another knew it was no use. Nothing he could say would make her feel better tonight.

Tomorrow he would tell her about her sister. If he told her now, she would demand they leave immediately and that wasn't the safest course of action. It could wait until tomorrow.

Tension filled the carriage on the short ride home. He wondered if she planned to resume their argument once they reached the house. They rolled to a stop. The coach door opened and Braden scrambled down. He held out his hand to assist Tia. She took it only long enough to reach the ground, and then pulled away as if she'd been burned.

She strode in the house and straight to his study.

"Good evening, my lord," Nelson said, taking Braden's hat. "It appears Miss Featherstone has returned. Shall I have the same bedroom made up for her?"

"Yes. Thank you, Nelson."

"Of course, my lord."

"It might get loud in the study. She was not particularly happy to be found." Braden shot his butler a grin. "Just ignore the noise and send the servants to bed once her room is made up. I will snuff the candles before I head up to bed."

"Of course, my lord. Good luck."

"I will need it." Braden headed to the study, but then stopped at the threshold. Tia poured a glass of brandy and tossed it back like a sailor. Then she poured herself another. "Drinking like that won't solve your problem."

She gulped down another and then turned to stare at him. "You're still standing there, so I suppose you are right."

"I am not your problem, Tia."

"Do you see any other person here trying to bring me back to a life I don't want?"

After pouring herself another, she sat down and sipped from her glass of brandy. Braden walked over to pour a snifter for himself. "The estate needs you. Your family needs you."

She pointed to him as she shook her head. "Now, that's where you are wrong, my lord. My mother doesn't need me. She is the one who thought I should take over your estate alone, while my sister was able to stay and continue to learn from her."

"Perhaps she felt you were ready to leave the nest."

"Ha! She wanted me gone." Tia took another sip of her brandy.

Braden collapsed into the chair across from her with a heavy sigh. He supposed he should be grateful she seemed to have moved away from his ruination of her. "If she wanted you gone so badly, why did she storm into my study and insist I run off to London and find you?"

She pressed her full lips together with a shake of her head. "I don't know. Perhaps it was a show to make you believe that she cared. Or maybe it was because she doesn't have time to take care of your tenants."

"Tia, I know deep in your heart that you do not believe such nonsense. It's the brandy talking."

"Hardly." As if to prove him wrong, she took another long drink of the heady spirit. "Mia was her favorite. Always has been."

"Is that why you left?" he asked softly. Perhaps her departure had nothing to do with Jonathon.

She rolled her eyes before finishing her drink. "No. It was all about your brother." She cocked a reddish brow at him. Her eyes held a glossy spark, showing the effects of the brandy. "I love your brother, can't you see it? Isn't that the real reason you chased after me? To stop me from seducing him." She rose, slightly unsteadily, and then poured herself another brandy before refilling his glass. A few drops landed on his breeches. "Of course," she began again, "I would never be acceptable as his wife, therefore the only logical explanation of why I went after him was to become his lover, right?"

Braden usually found drunken women rather unappealing, but there was something about Tia's current state of drunkenness that was quite humorous and slightly endearing. "I believe you may have had enough to drink for the night, Tia."

"When did I say you could call me by my given name? It's dreadfully scandalous, you know." She took another sip and dropped back into her chair.

"You are going to have a horrible headache tomorrow."

"Good," she said with another sip. "With any luck, I will be retching all over you in the coach. Perhaps that would make you turn back for London."

Braden tilted his head back and laughed. "Let us hope you have no luck, then. I would prefer to have a vomitless trip."

She sipped the rest of her brandy. Rising slowly from her chair, she released the pins holding her glorious red curls. "Perhaps there might be another way to convince you to stay here for a few more days."

The drunken seductress. He had never met one he couldn't push away . . . but as his cock rose tight against his breeches, he doubted his willpower. She approached him slowly. He wondered just how far she would take her act.

"So tell me, Middleton, what would it take?"

"You tell me, Tia? How far would you be willing to go?"

Slowly, she stripped off her elbow-length white gloves. "As far as it takes." She strained to reach the three buttons on the back of her gown.

"Would you like some assistance?" he asked with a half-grin. He was playing a dangerous game with a woman whose mind was hazed from alcohol, and yet he couldn't stop himself.

" I have it." She put her arms down and shook them out. She closed her eyes for a long moment before opening them with an overly bright smile. "I'm just a little dizzy."

"Brandy will do that to you."

She let the blue silk fall to the floor. "And what will you do for me?"

Bloody hell, the woman had a body made for a man's touch. Her full breasts pushed up from the stays. Her nipples were already straining against the white cotton of her shift.

"You're not moving," she commented.

"No, I'm not." He could barely move with his shaft so hard. "This is all up to you, Tia."

Her erotic smile almost made him come. "Is it?"

He shouldn't encourage her. A sane man would stop her now before things went too far. "Think long and hard before coming any closer. I cannot promise to be a gentleman."

She giggled softly. "I have never heard you were a gentleman, my lord." She took a step closer. "A rake. A defiler of innocents. That is what you are."

"Never that," he interjected.

"A man who takes whatever he wants." She straddled his lap and innocently pressed herself against him. "A man who knows how to pleasure a woman," she whispered near his ear.

"Now that I am," he said closer to her ear before running his tongue along the outer shell. "I can bring a woman to the wondrous heights of a climax several times in one night."

She shivered. "How wondrous?"

"Too wondrous for words." He kissed the long length of her neck until she moaned softly. "Tell me the truth, Tia. Did you enjoy that brief kiss on the dance floor? Did it excite you? Did the idea of such a scandalous thing make you wet?"

Her head fell back as he moved his lips along her jaw. "Yes," she whispered. "I hated you for it, though."

"Good, you should have. But no one will see us here." He cupped her cheeks with his hands and brought her lips to his. Perhaps he'd had too much brandy because he couldn't remember the last time an innocent kiss made him react so passionately. He moved his hands to her back to press her soft breasts against his chest. The urge to rip her clothes off and take her right here was becoming the most important thing in his mind.

He should push her away. Even as he had that morally righteous thought, her mouth gaped, allowing him entrance to her mouth. It was something he took full advantage of, and with a swift movement his tongue brushed against hers.

Her soft moan undid him. Suddenly nothing else mattered except being deep inside her warmth, showing her the pleasure a woman could feel with a man. She tasted like brandy as her tongue wrestled with his for dominance. God, she would be a spirited lover. One who could give as well as take. And damned if he didn't want her now.

Unable to stop himself, he lowered her shift until those beautiful breasts were exposed to the chill in the room. He pulled away from the allure of her lips to stare at her blue-veined breasts.

"How did that happen?" she said with a giggle, looking down at her exposed breasts.

"I did it."

"Why?"

The little slur in her voice told him this couldn't go on very long. He'd never forgive himself if he took her innocence when she wasn't able to fully give it. Still, it didn't stop him from drawing a taut nipple into his mouth and savoring the sensation.

Her hips pushed against his hard cock as she moaned softly. Dear God, he wanted to hear her moans as she climaxed. He had to stop this madness. Slowly, he drew away and stared at the wanton on his lap. Her red hair fell in curls to past her breasts. Her full lips were slightly swollen from the kisses she had enjoyed. Her eyes were half-shuttered as if she'd already come, but he knew that was just the drink.

Slowly, she lowered her head to his shoulder. "I don't think you're all that bad, Middleton."

"Oh, I am," he replied softly. "That and more."

Chapter 8

The sunlight hit Tia directly in the eyes, forcing a cry of pain from her. "Oh, who left the dratted curtains open?" Slowly, she cracked her eyes open and noticed it was only a slight part in the curtains that had caused the agony in her head. But the curtains that hung in Emily's guest bedchamber were pale yellow. These were blue. A beautiful dark blue velvet with gold roping along the edges.

"Where am I?"

She glanced about the room, but didn't recognize anything in particular, though it seemed strangely familiar to her. As if she'd been here before. But when?

She lay back against the bed and closed her eyes. What happened last night? She had danced with a few gentlemen, had only one glass of wine, and then . . .

"Middleton."

Pieces of the evening came back to her. She remembered dancing with him and how he kissed her in the middle of the dance floor. Then she agreed to come back to his house, didn't she? Or had he abducted her? She shook her head slowly as pain hammered her head. Brandy. She should have known better. They came back to his study and she had several glasses of brandy. Had Middleton been a gentleman, he would have stopped her.

What happened after the brandy?

A thought niggled her mind. Something profound happened after she drank all that brandy, but what?

"Miss Featherstone, may I come in now?"

"Yes."

Mrs. Abbott walked in with some gowns in her hands. "You have a visitor."

"At this hour?"

"It's noon, Miss Featherstone."

Tia sat up in bed and then rubbed her forehead. "Noon? Why did I sleep so long?"

"The viscount told me to let you sleep. That you'd had a difficult night."

Mrs. Abbott dropped some pins on the nightstand. "Mary found these on the floor of his lordship's study."

Tia's eyes grew large. "His study?" Memories of removing her pins and then her dress flooded her mind. "Oh God, did I . . ."

Mrs. Abbott gave a disapproving look. "Only you and he can answer that question."

"I couldn't have. I wouldn't have done that . . . not with him!"

"You don't remember?" Mrs. Abbott put away the dresses and then pulled a green muslin out to wear.

"No, I was angry with him. We came back here and I drank too much brandy. It's all a blur."

"Then you'd best ask him."

"But I would remember if I lost my innocence, wouldn't I?"

The housekeeper shook her head. "I suppose you would."

"Don't you know?" Tia knew she was starting to sound frantic. "You were married at one time."

"No, Miss Featherstone. Housekeepers just get to call themselves as if they are married as a sign of respect."

"Oh."

"Now come along, you have a caller."

"Who is here?"

"Lady Eldridge. She returned the dresses you left at her house." She helped Tia out of bed and removed her shift before placing a clean one over her head. "You gave us all a scare leaving like that. I thought for certain his lordship was going to sack me."

"I'm dreadfully sorry about that, Mrs. Abbott. I never imagined how it might affect you."

"No, you didn't."

Tia stared down at her hands. If Mrs. Abbott had lost her position because of Tia's impetuousness, she never would have been able to forgive herself. "I am sorry, Mrs. Abbott."

"Just see that it doesn't happen again." Mrs. Abbott draped the green muslin over Tia's head. "I cannot afford to lose this position."

"I understand."

"How did he find you?"

"We were at the same party."

Mrs. Abbott laughed. "How did you get in Lady Eldridge's good graces?"

"I met her that day at the park. She wasn't terribly feeling well, so I offered to assist her. Then she offered to let me stay with her. I think she wanted a friend."

"And she let you attend a party? You?" The housekeeper put up Tia's hair into a soft chignon.

"Yes."

"Hmm." She placed one more pin in Tia's hair. "You are all set. I already ordered tea."

"Thank you, Mrs. Abbott."

Tia walked down the stair slowly so her stomach wouldn't roil. Her head ached with every step. She walked into the salon and smiled at Emily. "Emily, I am surprised you are here."

"Oh, Tia," she said, then rushed to hug her. "Are you all right? You look dreadfully pale. Has he hurt you?"

"Shh, Emily." She pulled away and sat down. "I am fine, but feeling the effect of too much brandy."

"He got you foxed?"

"No, if my limited memory serves me, I did that all on my own."

Thankfully, Emily reached for the tea and poured. "Here. This might help."

The tea washed over her tongue and warmed her belly. "Thank

you. And you should not have returned those gowns. They were yours and the few new ones your husband paid for."

Emily waved a hand at her. "Nonsense. You need something to wear and my husband will never miss the money."

"Thank you again." Tia sipped her tea. "I suppose I am all anyone is talking about."

"That would be true. Everyone assumes you are his mistress since many know you went home with him. It's not good, Tia. You will never be accepted in polite company."

"I know. He did that on purpose to get me to return to the estate and my position there. I have no choice now. I'm only surprised that he didn't wake me at dawn for the drive back."

"I heard another rumor that I thought you might be interested in hearing. There was some scrape at a gaming hell last night and they say Mr. Tavers was involved."

"Jonathon? At a gaming hell?" Oh dear, if that were true, things might be worse for him than she imagined. "Which gaming hell, do you know?"

"The Red Door."

Tia had never heard of such a place, but she knew nothing about the gaming hells. "Where is it located?"

"Why? You cannot go to a gaming hell."

"Perhaps Middleton would like to know."

Emily sipped her tea with a frown. "I see. I don't know for certain, but I heard it was near St. George's. I am certain Middleton is aware of the place."

"I will make sure he knows." She wasn't certain about that. But if she could just manage to find out more about this place, it might help her find him.

"If you need to leave, you are welcome back at my home."

"I doubt your husband will want me back at his house," Tia reminded her.

"Leave that to me." Emily gave her a secret smile.

Tia could tell something must have happened. "Are things better between you?"

"Yes. His mistress decided to move on to another man. And since I told him I'm with child, he is convinced I am having his heir."

"Emily, is it true that the other man you believe might be the child's father is Mr. Tavers?" Tia hated asking the question, but had to know.

"W—where did you hear such a thing?"

"From the earl. He told me he didn't want you near Mr. Tavers."

Emily blinked back tears and nodded. "It was late June. He was so sweet, Tia. I couldn't help but fall in love with him. And he told me he loved me too."

June. He came out to the Middleton Hall in late June. After he had gotten Emily with child. Tia blinked back her own tears as sadness and frustration overcame her. The man she thought she loved had already given his heart to Emily. Jonathon had only been giving her false praise to befriend her.

It should bother her more that the man she loved had gotten a woman with child. And yet, for some reason it didn't. She had loved him, hadn't she? Shouldn't she feel more angst? Feel a torrent of anger toward him? Shouldn't she be ready to throw herself off a bridge because she had lost the love of her life? Or perhaps she had read too many romance novels and only thought herself in love with him.

"I really must leave now. I will call on you when I can." Emily rose and left Tia with her headache.

Braden stared at the papers in front of him, but he saw nothing. His mind constantly played back his interaction with Tia last evening. She was far too dangerous to his sanity. The only option was to get her back to the estate as soon as possible. If she hadn't fallen asleep on him, he wasn't certain what he might have done. He couldn't remember the last time he felt such a strong desire for a woman. If ever.

But he couldn't touch her. Not just because she was his wise woman. He had promised himself that he was done with his rakish ways. No matter how tempting he found her.

"My lord, Mr. Brady is here."

"Thank you, Nelson. Show him in here."

He wondered why the runner would call on him this morning. He'd already sent a note around, stating he'd found Tia. Perhaps he owed the man more than he thought.

"Good afternoon, my lord," Mr. Brady said as he entered the room. "I have news for you."

"Did you not get my note? I found Miss Featherstone." Braden pointed to a chair. "Have a seat."

"Thank you, my lord. You misunderstand, sir. I have news of your brother."

"You do?" Braden's heart pounded in his chest. "Is he alive?"

"As of last night he was, my lord. There was a scuffle at the Red Door between Mr. Tavers and Mr. Chambers. Poor Mr. Chambers took the worst of it, from all accounts."

"Do you know where Jonathon is now?"

Mr. Brady shook his head. "He was seen walking down Maddox Street, but that was all we have. At least we know for certain that he is in town."

And he was alive. "Do you know what the fight was about?"

"Mr. Tavers accused Mr. Chambers of cheating. A few of the men agreed that they had seen Chambers cheat, but the man would not back down."

"Thank you, Brady. I will go there tonight to see if anyone knows anything."

Brady rose and nodded. "Good day, my lord. As soon as I know of anything else, I will let you know." He hesitated a long moment. "Might I ask a question, my lord?"

"Of course."

"How did you find her?"

Braden smiled. "Do not feel badly, Brady. It was purely by chance. She had been with a new friend for a fortnight and never left the house. You would not have found her. I only found her because we were at the same ball."

"Thank you, my lord." Relief flooded the man's face. "Good day."

Braden sat back in his chair and stared at the ceiling. The Red Door. He should have known Jonathon would turn up there. And he should have told Adams what was happening with his brother. Braden was still troubled that the co-owner of the hell hadn't notified him of his brother's exploits. Adams knew he was concerned about Jonathon.

"Nelson?"

"Coming, my lord." Nelson's quick footsteps echoed down the hall. He stood at the threshold.

"Is she up yet?"

"Yes, my lord. She had a visitor, Lady Eldridge, who left a few minutes ago. She is eating luncheon in the dining room."

Braden's lips twitched, wondering how her stomach felt this afternoon. "I suppose I should join her."

He found her all but slumped over at the table. Her hands shook as she sipped her tea and by the looks of her mostly full plate, she hadn't eaten much of anything. "Good afternoon," he said in a booming voice.

"Shh," she said, holding her finger to her lips. "There is no need to be so loud."

"Don't tell me you have a headache." Braden sat down with a grin.

"Do be quiet, my lord." She stared at her tea, but made no move to drink it. "I forgot to ask last night if your arm has healed well."

"It has, thanks to your excellent ministration."

She started to nod and then stopped. "You are welcome. If you would like me to check it, I will do so."

"There is no need. So," he drawled, "are you ready to leave yet?" He had no intention of leaving London right now, but he did intend to put her in his coach and send her back to the estate.

"Not today, I beg of you, my lord." She looked up at him with dark circles under her eyes.

"I did warn you not to keep drinking all my brandy."

"Again . . . do be quiet. I realize whose fault this is." She sipped her tea slowly. "And I will never drink brandy again."

"Ah, spoken like a truly reformed woman. Perhaps you should go one better and say no spirits at all?"

"Why do you insist on talking when you know I feel dreadful?"

He laughed only slightly softer.

She bit down on her lip. "My lord, might I ask you something in private?"

Braden glanced at the footman and then nodded his head toward the door. "What is it?" he asked once the footman closed the door.

Her cheeks reddened like apples. "My mind is a little blurred from all the drink. What exactly happened after we returned home?"

He chuckled. "You don't remember. That is famous. I kept telling you to stop drinking my brandy, but you must have been feeling quite rebellious because you would not stop."

"Yes, I know. But what *happened?*"

"What do you think happened?"

She fisted her hands. "I don't know. I took the pins out of my hair. And I only know that for certain because Mrs. Abbott told me a maid found them. Did we . . . ?"

"Did we what, Tia?"

"You know what I want to hear," she said with a groan of frustration.

"Are you done?" Braden asked, glancing to the still untouched food.

"Yes, why?"

"One of the best ways to get your memories back is to return to the scene." He rose from the chair and held out his hand for her. "Come along. Let us return to the study."

Once they reached the study, he closed the door behind them. "The first thing you did was—"

"Pour myself a glass of brandy. I remember that much."

"And after gulping it down like a sailor, you poured yourself another and then a third."

"And I believe there might have been a fourth one in there somewhere, but that's where it gets fuzzy," she said, collapsing into the same chair she sat in last night. "I know we were talking, but I don't remember the topic of conversation. I'm assuming it was your dreadful behavior at Lady Whitfield's party."

Braden sat in the chair across from her. "Actually, we discussed your sister and family some."

She frowned, but said nothing for a long moment.

"And then you attempted to seduce me."

"You're mad," she said with a laugh.

"Stand up, Tia." For once, she did as he requested without question. "You stood in that very spot and loosened your hair for me."

"While you sat in that same chair," she muttered. "Oh dear God, I remember. I acted like a wanton last night." Her hands covered her mouth as she sank back into the chair. "But I still don't remember what happened after you . . ."

"After I what?" He wanted to know exactly what she remembered.

"We kissed. You kissed me everywhere," she said breathlessly. "My ear, my jaw, my mouth—you put your tongue in my mouth!"

"Had you never been kissed like that before?" The woman was in her middle twenties. How could she not have been kissed by some beau?

"No," she whispered. "Your brother kissed me once, but it was nothing like that." She stared at the carpet as if unable to meet his eyes. "Did anything else happen?"

Braden struggled with telling her the truth and letting her believe nothing else happened. "Nothing important."

"Let me be the judge of that," she said in a harsh tone. "Something did happen."

"Let us just say we went a little farther than kissing."

"You took my virginity, didn't you?"

"No," he said in a righteous tone. "I would never have relations with a woman who was incapacitated by brandy. When I make love to you, Miss Featherstone, you will be sober and begging me to please you."

"How dare you! I will never let you make love to me."

He rose and pulled her up against his body. "You were begging me to pleasure you last night. And I have never been so tempted to take a drunken woman to my bed. But I did not."

She blinked back tears. "Thank you for that, my lord."

"Tell me something, would it have been all that awful if we had?"

"The worst, my lord. The worst." She broke away and raced from the study.

"Far from it, Miss Featherstone. Far from it."

Chapter 9

Tia ran to the relative safety of her bedchamber. After collapsing into the bed, she finally let her tears fall. He kissed her last night. And not just that punishing kiss on the dance floor. She remembered the sensation of his tongue swirling against hers. How it made her tingle from her breasts to her loins. He was right. She had tried to seduce him.

What had she been thinking?

Had the alcohol muddled her mind so thoroughly that she couldn't remember right from wrong? Was it lust that had spurred her actions? Or perhaps frustration at her situation?

She closed her eyes and one final memory returned to her. "Dear God, I let him suckle my breasts," she whispered. How could she have forgotten that most amazing sensation? It had made her moist and she had rubbed herself against him, trying to get some relief from the growing feelings in her body.

He must think her nothing better than a strumpet. She had promised herself that she wouldn't give into temptation. She wanted marriage, not just a bastard child to raise on Middleton's estate. The tenants didn't care if she married or not, they only wanted her to have a child, a girl, to teach the healing ways. But she cared.

She had cared.

Now, after feeling those sensations, would she ever be able to resist him? She had to fight him. He wouldn't give her what she wanted most—love. Middleton would be happy to bed her and forget her. Jonathon had told her more about his brother than she should know. How after their father died, Braden did what he had to in order to bring extra money into the house until their mother recovered from her grief. Tia knew he'd stolen from people. And had probably done worse than that.

After hearing Emily's words, Tia had to wonder if Braden could have succumbed to murder to help his family, even if it was just he and Jonathon now. Could she be living under a killer's roof?

Would a killer have stopped a drunken woman from seducing him? She didn't think that he would. But being a gentleman and a murderer were two different things. Only last year, she'd read in the paper about an earl who had killed his own wife. Surely, most people would have thought him a gentleman until that night.

A shiver of fear raised gooseflesh on her skin.

She shouldn't stay here any longer. She had to get out of this house. But she had nowhere to go and no money. If she asked, Emily would give her enough to get back to Middleton Hall, but she was no better there on his property.

Or you could just ask him if he killed his cousin.

She almost laughed aloud at her conscience's attempt to redeem him. And if she left, she would never be able to help Jonathon. She wanted to hate Jonathon for making her believe he had an interest in her, but she couldn't. He had far too many problems. It was probably best that she let the idea of loving him go. But she still wanted to help him. He needed to find a way of fighting the demons inside him.

With a sigh, she resigned herself to her fate. She had to reason with, or convince, Middleton to stay here a few more days so she could investigate the Red Door.

And as her mother always told her, there was no time like the present. Tia walked to the basin and washed her face. Looking up into the mirror, she pinched her pale cheeks for a little color and arranged her hair. She also pulled up the bodice of her dress to cover herself more. The last thing she wanted was to make him think she was a strumpet.

Determination swept over her. She could do this. No, she *would* do this. She walked out of the room and down the stairs. Finding Nelson in the salon speaking with a maid, Tia waited until he finished.

"Mr. Nelson, where is Lord Middleton? I need to speak with him."

"In the library, miss."

"Thank you."

She strolled down the hall to the library and found him staring at a map of London. "Going somewhere?"

"Yes. Now what can I do for you, Miss Featherstone?"

"I wanted to ask a favor of you." She walked over to the shelves lining the walls and stared at all the books. She slid a finger down the buttery leather binding of one book.

"Go on," he said, not looking up from his map.

"I was hoping you would agree to let me stay here a few more days."

"No."

"That's it? *No.* Don't you want to know why?" Tia tried her best to keep her frustration out of her voice.

"No."

"Is that all you have to say?"

Middleton sighed before moving away from the desk. Several lines creased his forehead as he frowned. "Yes. That is all I have to say on this subject. You are leaving tomorrow morning."

"What do you mean, *I* am leaving? Won't you be coming with me?"

"No, I have some business to attend to here. I won't be back until it is complete."

Her mind spun with emotions. If he wasn't leaving, there was no reason she had to go either. "Then I will stay until your business is finished. I promise I shall behave this time. I won't leave the house without a maid. I will let you know exactly where I am going at all times."

He crossed his arms over his chest as he leaned against the desk. The movement only accentuated the breadth of his shoulders. "You are a terrible liar, Miss Featherstone."

She stared down at her hands. "I cannot leave yet."

"Sit down. There is something I haven't told you and I believe it will change your mind."

"What is it?"

"Sit down, Miss Featherstone," he commanded.

Tia took the closest seat. "What is wrong?"

"Before I left to find you, your mother informed me of an . . . an incident with your sister."

"My sister? What happened to Mia?" Her eyes opened wide as her mouth fell open. She had felt as if something had happened to Mia, but she'd ignored the sensation. She should have known better. They were always sensitive to each other's feelings.

"Yes."

Her mouth went dry. "What happened?"

"Your sister was abused by a man. She will be all right. She is staying at Hartsfield Park until they catch the man who did this to her."

And this was precisely why Tia had never given her affections away as her sister did. It led to nothing but trouble. "I see," was all she managed to say. "It was that new man she was with, wasn't it?"

"Honestly, I don't know." Middleton walked over and handed her a handkerchief.

Tia hadn't realized she was even crying. "I told her not to see him. She wouldn't even tell me his name. Only that he was new to the neighborhood."

"Come here." He helped her to her feet and brought her into the safety of his arms. "I'm sorry, Tia," he whispered. "But you needed to know why I was insisting you return."

"When did this happen?"

"The day before I left."

"But that was almost a month ago. Why didn't you tell me when I was here a fortnight ago?" At that point, she might have been able to help her sister. But now it seemed unlikely that Mia needed her.

"I didn't have the chance. After being shot and then drugged with laudanum, you were gone when I woke."

"What were her injuries?"

"I'm not completely certain. I believe her ribs were either cracked or bruised and she was hit on her face."

Tia's analytical mind took over. "Even if her ribs were cracked, she'd be healing quite nicely by now."

Middleton pulled back slightly. "True, but you still need to go to her."

"And I will, but in a few days' time. There is something I must do first."

"Oh? And what would that be?" he asked in a harsh tone. "I can only assume it has something to do with my brother."

Tia closed her eyes. There was something in his voice that tugged at her heart. She couldn't explain it, but there was a desperation she'd never heard before. "Yes," she whispered.

"Stay out of my brother's life. You don't know the real Jonathon. The man you met at Middleton Hall was an illusion."

"You're wrong." Tia backed up when he glared down at her with his icy cold eyes. "I know you are. Jonathon and I talked for hours. I did know the real Jonathon."

"He would not have told you everything." Middleton stepped closer to her. "He knew how to woo a woman and that is all he was attempting to do with you."

Tia's anger surged. She'd had enough of Middleton speaking so poorly about a man who only needed help. She was angry with herself for believing his brother's fine words. Before she could stop herself, she slapped his cheek harder than she had ever hit another person.

"Bitch," he swore, then pulled her up against him, holding her wrists behind her. She struggled against his strength. "You are getting on a coach tomorrow for the Midlands."

"I'm sorry I hit you," she whispered. "I—I don't know what comes over me when you're near. I want you to understand my feelings and stop disregarding them." Her breasts were crushed against the hard muscle of his chest. She could feel every breath he took as his chest rose and fell. Staring into his blue eyes, she felt herself sinking into a pit that she knew would be dark, but she couldn't help herself. There was something about this man that she had never felt with another.

"You are going home."

"I will do anything to stay," she cried.

He pushed her away from him. "Do not say things you don't mean."

"I meant it. I'll do anything."

Middleton closed his eyes as if fighting some unknown demon. "There is only one condition to you staying."

"What? I will meet your conditions. Anything."

"You will be my mistress."

Braden knew how wrong it was to ask that of her. Surely, this would force her hand. She wouldn't give up her innocence to find his brother. This would get her out of his hair . . . and his life, at least for a short while.

"You cannot be serious." The wavering tone of her voice gave him a shot of confidence.

"I am. For as long as we are in London, you will warm my bed. You will be a willing lover. Anything I want from you, you will do." He leaned in closer and whispered, "Anything."

"I . . ."

"Make your decision. The coach in the morning or my bed tonight."

She pressed her lips together. "This is dreadfully unfair."

"So is life, Tia. Now make your decision."

"I need a few moments to think on it. I can't make such a life-altering decision in just a few seconds."

She turned away from him, but Braden knew he hadn't frightened her enough yet. He wrapped his arms around her, bringing her up against his chest. He pressed light kisses on her neck. "What is your decision?"

"I can't make a decision so quickly," she said.

"Of course you can," he whispered near her ear. He ran his tongue along the outer shell of her ear until she shivered. "Tell me."

Make the right decision, he willed her. *Turn me down. I don't deserve the pleasure your body will bring.*

"I don't know!"

"Yes, you do." He rubbed his thumbs across her breasts until her nipples tightened. He was certain she would back down. She didn't want to make the same mistakes as her sister. "Your body knows."

"Just give me a few minutes," she begged

Braden slowly moved away from the sweet heat of her body. "Very well, I am a fair man. You have until dinner, but no longer. I want your answer then. If you choose me, we will have plans for the evening. If not, you will be locked in your room until morning."

"I understand," she said quietly.

"Good."

"What would our plans be if I decide on you?"

"A gaming hell. I have an urge to gamble. As my mistress, you will go wherever I desire. Even if that means attending a ball or party. Every person will know you are my mistress and the men will dream about what we do in bed."

She pressed her lips together as her face went pallid. "I understand. But back to this evening. What gaming hell did you place on visiting?"

"The Red Door."

Her face lit up. "The Red Door?"

Oh hell, what had he done? Why would she have an interest in the place? She couldn't have heard about Jonathon's scuffle last night. *Lady Eldridge.* Emily might have told Tia about it. Damn. "It was just a thought. I may actually try a different place tonight."

Seeing her crestfallen face, he knew he was right. She had heard the news.

"Middleton, may I ask you something?"

"I'm quite certain I should say no, but go ahead."

"I was very foxed last night and while I remember some of the embarrassing things I did, the one thing I can't completely remember was the kiss we shared. Before I make my decision, I would like a kiss." She cleared her throat. "A real kiss."

"A real kiss?"

"Yes. Like last night."

He couldn't do this. Kissing her again was madness He'd never be able to resist her. Was there some way he could kiss her that would repel her? He had never been taught how to disgust a woman.

"Make your decision," she said, almost as forcefully as he had to her.

"Very well."

She walked into his arms and wrapped her arms around his neck. Her breasts pushed against his chest, sending blood to a part of him that he needed to control. He lowered his head and kissed her softly. Even such an innocent kiss was enough to make him hard. There was no way of resisting her when he wanted her naked body wrapped around his.

Instead, he decided on another tactic: passion. He moved them back a few steps until he had her pressed between the wall and his body. Then he slid his tongue across her full lips until she opened for him. The sensation of her tongue on his sent a primal longing through him. Pressing his hips against her, he heard her moan as she realized how badly he wanted her.

He had to keep some amount of control, but just enough to realize when she became frightened of the passion he was stoking in her. A low moan erupted from her as he moved his thumbs across her breasts. God, he'd give anything to see those beautiful orbs again. He could feel her start to retreat and knew the timing was about right.

She trembled in his arms when he wouldn't release her. He pressed his body to her once more, showing her his strength and desire. Finally, her arms pushed against his chest and he knew she had reached her limit.

Now she would go home and leave him to find his brother.

He leaned away from her, trying not to smile. Her face was flushed and her breathing erratic. "Was that suitable?"

"Yes," she whispered, her eyes as large as a doe's.

"Let me know your decision by dinner."

"I already have my answer."

This time he did smile. "Excellent. I shall have Mrs. Abbott pack your things."

She tilted her head down and looked up at him shyly. "My answer is yes."

Bloody hell, no! "Tia, think about what you are saying. This is serious business, not to be thought about in the throes of passion."

"What better time to choose a lover?"

"But I won't just be a lover, I'll be your master. As my mistress, you will have to make sure my every desire is satisfied. Day or night. Anywhere I decide." Could she not be as innocent as he'd thought?

"I understand. And again, my answer is yes." She took a step closer and whispered, "Shall we start now?"

He took a step back. Dear God, her mother would kill him. And right now, he wasn't sure he even cared. "Yes."

Chapter 10

*N*ₒw? Did he really say now? Tia's heart pounded in her chest and not just from that amazing kiss. She had sensed he was trying to scare her with passion, but she'd been positive he would retreat from his position if she advanced. What was she to do? She couldn't really fall into bed with him. That wasn't the plan.

"I—I." Oh God, he was coming closer to her. The passion of his kisses had shown her how weak she was around him. If she wasn't careful, she might let him do whatever he wanted to her. And quite happily.

"Yes?"

"Perhaps we should wait until later, after . . ." After what? She had to think of something quickly. "After we return from gaming." And then if they'd found Jonathon or enough information about his whereabouts, she might be able push Middleton off another night. "I don't wish for either of us to be tired while gaming. It's a recipe for loss."

His molded lips twitched as if he found some aspect of this situation amusing. She certainly did not. Her innocence was on the line here. There had to be a way of dissuading him.

"I see. I suppose I can grant you that one boon. For one in return."

"One in return?" she whispered.

"Oh, yes, I will tell you later, when we are naked."

Tia swallowed hard. "Naked?"

Middleton smiled, fully revealing a row of white teeth that looked like he wanted to gobble her up. "That is how this is done . . . at least most of the time." His brows rose at her seductively.

"Most of the time?"

"You are repeating everything I say like a parrot."

Stop looking at that handsome face and concentrate, she scolded herself. She blinked and then moved away. "If we are to go out tonight, I should get ready."

"Yes, do that. I have an errand to run, so I will return in a while."

She nodded and raced out the room. Once she reached the sanctuary of her bedchamber, she flopped on the bed. "What have I done now?" she said into the pillow.

None of this was supposed to have happened. But now she felt as if she were getting closer to finding Jonathon. And once he was found, she could get him back to the doctor her mother had recommended. Briefly, she wondered that if she told Middleton what she knew, perhaps he could help her with Jonathon.

No. Middleton was too caught up in his business to worry about his brother. He probably assumed Jonathon was just off in town having the time of his life. Instead, he might be jeopardizing his life.

She sat up, determined to formulate a plan for both the gaming hell and trying to keep Middleton from his lascivious plan for her after the gaming. She touched her fingers to her lips, gently caressing them like his kisses. Did she want him? A part of her certainly seemed to like his touch and wondered what it would feel like to have him deep inside her. A quick shiver raced down her back. The idea of Middleton inside her, knowing her body, excited and frightened her.

Tia knew no one would care if she had an affair with him. Except, quite possibly, Jonathon. He had warned her about his brother's reputation with the ladies of the Society. She smiled, remembering how he had warned her about his own reputation. Not that she had anything to worry about with him.

If it came to it, could she let Middleton make love to her? God knew the man was handsome enough for any woman. With his dark looks and darker clothing, he lent the impression of a devil ready to strike. She closed her eyes and imagined him caressing her body—his fingers playing roughly with her nipples before working their way down her belly to split her folds. Just thinking such lurid thoughts made her wet with desire.

What would be the worst thing that happened if she let him make love to her?

She blinked her eyes open with that horrific thought. She could be more than ruined. She might end up with child. His child. His heir, quite possibly. And while back at the estate no one would mind much if she had a bastard child, she'd never wanted that for herself. She wanted love, marriage, a friendship that lasted like her parents' marriage.

Those things would never be possible with Middleton.

Tia finally put away her musing and walked to the linen press. What did one wear to a gaming hell? She had no idea. Emily had bought her two day dresses and the one silk gown Tia had worn for the party. Emily had wanted to buy her more, but Tia refused to let her spend any more money on her. Even the day dresses were too fancy to wear out at Middleton Park when she called on the tenants.

She pulled out the silk and held it up to her. Was this too extravagant? Perhaps the yellow day dress would be best. Reluctantly, she placed the silk back into the linen press and withdrew the yellow muslin. It was far prettier than most of the dresses she'd owned prior to Middleton destroying them out of an insect fear.

Staring into the looking glass, she smiled. The yellow would be perfect. She walked over to ring for Mrs. Abbott, when the door to her bedchamber swung open. Without even a quick knock to bid entrance, Middleton strolled into her room with his hands full.

"Just as I expected," he said, seeing her muslin dress on the bed. "You have nothing to wear. Well, I have solved that dilemma." He placed the packages on the bed. "Miss Barnes, please come in."

Miss Barnes? "Middleton, what is going on? You walk into my room uninvited and toss packages on my bed."

He turned to her with a smile. "Actually, all those things are mine. I'm just letting you use them."

Tia shook her head. "What?"

He pointed to the bed. "The bed, the room, the packages. They are actually all mine."

"Of course they are."

"Miss Barnes, please come in here. Don't be shy." He ambled toward the threshold. "I know she sounds like a termagant, but she is really not that horrible."

"Who sounds like that?" Tia demanded with her hands on her hips.

He glanced back at her with a smirk. "You have to ask?" He walked out of the bedchamber and returned with a young girl of no more than twenty. "Tia, this is Miss Barnes, your lady's maid while you are staying with me."

Tia's mind spun at dizzying speeds. He hired a servant just for her. Guilt overwhelmed her. "My lord, you shouldn't have done such an extravagant thing. Mrs. Abbott—"

"Is the housekeeper who needs to focus her attention on the duties of the house. Miss Barnes worked as a lady's maid before, so she shall do just fine. I actually borrowed her from my cousin, Alistair. His oldest sister, Constance, married earlier this year, so he didn't need two lady's maids."

"It is a pleasure to meet you, Miss Barnes."

She bobbed a quick curtsy. "And you, ma'am."

"I shall leave you two to get ready. I would like to leave by eight." Middleton nodded and then left.

"What should I call you, ma'am? Lord Middleton didn't explain things to me."

"You may call me . . ." What did a maid call a woman in these circumstances? "Tia."

The girl shook her head violently. "I can't do that, ma'am. It's not proper."

"Then Miss Featherstone."

"Very good, Miss Featherstone. And you may call me Mary."

"It is a pleasure to meet you, Mary." Tia hesitated for a long moment. "I'm honestly not used to having a maid."

"I understand, ma'am." Mary moved the bed and unwrapped the packages. "Oh my, Miss Featherstone."

Tia glanced over and her mouthed gaped. Mary held up yards of brilliant red silk that shimmered like rubies. "He wants me to wear that tonight?"

"I believe that is his intention."

Wearing that dress branded her as a harlot before she'd even done anything worth mentioning. A few passionate kisses and slightly more shouldn't qualify her as a strumpet. Slightly scandalous, perhaps. "Let me try it on."

Mary helped her undress and then slid the red silk over Tia's head. The fabric caressed her skin as it glided down her body. It was far too much. Not just the money for the dress, but the idea of wearing something so decadent.

"It is beautiful, miss." Mary pinched an inch of fabric at Tia's waist. "But a little large. I can take it in quickly."

"Yes, this is the most beautiful gown I have ever worn." Once Mary had her buttoned, Tia moved to the mirror and gasped. With her red hair, she didn't think the gown would flatter her features. But Middleton found the one shade of red that complemented her hair and fair skin. But it was the low-cut bodice that made the decision for her. Her breasts were all but heaved out of the dress. One good breath and everything would be on display. "No," she whispered. "As beautiful as this dress is, I shall wear the blue silk."

"As you wish, miss."

A little shiver of fear raced down her back. She wondered how Middleton would take her act of defiance. Some men beat their wives and mistresses. Was he one of those men? Jonathon had never mentioned it, but he might have wanted to protect his brother.

After dressing, she quietly made her way down the stairs. "Nelson, where is Lord Middleton?"

"In the salon, miss."

"Thank you." She steeled herself against the bluster of his anger and walked toward the salon. When she reached the threshold, she stopped. He was facing the window with a glass of sherry in his hand. She took one more step and the floor creaked under her foot. He turned around and smirked.

"Well played, Miss Featherstone." He saluted her with his glass.

"I beg your pardon?"

"The dress," he said as he approached her. "But I don't appreciate it when my commands are ignored."

She sent him a smug grin. "But you never explicitly said to wear the dress. You only placed the packages on the bed and said you had solved my dilemma, assuming I had one to begin with."

He black brow furrowed for a moment before his smile returned. "Touché. I believe I shall have to let you win this battle. And the next time I will be very clear in my expectations."

"Do try, my lord."

"Shall we depart?"

Tia frowned. "Depart? I thought we would eat first?" She had been so eager to leave for the gaming hell to discover any information about Jonathon. But now, apprehension filled her. Leaving this house with him sealed her fate.

"We are going to a small soiree first. We can eat there."

"A soiree?"

"Yes. I thought it would be a good chance to introduce you to some of my friends." He placed his glass on the table. "Shall we?"

"I—I—"

He drew her up against his chest. "Unless you have had a change of heart?"

Tia could feel the heat from his body warming her chilled skin. She had to do this . . . for Jonathon. "I am ready."

She could have sworn she saw a look of disappointment cross his face. Could he be frustrated that she didn't give up this mad idea? She shook her head. That was an odd idea indeed. He was the one who suggested the arrangement in the first place.

"Let us be off," he said quietly.

Her entire body started to quake as they left the house and he helped her into the carriage. Every person she met tonight would know she was Middleton's mistress. A sense of helplessness invaded her. There was no going back after tonight.

She wondered what Mia and her mother would think of her actions. Mia would tell her to take the man to her bed and enjoy it. Her mother's advice might be of a more practical nature, with the warnings of the consequences of her actions. Since neither were here, it was up to Tia to decide her fate.

"What are you fretting about?"

"Everyone will know," she whispered.

"Yes, they will. That is what I told you before you agreed to this plan." His harsh voice told of his own frustration.

"I know you did," she said softly. "But now . . ."

"Now it's real."

She nodded slowly. Warmth filled her hand as he clasped it between his. He squeezed her hand gently.

"It will be all right, Tia," he murmured near her ear.

If only she could believe him. "Thank you."

He brought her gloved hand up to his lips and kissed her hand. A long moment of silence filled the carriage, stifling the air around them. Finally, he asked softly, "Are you in love with Jonathon?"

Was she? Two days ago, she would have said yes without a thought. But after learning about his relationship with Emily, Tia doubted he had any true feelings for her. And she wondered if she ever truly loved him.

"Forget that I asked," he muttered.

"I was thinking about your question."

"It wasn't difficult. Either you are in love with him or you are not." He pulled his hand away from hers and crossed his arms over his chest.

"I learned something about him this morning and it may have influenced my feelings for him. Yet, I don't know for certain that it's true." And why did he care how she felt about his brother?

"You're being very cryptic, Tia."

"A woman is with child and it might be Jonathon's baby."

He leaned his head back against the velvet squab and sighed. "I'm not terribly surprised."

"Oh? I had always heard you were the lascivious rake in the family."

He inched away from her. "Perhaps I am," he replied coldly.

Why did his answer make her want to question him further? The tone of his voice had changed. His entire demeanor had stiffened. Were the rumors of his behavior exaggerated? She doubted he would tell her the truth.

Instead, she moved her gaze to the window. "Where are we going?"

"Mrs. Ellsworth's house."

"Is she someone important?" She should know these things if he wanted her to attend with him.

"No. She's not important at all."

"Then why are we going?"

"Because I said we were going," he answered tightly.

Tia released a soft sigh. Apparently, he felt no need to make her feel comfortable at the party.

"Is there an issue?" he asked.

Before she could answer, the carriage slowed to a stop. The door opened and Middleton jumped out. So much for letting him know how she felt about the situation. He held out his hand to help her down. As she attempted to pull away, he clasped her hand tighter and then folded her arm around his to escort her inside.

Only a few carriages lined up to release passengers. She wondered where all the people were for the party. It was close to nine. The party should be crowded by now. The door opened as they walked up the steps.

Tia heard a few voices resonating from a back room. The butler glanced at them both and gave a quick nod. Middleton escorted her down the corridor. The room opened before them and Tia's mouth gaped. There were only about twenty people in the room. The women were clad in garish gowns that barely covered their breasts and several sat on the laps of gentlemen.

"You took me to a whorehouse?" she whispered to Middleton.

He looked down at her with a grin. "This is no whorehouse. Come along and I shall introduce you."

He started to tug her toward the people in the room, but Tia wouldn't budge. "I have no desire to be introduced to anyone in this room."

"I believe I told you earlier that if you chose to become my mistress, you would go where I wanted you to and act appropriately."

Tia wanted to turn around and leave him and these people, but knew she had to try to help Jonathon. "Very well."

"Excellent."

He escorted her into the room and brought her to a woman in her early forties. "Mrs. Ellsworth, this is a friend of mine, Miss Featherstone."

The woman scanned Tia from head to toe, before nodding her head with a slight smile. "A little different from your usual, Middleton. But glad to see that horrid rumor of your reformed ways was false."

Tia glanced up to see Middleton tighten his jaw before replying, "I guess a true rake can never be reformed."

Mrs. Ellsworth only laughed. "I haven't met one yet."

Middleton nodded and pulled Tia away from the rude woman. Tia wondered at her remarks, though. Before she could question him, Middleton introduced her to several other couples who all seemed as rude as Mrs. Ellsworth. Tia couldn't understand why he would even want to attend this party.

"Excuse me," he said softly near her ear. "I need to speak with a friend of mine alone for a minute."

Tia's shoulders sagged. The idea of making idle conversation with any of these people was enough to make her feel ill. She sipped her wine, praying no one would attempt to speak with her.

"So you are Middleton's latest."

Tia turned at the sound of a woman behind her. She pressed her lips together to keep her mouth from gaping. The woman was petite with delicate features and perfectly coiffed blond hair. She was, from what Tia had heard, what every man wanted in a woman.

"I suppose I am," Tia finally remembered to reply.

"I am Lady Penelope Harty."

Tia gave a quick curtsy. "Tia Featherstone."

Lady Harty's brows rose slightly. "You do not seem his type at all."

Tired of hearing the same comment from several people, she asked, "And exactly what does that mean?"

Lady Harty giggled in a high-pitched tone. "Oh my, surely you know of his reputation?"

"Apparently I do not."

"Why, after I jilted him, he seduced nearly a hundred women in only a matter of a few weeks. It was dreadfully scandalous."

Tia closed her eyes. She'd heard the rumors of his lascivious behavior, but this was far worse than anything she had imagined. "And why did you jilt him?"

Her cheeks reddened. "I was forced to marry an earl. Middleton was just Mr. Tavers at the time of our relationship."

An older man who appeared to be in his late fifties and dreadfully overweight waddled up to Lady Harty. "Introduce me to your new friend, Penelope."

"Miss Featherstone, this is my husband, Lord Harty."

Tia curtsied quickly. The lewd look Lord Harty sent her made her feel uncomfortable. She made a fast excuse and sought the security of Middleton. She scanned the room for him, but did not see him in the small group.

Oh, God, he wouldn't have left her here alone, would he?

Chapter 11

"What are you about, Middleton?"

Braden stopped in front of his friend Jack. "I have no idea what you are talking about, Jack."

"Your vow?"

"It wasn't exactly a vow, Jack." Braden shifted uncomfortably in front of his friend. Why did he suddenly feel like a schoolboy reprimanded by the headmaster?

Jack started to walk away, shaking his head as he went.

"What did I do?" Braden asked.

Jack stopped and turned back around. "You have to ask? After Penelope and all those other women, you swore you were going to reform. I believe your words were something to the effect of 'no more women, I want a wife.' "

Braden clenched his teeth together. "She's not my mistress."

Jack choked back a laugh. "You kissed her in the middle of Lady Whitfield's party. She left with you. And you have the nerve to bring her here." He leaned in closer and whispered, "Whether you bedded her or not doesn't matter and you know it. In the eyes of everyone in town, she is your mistress."

"It's a long story, Jack," Braden said with a sigh. "I never meant for anyone to think she was my mistress." And she was supposed to be back at the estate by now. Jack's words only reinforced the guilt Braden had been feeling since she agreed to his foolish plan. *Dammit!* She wasn't supposed to agree. Now he was in too deep.

"Well, it's a little too late for that."

Braden grabbed a brandy and walked toward the library after a quick glance back at Tia. She would be fine for a few minutes while he talked to Jack. His friend followed him into the deserted library.

"Do you plan on telling me what happened?" Jack asked, before sipping his own brandy.

"Tia is my wise woman."

"Your what?"

"My wise woman. She works on the estate healing, delivering children, and so forth. She left to chase down Jonathon." Braden took a sip and let the heady liquid rest on his tongue for a minute before swallowing. Slowly, he told Jack the rest of the story.

As he finished, Jack chuckled. "So she beat you at your own game."

"Apparently, she did. Now, what am I supposed to do?"

"Nothing. When you arrive home tonight, you tell her to go to bed . . . alone."

Braden knew that was exactly what he should do. But his body wouldn't listen. One certain part of his body, in particular, wanted nothing more than to leave this damn place and take her home to his bed right this moment. "I know," he muttered.

Jack chuckled again.

"What the bloody hell is so funny?"

"I'm just happy that this is your problem and not mine."

Braden shook his head. "I won't ask what you would do."

Jack tilted his head back and finished his brandy before saying, "There is no need. You know what I would do. And it certainly isn't taking her to a gaming hell or telling her to go to bed alone."

Braden placed his half-full snifter on the table. "I need to find her and get her away from these dreadful people."

"Good luck," Jack muttered with a laugh.

Braden left the library and walked back into the salon. He soon spied Tia speaking with his cousin, Alistair. No good would come of that. Braden strolled up to them with a tight smile. "Good evening, cousin."

"Good evening, Alistair."

"And how are you, Middleton?"

"Quite well now," he answered and wrapped his arm around Tia. "I see you have met Miss Featherstone."

"Yes, we met at Lady Whitfield's party." Alistair smiled. "We even shared a dance."

"Did you now." Braden slid a glance at Tia's face. Her cheeks had reddened slightly. Had they shared more than a dance?

"Yes," Tia finally spoke up. "We did share a dance."

"Of course," Braden said.

"Good evening to you both," Alistair said with a quick nod.

"Stay away from him," Braden warned Tia once his cousin was out of earshot.

She looked up at him with wide eyes. "Why? He seemed quite lovely to me."

She had no idea about the perverted nature of most of the people in this room. It had been a terrible mistake to bring her here tonight. "He may not be all that he seems."

"I believe the same could be said of you," Tia retorted.

"So it could." Braden clasped her elbow. "We are leaving now."

"As you wish."

They walked out of the room and out to his carriage. Silence filled the carriage as they rode toward the Red Door. It was time to tell her everything. She deserved that. And he needed her help as much as he hated the idea of needing another person.

"I supposed if we are to be lovers, we should be honest with each other."

Tia looked over at him. Curiosity filled her. She knew what she hadn't been honest about, but what was he hiding? "What do you mean?"

"My business and reason for staying in town is to find Jonathon."

She looked up at him, but tears blurred her vision. Perhaps he wasn't the monster that so many tried to portray him. "It is?"

"Yes, he needs help, Tia."

"I know."

He released a long sigh as if he didn't want to say more, but must. "Did he tell you about the opium?"

"Yes," she replied slowly. A part of her felt it was wrong to break Jonathon's confidence, but she obviously couldn't help him alone. "That is why I was trying to find him. He told me a few days before he left that he had to go back to London. That someone needed him. I assumed it was a lie and that he was still having issues getting away from the drug. I tried to convince him to stay at the estate where the temptation would be less, but he wouldn't listen."

"I'm worried, Tia. The runner and I have checked all his usual haunts. No one has seen him. Until I heard about the fight at the Red Door, I was beginning to think he might be dead."

She stared up at his handsome face, unable to look away from the pain she saw. "It will be all right, Middleton. We will find him. I know of a doctor who is in town and helps people who really want to stop eating opium. But it's very difficult for most people."

"Does he have success?"

"Yes. But not in every case."

"Thank you," he whispered before kissing her hand again. "Is there any place he might have told you that I should know about?"

Tia shrugged. "I checked all the places he talked about with me, but no one had seen him." This time, she squeezed his hand. "We will find him, Middleton."

He stared down at her intently. "Call me Braden."

She glanced away and shook her head. "It wouldn't be proper."

"In the eyes of everyone we meet, you are my mistress."

She stared at her hands. "I suppose you are right. But I would not feel comfortable calling you by your Christian name in front of others."

"Then do it in private."

"I could do that," she whispered.

"And yet, you still haven't uttered my name."

"Braden."

"Much better." The carriage slowed to a stop and he jumped out. Holding out his hand, he said, "Come along, Miss Featherstone."

She took his gloved hand. "As you wish."

"I wish for many things," he whispered in her ear. "Many things."

The heat of his breath tinged her ear. The way he said those words made her heart leap and her desire heighten. How could she want this man? He was the exact opposite of his brother in looks and demeanor. And yet, Jonathon's kisses never made her weak in the knees as Braden's did. She wondered what would happen when they arrived back at his home later this evening. Would he take her in the study up against the wall? Perhaps in a chair. Or maybe he would make love to her in his large bed, slowly teaching her the ways of desire.

She shook her head to clear her thoughts away from the desire she felt for him. It was wrong to want a person strictly for his body. Although, her sister had done exactly that with two men. Even now, Tia wondered if Mia was sharing the earl's bed. It wouldn't surprise her at all.

Middleton wrapped her arm around his in a very protective movement. She wondered if that was for show or because he felt a need to protect her from something or someone inside. They approached the large red door to the gaming hell, but the door remained shut. Middleton took out a card and slipped it into a small slot near a peephole in the middle of the door.

The heavy door creaked slightly as it opened before them. The entrance was dark with only two candles spreading light down the hall. As they walked down the mysterious corridor, the sounds of merriment emanated from the room in front of them. Two brutes stood sentry at the double doors. The hulking men opened the doors with a bow to Middleton.

"Good evening, my lord."

Middleton remained silent, but nodded in reply.

"Enjoy yourself, my lord," one man said with a nod.

Tia clenched her jaw to keep her mouth from gaping at the lavish sight in front of her. Crystal chandeliers hung from the ceiling. The walls were papered with red and gold striped silk wallpaper. Liveried footmen carried gold trays filled with assorted drinks for the guests. The men outnumbered the women in attendance, but both were equally dressed in their finery.

"You might want to close your mouth. People will stare," Middleton whispered with a short laugh. "Come along."

"Do you really expect Jonathon to be here tonight?" she asked softly as he led her to the hazard table.

"No, I don't. I am hoping someone might know where he's staying so I can talk to him."

"What do you want me to do?" They stood near the hazard table and watched the play. Tia had no idea how people played the game or won money at it, but it was fascinating just the same.

"Stand next to me and smile. Perhaps, if you should have the opportunity, speak with some of the ladies here tonight. My brother was known for his excesses with women. Someone might have seen him."

"Your brother was known for his excesses with women?" Tia whispered. "What about you?"

He leaned in closer until she could smell the spicy scent he wore. His icy blue eyes glared at her. "Trust me, I am even worse than Jonathon."

"I had no doubt about that."

"Oh?"

She smiled up at him. "Jonathon would never coerce me into becoming his mistress," she whispered so softly that no one standing near would hear their conversation.

His white teeth gleamed in the candlelight. "It was your choice, sweetheart. There was no coercion involved."

Tia's brows rose. "Indeed." She knew he was right, but would never admit it to him.

"Besides," he said with a smirk, "I don't believe you have become my mistress yet."

But after tonight, she would be. And the idea frightened and excited her at the same time.

"Middleton," a loud voice boomed from behind them. "I'm surprised to see you here after your brother's scuffle last night."

Tia and Middleton turned to see an older man, near to fifty from the looks of him, standing behind them.

"Kettering," Middleton said with a bow. "I was looking for my brother."

The man laughed. "Hardly think he would have the nerve to show up here again."

"Were you here last night?"

"Of course. Saw the entire thing." Kettering stared at Tia as if he'd never seen a woman before tonight.

"What happened?"

"He was at the faro table. He looked pretty deep in his cups. Another man I don't know started to antagonize him. Your brother threw the first punch and then they were hitting each other. Adams had both men thrown out. He told them never to set foot in here again."

Middleton frowned deeply, creating lines across his forehead. "You don't know who the other man was?"

"Never saw him here before last night." Kettering slid a glance toward Tia. "Now, you must introduce me to your companion."

"This is Miss Featherstone." Middleton looked at her and said, "Lord Kettering."

"My lord," Tia said with a quick curtsy.

"My, she is a fetching gel," Kettering said and then licked his lips as if he wanted to devour her. "Do let me know when you tire of her."

Middleton stiffened. "That might take a very long time, Kettering."

The man wiggled his white brows at her. "Might be worth the wait."

Tia felt her cheeks burn from the disgusting man's scrutiny. "My lord, I believe Lord Middleton is right. I have no desire to leave his bed any time soon. He had to beg me to accompany him tonight. I would have preferred we stay at home . . . in bed."

Middleton's lips twitched.

"I see." Kettering glanced at them both and nodded. "Good evening, then."

"Well played, Miss Featherstone. Perhaps tomorrow night we shall stay at home. In my bed."

Tia's cheeks burned from the hot gaze he sent her. "So who exactly is this Adams man? Perhaps we should find him and see if he has anything to add."

"Nice way to change the topic, Miss Featherstone." He led her away from the hazard table. "Philip Adams is one of the owners of this establishment."

"Oh, is he here tonight?"

"Right over there," he said, leaning his head to the right.

"That man standing against the wall?" The man looked more like one of the hulks guarding the doorway. He was well over six feet with large muscles and as they walked closer, he displayed even white teeth and dimples in both cheeks.

"So, you ejected my brother last night, Adams?"

"You would have done the same, Middleton." Adams scanned her with a frown. "I thought you were through with that."

"Long story."

"I'm quite certain it would be an entertaining one at that." He turned toward Tia with a grin. "Philip Adams, at your service."

"Tia, this is Mr. Adams. This is Miss Featherstone."

Adams lifted her hand and kissed it softly. "A pleasure indeed. I can see why you might have given up your vow."

Braden clenched his jaw and smiled slightly at his friend and business partner. "It was hardly a vow." Of course, that was exactly what it was and now that both his friends had reminded him of it in one night, he felt his frustration growing. He had to get the conversation off Tia.

"Who was the man Jonathon was fighting?" Braden asked.

"Evan Chambers."

"Yes, but *who* is he? I have never heard of him before the runner told me his name."

"No one of any significance. The third son of Mr. Richard Chambers. A banker in town."

A banker? Dear God, had Jonathon tried to get a loan to carry him until his allowance next month?

"Chambers?" Tia whispered.

Braden looked down at her pale face. "What do you know about him?"

"Your brother told me Chambers was the one who encouraged him to take the . . ."

"The what, Miss Featherstone?" Adams demanded. "You need to tell him what you know about this mess. And your involvement."

"My involvement?"

"Her involvement?" Braden asked at the same time. Tia had better not be involved in this situation. She had access to opium for medicinal purposes. If she had anything to do with his brother's addiction, he would never forgive her.

"Perhaps we should take this out of earshot of others," she wisely recommended.

Her suggestion only raised Braden's suspicions of her. "Very well, let us talk in the office."

Adams slid back a door and they entered a dark corridor. He led them back to an office where two people sat counting money. "Liam, go check on the faro table. Mr. Blackwood seems to be winning an unusually large amount. Simon, give Weathers a break at the front door. Tell him to get some supper."

"Yes, sir," they answered in unison and quickly departed the room. Both gave Braden a quick nod.

"Now, what exactly is your involvement in this situation, Tia?" Braden asked as he closed the door to the office.

"Nothing. Jonathon and I had become close friends while he was staying at the estate."

"She's from the estate?" Adams asked.

"Not now," Braden replied.

"As I was saying," Tia said with a pointed look at Adams. "We had become close friends. That's when he started to confide in me about his past. He told me about . . ." She paused and gave Braden a questioning look.

Braden nodded, understanding she wasn't sure if she should speak of this in front of Adams.

"He told me about the opium. He admitted that his intake had become out of hand, but you were helping him. I asked him how he had started, assuming it was due to a physician giving him too much when he was hurt in some manner. But he told me it was a man named Chambers. He had told Jonathon how enjoyable it was when he ingested the drug."

Braden closed his eyes. Like Tia, he had assumed it was a physician who had started the intake of the drug. "Is there anything else you haven't told me?"

Tia shrugged. "I do not believe so. I had forgotten about Chambers until I heard his name."

"Where can I find him?" Braden asked Adams.

Adams wrote down an address. "That is his father's address. I don't know where Chambers is staying while in town. I'm sure his father could tell you."

"Thank you. If you hear anything, please let me know."

"Before you go . . ." Adams unlocked a drawer, pulled out an envelope, and handed it to him. "For last month."

"Thank you."

Tia glanced between them both, but kept silent. Braden assumed she wanted to question him about the envelope, but perhaps realized she had no right.

"Good evening, Miss Featherstone," Adams said with a quick bow. "It was a pleasure meeting you."

"And you, Mr. Adams."

"Come along, Miss Featherstone," Braden said tightly. "We should be leaving now." And going back to his home, where she would expect him to make love to her.

Oh, dear God, how was he going to resist her?

Chapter 12

Tia's hands trembled as she clamored into the carriage. But as she sat back against the leather squabs, she noticed a difference in Middleton. He sat across from her stiffly with his arms over his chest. His lips were pressed into a tight line, as if he were angry about something. Perhaps he'd hoped for a more positive outcome tonight.

"Are you all right, Middleton?"

He closed his eyes and nodded. "I am fine. Only worried for my brother."

"I understand." She didn't know how she could have missed the concern on his face. She wanted to ease his burden and reached over to touch his knee. "At least now we have some information."

"And yet, we still do not know where he is," Braden replied in a harsh tone.

Taken aback by his demeanor, she removed her hand from his knee and sat back. Not knowing what else to do, she glanced out the window as the dark streets of London flew past. The man was nothing but contradictions. At times, he treated her rather rudely and other times seemed almost protective of her. He could be cold and not talk to her and then speak of his brother's issues. Yet, he never talked about his past.

She doubted he would tonight, but maybe he could tell her more about Jonathon. It might give her some insight into how his problems started. "What was Jonathon like as a child?"

He turned his head and scowled at her. "Back to your infatuation with the boy?"

"No," she replied, wondering why he always pushed her away. "I thought if I learned about his past, it might help determine why he started with the opium."

"He was a fine young boy. The light of my father's eyes."

"And you weren't?" she whispered.

"No."

"Your mother's, then?"

"No." He glanced away. "I thought we were discussing Jonathon, not me."

"It might be good to hear about your childhood too. I should think it had an impact on Jonathon's upbringing." Perhaps that would get him to tell her about his childhood.

"Not likely. When I was home, my parents spent their time away from me as much as possible. Once my father died, I had to find a way to support my mother and brother."

"How old were you?"

"Ten."

Tia closed her eyes, trying to imagine how difficult it must have been for a ten-year-old boy to find a position to bring money in to support them. "How did you do that?" she asked in a soft tone.

"Doing unspeakable things." The carriage rolled to a stop in front of his house. Middleton jumped out of the carriage and held a hand out to assist her. They walked up the steps in silence.

"Good evening, my lord, Miss Featherstone."

"Nelson, have a brandy poured in my office. I have some papers to look over," he said harshly.

"Would you like company?" she asked hesitantly.

"No, go to bed."

"You're not coming to bed?" Wasn't tonight when he had said he would make her his mistress, make love to her, and show her how to please him? She should be happy he wanted to work and she wouldn't be forced to accept him into her bed. Except a part of her wanted just that. As much as she'd told herself he was all wrong for her, there was an attraction she'd never felt for another man. A very dangerous attraction.

"Go to bed, Miss Featherstone." He walked down the hall before she could reply.

Feeling rejected, she walked to her bedchamber, where Mary waited for her.

"How was your evening, miss?" Mary asked as she helped removed Tia's gown.

Tia shrugged. She had no idea how to describe all that had happened tonight to the maid. Perhaps someone born and raised in Society might understand the oddities at the party tonight. But she doubted either a lady or a maid had been in many gaming hells. Few even let women inside their hallowed halls. "It was fine," she finally replied, stifling a yawn.

Maybe it was best that Middleton didn't want her tonight, although his rejection stung her pride. What was wrong with her that he didn't want to make love to her? She shouldn't care, but she did. "Ow!"

"Sorry, miss. I didn't mean to jab you with the pin," Mary said quickly.

Tia slid a glance toward her maid as she hurriedly put all the pins in a decorative jar. Mary appeared a bit nervous tonight. "Are you all right, Mary? You seem to be in a rush."

She inhaled and then blew out a breath. "No, miss. I am well. Just tired and wishing for my bed."

"Once you remove my stays, you can go to bed. I can manage the rest."

"Thank you, miss. You and his lordship are most kind." Mary swiftly untied her stays, put the clothing away, and said, "Good night, miss."

"Good night, Mary." Tia put on her night rail, then sat at the small dressing table and removed the pins from her hair. She wished she knew for certain if Middleton would be joining her. If he did, she wanted to leave her hair down. Not knowing for certain, she quickly put her hair in a queue. Unable to sleep, she picked up a book and stared at the words.

The sound of Middleton's voice carried from the study and made her pause from her reading. Who would he be yelling at? It was nearly one in the morning! She picked up a shawl and tossed it over her shoulders before heading down the stairs. Nelson met her at the door to Middleton's study.

"Who is here, Nelson?"

Nelson shook his head. "I only went downstairs a few moments ago. There was no one here."

Tia bit down on her lower lip and listened to Middleton's rant.

"You should be ashamed of yourself. You were doing so well at the estate, only to return here and revert to your foolish ways!"

A short bout of silence followed.

"How dare you say that to me, your own brother? You are the one who brought shame to this family, not I."

Tia's mouth gaped. "It's Jonathon, Nelson. He must have come in after you went downstairs."

Nelson's brows furrowed as he shook his head. "I'm quite certain the footman at the front door would have notified me."

She reached for the handle and stopped when he said, "Miss, if that is Mr. Tavers in there, I doubt his lordship would like you to interfere."

"You might be right, but my concern is I don't hear Mr. Tavers's part of the conversation. He might be hurt." Without another thought, she opened the door and entered the room.

"What are you doing here?" he demanded.

Tia scanned the room. "Where is Jonathon?" she whispered.

"Right over there," he said, pointing to an empty chair by the fireplace. "And what would make you think coming down here with no clothing on was a good idea? Anyone might see you!'

Panic surged through her mind as she tried to determine what was causing his delusions. There was no one else in the room except Nelson, who stood at the threshold staring at them both. How much brandy had Middleton ingested in an hour? "I am wearing my shift, Middleton."

"Sweetheart, you have a shawl covering your nakedness and nothing more. Now Jonathon and my own butler can see your beautiful body." His voice changed to a husky, slurred tone as he approached. "Maybe that is the way you like it? Do you want people to watch as I fuck you?"

She slapped his face and then drew back in horror. His eyes were dilated almost completely. He was not drunk. "Middleton, open your mouth."

"All right," he said and then closed his eyes and opened his mouth.

"Are you thirsty?" His mouth appeared terribly dried out. Her suspicions increased. "Nelson, light a few more candles for me."

"No," Middleton said, drawing back toward a darker corner. "It's too bright in here already."

"Oh, God, not again." Tia turned toward Nelson. "Find a couple of footmen and get his lordship to bed now."

She started to run from the room, but Nelson caught her arm. "What is wrong with his lordship?"

"I think he's been poisoned." She pulled away from his grip. "I have to get my bag and make sure I have what I need." She ran from the room, lifting her night rail up to her knees as she raced up the stairs. "Get Mary too. I may need her."

"Of course, miss," Nelson shouted up to her as he hurried to wake an extra footman.

Tia hurled open the door to her room and found her bag of herbs and things next to the linen press. Strange, but she didn't remember moving it there. Perhaps one of the maids had been tidying up today. With a shrug, she picked up her bag and followed the footmen attempting to carry Middleton to his room as he laughed like a child.

Her heart pounded in fear as they laid him on his bed. She was certain what had caused the poisoning, but had no idea who would try to kill him.

"It's bloody hot in here," he grumbled and then again as the footmen struggled to get his clothing off. "Would someone please extinguish those candles?"

"I need one or two on for now, my lord," she said softly.

"Beg your pardon?" he said. "You're speaking too low."

"It will be all right, Middleton. I'm going to help you."

He laughed. "Nothin' wrong with me."

She touched his forehead and he felt heated. This was happening all too quickly. She had only dealt with one other case like this and . . . She refused to think about what happened. Once the footmen had finally undressed him to his drawers, Nelson looked over at her.

"Miss, it's quite improper of you to see him like this."

Tia laughed softly. "Mr. Nelson, I have been doing this work since I was a child." She wanted to speak about the ailment, but not in front of the footmen. Right now, the only person she trusted was Nelson. "Please dismiss the footmen. If we need them, we can call for them."

He did that and then came back into the bedchamber. "What is wrong with his lordship?"

"Belladonna."

"What is that?"

"A poisonous plant."

Nelson's eyes narrowed. "Who would do such a thing to him? He is a far kinder master than the previous viscount. And where would someone get such a plant?"

Tia had a dreadful premonition about where the drug came from. If she was right, it meant someone in the house had done this to him. Her hand shook as she opened her bag, praying she had what she needed. Finally, at the bottom, she found the small bag of black powder. "Nelson, I need a glass of water."

"Yes," Middleton mumbled. "Dreadfully thirsty."

"Yes, miss." Nelson walked to the basin and filled a glass. He handed it to her and then asked, "What are you doing?"

"Giving him charcoal. It helps to absorb the poison in his belly." And hopefully this time, it wouldn't be too late. She took the glass and stirred in a teaspoon of the powder. "Help him to sit up."

Nelson moved behind him and lifted him into a sitting position. Tia helped Middleton drink the liquid down.

"Nasty bitch," Middleton muttered. "Why is it so dark in here?"

"Oh God," she whispered. She held up two fingers in front of him. "How many fingers am I holding up, Middleton?"

"Too blasted dark to tell," he replied.

"What is wrong?" Nelson asked.

"He's lost his sight." Seeing Nelson's shocked face, she continued, "It should come back as the poison leaves his body."

"Now what?"

"We wait." She looked up at the older man's face. "Go to bed. There is nothing else you can do for him now. I will stay with him."

"Can I trust you?" he asked seriously.

She tilted her head and looked at him. "Would I be trying to save the man I poisoned?"

"I suppose not."

"Nelson, what happened to Mary? I asked that she assist me."

"I am not certain. I will check on her." He moved to the door. "If there is any change, you will let me know immediately."

"Of course."

It was a long night spent in worry for her. Middleton worked his way through many of the stages of belladonna poisoning, from the blindness to the retching. Finally near dawn, he fell asleep. But when she wasn't busy, the memories of the last case she saw of this poisoning haunted her. Angry with herself, she pushed away the scarring memories and gave her attention to Middleton.

His lips looked less cracked than before, but his fever was still raging. She prayed the charcoal was working. In another hour, she would give him more. She pulled her bag up from the floor and searched inside until she found her vial of belladonna. In small doses, it was good for some female issues, along with other assorted complaints. But it was never to be used in higher doses because it was so poisonous. Picking up her near-empty vial, she knew the poison had come from her bag.

A tear fell down her cheek. If she hadn't run from her position at the estate, this might not have happened. It was her fault and if he died like that poor child, she would never be able pick up that bag of herbs again.

"Yes," Middleton started to mumble. "Yes, please." He writhed in the bed as if his fever was getting worse.

Tia felt his forehead as best she could while he tossed back and forth, but he felt no different from before. He might be hallucinating still.

"No," he said this time. "Not right. God, but I want her."

Tia wondered whom he was imagining in his dreams. Penelope, perhaps? Although Tia had no idea what he saw in that bitch.

"Yes, put your hand on my cock." His own hand reached between his legs, stroking his thickening member.

Tia stared, mesmerized by what she saw, and briefly thought she should look away . . . but couldn't.

"Your mouth," he muttered. "That's it."

Her eyes widened as his hand continued to stroke his hard cock. A part of her wanted to slide the light sheet down below his hips. She refused to do such a thing to a man hallucinating about another woman.

"Yes, just like that," he groaned. Suddenly his back arched and his hand stilled. "Oh God, Tia," he whispered. "So good."

She jumped back out of her chair, covered her mouth with her hand, and stared at the man who had been having an erotic dream about her. *Her!*

Braden slowly opened his eyes and then shut them quickly. The light from the candle burned like the sun beaming into the room in July. What time was it? And why did he feel like he'd overindulged the night before? He tried to think back to last night, but nothing came to him.

Something didn't feel right. His head ached and he felt as if he'd been run over by a carriage. His muscles felt weakened and tired. He forced his eyes to open slightly again. This time wasn't as bad as the first, but it still pained him. Everything seemed overly bright.

There was an empty chair moved nearer the bed, as if someone had been watching him sleep. How odd. A door creaked open and Tia walked over to the nightstand and placed a glass of water down. Odd, he never remembered that door making a noise before. Nelson would need to know about that. He wanted to speak, but his mouth couldn't form the words. What the bloody hell was wrong with him?

He watched as she put black powder into the liquid and fear overcame him. What in God's name was she giving him? Poison? She came closer to the bed with the glass in her hand.

"Are you truly awake yet? Or just dreaming with your eyes open?"

Why was she shouting at him? He tried to move his hands over his ears, but they seemed stuck in their position. Did she tie him down? She lifted his head to drink the potion. His damned body wouldn't help him knock the glass out of her hand. The vile liquid seeped down his throat until he coughed.

"Shh," she shouted. "There's nothing more you can do but sleep. It will be over soon."

His wise woman was really trying to kill him. And there was nothing he could do about it.

The next time he awoke, daylight filled the room and instead of the light burning his eyes, it felt nice. His head seemed clearer than the last time. Had her poison not worked on him? Scanning the room, he found her sitting in the wingback chair next to the bed, with her head in the crook, asleep. He tried to sit up until the weakness of his body forced him back down on his pillow.

"Can you hear me all right?" she whispered, blinking the sleep out of her eyes.

"You'll hang for this," he muttered.

"For saving your life? All right, if I must," she said with a slight laugh.

"I saw you giving me that black liquid." His voice sounded gravelly to his ears.

"Yes, charcoal to absorb the poison." Her hand went to his forehead and then she smiled. "Your fever has broken. Can you see me?" She stared into his eyes with a frown. "Your eyes are still slightly dilated but they look much better."

"What are you talking about?"

"Can you see me? The belladonna gave you temporary blindness."

"Belladonna? Why would you give me that?" he asked as anger invaded his mind. How dare this woman try to poison him and then say she saved his life?

She had the gall to giggle at him. "I most certainly didn't give you belladonna. Although, I'm afraid it may have come from my bag of herbs."

If she hadn't tried to poison him, then who had? "Who?" he whispered.

"We're not certain yet. Nelson is looking into that while I take care of you."

"I thought you didn't enjoy caring for people any longer."

She stared down at her hands for a long moment. The expression on her face seemed pained, as if she were reliving something she wanted to forget. "I wasn't about to let you die, my lord."

"Why not?"

She pressed her lips together, as if trying to formulate an answer. "There is nothing worse than watching a person die who is far too young." She stood up and went to the basin to pour more water.

"How did you know it was belladonna poisoning?" he asked.

"You never forget it once you've seen it."

He wondered what she meant by that. If only he felt like himself, then he might be able to sort through the hazy questions in his mind. "Can I eat something?" Far from the curious questions rolling through his mind, but he was hungry.

She turned away from the basin. "Of course. But I must start you on something easy, like broth. If that stays down then we'll see about some toast."

"I'm starving, woman."

Her smile lit the room. "And that is an excellent sign. Let me get someone to bring up some broth."

As she left the room, his mind tumbled through the questions. Who did this to him? Who wanted him dead?

She walked back into the room with a smile on her face. "Nelson is very happy to hear you are feeling better. You gave him quite a scare."

A horrible thought came to him. "Perhaps I shouldn't eat food prepared here."

"Nelson already had that same thought. Every one of the servants will have to try the broth and only then will Nelson himself pour it into a bowl for you."

Braden smiled slightly. "He's a good man."

"Yes, he is. You should do something special for him."

"Such as?"

"A bonus," she said lightly.

He nodded slightly. "Bring me the envelope from Mr. Adams."

"Of course." She searched his linen press until she found the jacket he'd been wearing that night. "I have found it. Do you remember anything after we left the Red Door?"

"No. The last thing I remember is telling you that we were leaving. After that, everything is blank. Will it come back?"

"Most likely, not." She handed him the heavy envelope.

He dumped the contents on the bed before pulling out a twenty-pound note. "Hold this for me."

She took the note and her eyes widened. "Twenty pounds! That's a bloody fortune. And why did Mr. Adams give you so much money?"

He tilted his head with a lopsided grin. "Not one of those gossips told you I was part owner of the Red Door? That is why Jonathon was there. He knew he wouldn't be turned away."

"I had no idea."

A loud rap on the door announced his first meal in several days. Mr. Nelson approached tentatively. "Good afternoon, my lord. I do hope you are feeling better today."

"I am at that, Nelson. Thank you. Any ideas on who might have done this to me?"

Nelson slid a glance at Tia, who nodded slowly. "We believe it might have been Mary, my lord. She has not been seen since that night."

"And she had access to my bag," Tia added.

"Why would a woman I barely know want to kill me?" Braden asked. "Nelson, bring Mr. Brady around tomorrow. I want to get his opinion on this matter." Hopefully, the runner would have some insight on why a maid would want him dead.

Chapter 13

Braden awoke again the next morning, only to find Tia once more asleep in the chair next to him. He wondered if she'd had much rest at all since his poisoning. Sleeping in the chair, she hardly looked like a wise woman. Instead, she appeared almost angelic. Her red hair had come loose from its confinement and curls framed her freckled face. He'd never been partial to women with red hair and freckles before. Most of his women had been blond.

Still, there was something that drew him to her. It was madness. He couldn't seduce his wise woman. The complications from that union could be enormous and the first would be her mother. Mrs. Featherstone was a formidable lady, indeed. There were few people—much less women—who could intimidate him, but she came close.

As if realizing she was being watched, Tia blinked her doe-like eyes open. A slow smile lifted her lips. "How are you?"

"Much better. My eyesight and hearing appear to be back to normal. And if my grumbling stomach is any indication, I would love to eat something a little more substantial."

"Of course. You could try a sandwich."

"Very well, but only if I can have a full breakfast tomorrow. And get out of this damned bed," he replied with a smile.

"Breakfast, maybe. Bed, no." She stretched her arms over her head, accentuating her full breasts. "You should spend a week in bed to get your strength back."

Damned desire. He could spend a month in bed with her. He closed his eyes, but still couldn't get the image of her breasts pressing against the blue muslin. "Then you'll have to join me in bed."

Dammit! He wasn't supposed to say that!

She laughed almost nervously. "I doubt you're up to that just yet."

"You have no idea," he muttered as his cock thickened with anticipation. "I feel much better than yesterday."

"Get your strength back and then we'll discuss the matter," she said casually. "I will order you a tray and then I'll get dressed."

"My strength has recovered." Braden blew out a frustrated sigh. Seducing her wasn't an option if he planned to keep his vow to reform. But six months without a woman was killing him. Perhaps that was the only reason he found her so devastatingly desirable. She was pretty, but not his typical blond beauty. Yet, there was much more to her.

He had thought her selfish to leave his estate and the people who needed him. Now, he wondered if she hadn't run from something or the memory of someone. Could that really have been the reason she ran? She admitted she'd seen a poisoning with belladonna before. He closed his eyes. Had someone on the estate died from it? It seemed unlikely. He had never heard of the poisoning until she told him what had happened.

That left the possibility that she had left because of another reason. He doubted it was entirely his brother's departure. Once she'd discovered Jonathon might have fathered Emily's baby, she had given up her infatuation rather quickly.

A few minutes later, she returned and a footman carried in a tray laden with food. His eyes widened and his stomach grumbled.

"It is not all for you," she said with a smile. "I thought we might as well share a meal together."

He pushed himself up to a sitting position. "Excellent suggestion, Miss Featherstone."

"Would you like a shirt?" Her face reddened as she looked at his bare chest.

"No, I am just fine." Watching her cheeks redden, he said, "This can hardly bother you. I've been shirtless for . . . ?"

"Three days. That is normal for that type of poisoning." She removed one plate and then put the tray on his lap, then sat back down and took a bite of her sandwich. He couldn't help but stare at her. There were dark circles under her eyes as if she hadn't slept much because of him.

"Will it have any lasting effect?"

She shook her head as she chewed. "No," she finally answered. "You should be fine now. Just don't ingest anymore."

"I will do my best to avoid it." He reached for his sandwich and took a bite. "Does it really taste this good or am I just starving?"

"No, it really tastes this good," she said with a laugh.

It was the first time she actually seemed comfortable around him. And he liked it. There was something about her that warmed his heart. He wanted to see her smile more, dress in silks and fashionable clothing. This was not him!

Was this all just the effect of her saving his life?

That had to be the answer.

"What are you thinking about?" she asked. "You have been staring at me for two minutes without saying a word."

"It was nothing."

She stifled a yawn, but he noticed. Once luncheon was finished, he would insist she take a nap.

"I'll take your tray now," she said as he finished the last bite of his sandwich. She reached over him to lift the tray.

He brought his hand to her soft cheek. She paused and looked over at him. Her eyes widened in surprise. "Thank you," he whispered. "I wouldn't be alive if not for you."

She blinked quickly, then grabbed the tray and left the room. When she came back a few minutes later, her eyes were slightly red as if she'd been crying. He had no idea what was wrong.

"Tia, please come over here." He patted a place on the bed next to him. For once, she did as he requested without question. She sat down on the bed, but refused to meet his gaze. He turned her head toward him. "Why were you crying?" he asked softly.

"I was not crying," she replied, but then blinked several times.

"Were you worried about me?" He let his hand rest on her cheek.

"Of course I was worried about you. If you had . . . died, the blame would be on me. Everyone would assume because the belladonna was from my bag that I had something to do with the poisoning."

She was just a dreadful liar. "What is the real reason?"

Closing her eyes, she shook her head. "I lost a child to belladonna poisoning a year ago. It was all my fault. I had grown it because it can have some medicinal qualities in small doses. She ate a handful of berries on a dare. Her little brother survived by chance. But I had never seen the effects of the poison. By the time I arrived at the house, her fever was very high. I made a terrible assumption that it was just a summer fever."

Braden wiped the tears that flowed down her face. "I am sorry that you had to relive that with me." Slowly, he brought her down to rest against his chest. Her tears dampened his skin. "Shh," he murmured, caressing her hair. "Please don't cry."

"I'm sorry," she said with a little hiccup. "By the time I came back the next morning, she could barely breathe. She died an hour after I arrived. It wasn't until a day later that her brother admitted to eating the berries. I should have known. I should have known what the symptoms were before I decided to grow that damned plant."

"It wasn't your fault."

"Seeing you like that brought back all the memoires and I was terrified that I would lose you."

Braden shook his head. "It wouldn't be much of a loss for the world. There isn't much I can claim that I've done to make this a better place."

"You must have done something good in your life. You are trying to help your brother." She shook her head. "And your servants love you."

"Except one."

She wiped her tears away and nodded. "Yes, except one who poisoned you. But your tenants also have a great respect for you. No one liked the previous viscount." As if realizing where she was, she pulled back and stared at him.

"You were fine where you were," he whispered.

"I—I—"

Even knowing he shouldn't, he reached up and cupped her neck. He brought her closer and kissed her tenderly. Her soft lips responded to his gentleness. Before passion could overtake him, he broke away and softly said, "Thank you."

"I—"

"Go take a nap, Tia. You look as if you've barely slept since I took ill."

She nodded, but continued to stare at his lips. "You should nap too. By tomorrow, you shall feel much better. I'll come back at dinner."

"I look forward to that."

Tia left the room quickly and headed to her bedroom. She flopped on the bed, burying her head under a pillow. What just happened in there? If he hadn't been a gentleman and pulled away, she might have continued to kiss him. She might have encouraged him to do more than kiss her. What was wrong with her?

He even admitted he had done nothing with his life. He wasn't the type of man who fell in love. Even Emily had told her he was nothing but a rake. And whatever that vow was he had supposedly taken, apparently he wasn't keeping it.

But that handsome face drew her in. She wanted those lips on her mouth, her breasts . . . everywhere. He obviously wanted her, so why hadn't he taken the initiative yet? Dear God, he'd had an erotic dream about her. A part of her wanted to march into his room this instant to confront him.

She pounded her fists into the bed. In her entire life, she'd never felt such frustration running through her. Not even when she thought she loved Jonathon did she feel this way. There was only one way this madness would stop.

She had to have him.

After all, who was she to save her herself for marriage? She would probably end up married to some tenant farmer on the estate. He wouldn't care if she'd already been with Middleton. The man would presume they would get some preferential treatment because of that fact. Well, whoever that man turned out to be, she would set him straight. She wanted nothing from Middleton . . . except his body.

With her mind made up, she rang for a bath. After an hour of soaking in lavender-scented water, she dried off and walked to the linen chest. With a smile, she pulled out the red silk.

"What are you doing with that dress?" Mrs. Abbott said as she entered the room to assist her. "You are not going out tonight."

"No, I am having dinner in his lordship's bedchamber," she replied with a smile.

"Miss Featherstone, the man is still recovering from being poisoned. He will not be in the mood for such foolishness."

"Oh yes, he will." And if he were too weak to make love to her then, she would make love to him. How hard could it be?

"I suppose he might be all right. He did call for a bath not long before you."

"Excellent. Now help me into this dress."

Mrs. Abbott sighed and then assisted her with her undergarments. "Are you certain this is what you want? You'll be branded a harlot."

"I already am. I might as well find out what it is I'm supposed to have done."

"I wish I could say I see your point, but I don't. You know what can happen. He won't marry you just because you carry his child." Mrs. Abbott laced her stays tight.

"I am a wise woman, Mrs. Abbott. I understand how babies are made. I also have no expectation of marriage from his lordship. If I get with child, I will return to the estate and no one will mind as long as I teach my daughter the healing ways."

"And if it is a son?"

Tia couldn't think about that. "I will deal with that if it happens."

"As you wish." Mrs. Abbott led her to the table. "Now, we must do something with all this hair."

"Nothing tight."

"Of course not, but he will want to take your hair down slowly."

Tia wasn't about to ask Mrs. Abbott how she knew that. By the time Mrs. Abbott was through, Tia was shocked. Her upswept hair was still loose, so once a few pins fell out, all of her hair would tumble down her back. But it was the shocking bodice that forced a gasp from Tia's lips.

"Don't take a deep breath or they will tumble right out of there," Mrs. Abbott said with a giggle. "At least you have enough to keep that up. It would fall right off me with these little tits."

"Hush," Tia said, afraid if she laughed she would expose herself.

Footsteps sounded down the hall. "That would be the footmen bringing dinner," Mrs. Abbott commented. "Are you certain you are ready for this?"

Tia took one last look in the mirror. She barely recognized her reflection. The high-waisted red silk was accented by a hint of black lace at her bosom. The black lace also lined the bottom of the skirt and short sleeves.

"Come along," Mrs. Abbott said. "The footmen are leaving and you don't want to keep him waiting."

"Thank you for your help." Tia blew a long breath out. This was it. After tonight, she would know exactly what happened between a man and a woman.

She knocked on his bedchamber door with a shaking hand. Hearing his reply, she slowly opened the door and walked inside.

"Bloody hell," he muttered from the chair in the salon. "Are you going somewhere tonight?"

She licked her lower lip. "I thought it would be nice to dress for dinner. I'd heard you bathed, so I assumed you would be dressed too." If you could call black trousers, a white linen shirt, and black waistcoat *dressed*. He didn't even bother with a cravat.

"That is a bit overdressed, wouldn't you say?"

She couldn't help but notice how he clutched the arms of the chair. "I suppose it is. But I didn't want you to think I didn't appreciate the gown. It is lovely, isn't it?"

"Yes," he said hoarsely.

"Shall we eat before things get cold?"

"Yes."

He rose slowly and pulled the chair out next to him for her. She slid into the seat and looked at the two plates before her. "Be careful not to eat too much tonight. Your stomach might still be sensitive."

"I am fine now," he grumbled before taking his own seat.

"Did you enjoy your bath? It must have felt wonderful after being in bed for three days."

"It was fine. But my valet was off tonight, so I am still with this," he said, rubbing his hand across his beard.

"It rather suits you," she said softly, before taking a bite of beef.

"I'm not sure most women would agree. Some say it's rather scratchy."

"I didn't mind it." Heat crossed her cheek. "I meant that it wasn't all that bad the few times I felt it."

"So you like kissing men with beards?" A black brow rose in question.

She looked down. "At least one."

He resumed his eating and the conversation came to a halt. Tia tried to think of something to say, but nothing came into her mind. Perhaps he was in a hurry to finish eating and move on to other things.

She sipped her wine, hoping for a little courage. She was certain this was the right thing to do. Well, maybe not right, but not wrong, either. She had no false expectations from this. Men like Middleton didn't marry wise women. And that was all right. But she could be his mistress.

As they both finished dinner, he rose and walked to the brandy. "Would you care for some brandy?"

She giggled. "No, thank you. After the last time, I believe I will just finish my wine."

"As you wish."

Why did he seem so tense tonight? It wasn't as if this was his first time. She was the one who should be nervous, but it was excitement that flowed through her veins. "Is everything all right, Braden?"

"I am fine." He drank his brandy down in two large gulps. "Thank you for joining me for dinner."

"You are welcome." She slowly rose from her seat, eager to move to the bedroom.

"Good night."

Good night? "What do you mean?"

"I am very tired, so I believe I shall retire now. Thank you again for dining with me." He rose and walked to the door.

What was she supposed to do now? "I thought you might want to talk for a while," she said, walking up to him.

"No. I'm tired."

She smiled up at him in what she prayed was a seductive manner, then brought her hands to his chest and slid them around his neck. "Still too tired?"

"Yes, good night." He broke away from her and opened the door.

Stunned, she looked up at him with tears blinding her sight. "Good night."

Chapter 14

Braden slammed the door behind her, furious with himself for hurting her feelings. Why did he make that damned vow in the first place? So he'd been with too many women after Penelope. That didn't mean he had to stay a saint. And poor Tia had no idea why he'd just rejected her.

Guilt slid into his gut.

He could hear her crying from the other side of the wall. "Dammit." He had to talk to her. But the idea of seeing her in that gown would be his undoing. He'd never seen a more erotic and sensual sight than Tia standing in his bedchamber with that red silk dress. He'd wanted to rip it off her and take her to his bed. Instead, he had insulted her.

He had to try to explain to her why he had turned her away. Not that it would ease this agonizing desire he felt for her. He only hoped that she had changed into something less sensual. He walked to her room and stared at the door. Listening, he could hear her crying still, but no sound of anyone else in there. He slowly opened the door to her room and locked it behind him. The last thing he needed was Mrs. Abbott finding him in Tia's room.

"Tia?" She lay across the bed with that damned gown still on her.

"How dare you come into my room uninvited?" She hurled a pillow at him. "Get out!"

"Let me explain," he said softly, dodging a second pillow thrown toward his head. He walked up to the bed.

"There is nothing to explain," she replied as she rolled over on her back. "I understand perfectly. You don't want me as your mistress. Do not worry, I will not attempt to seduce you again."

He couldn't help but stare at her red eyes. But slowly, his gaze slid down her body until he reached her breasts. Laying back like that had cause one breast to move slightly, allowing a slight hint of pink areola to peek out from the black lace. His cock reacted.

"Just let me explain," he said before looking away from the temptation. He sat on the end of the bed facing the wall and not her. "After Penelope, I went a little mad. Some men drown their sorrows in drink. I drowned myself in other women." He raked his hand through his hair. "I was reckless and used more women than I can even remember. But trust me, the number was not near one hundred as I've heard rumored. Still, it was more than it should have been."

"What does that have to do with me?"

"After a couple of months, I realized what I was doing and stopped. I was drinking with Adams and another friend when I decided it would be best if I didn't have another woman until I married."

"That was your vow?" she whispered incredulously.

"Yes."

"Then why did you press me to become your mistress?"

"I thought you would be insulted and possibly scared off. That way you would go back to the estate." He sighed. "It was a rather insane plan."

"No more than me accepting, thinking you would back down."

He turned and looked back at her. She had scampered back against the headboard and covered herself with a pillow. He hated the vulnerable look he saw in her amber eyes. "I'm sorry I hurt your feelings, Tia. I never wanted to do that."

She nodded, but a lone tear fell down her cheek.

Staring back at her, he knew he had to make this right. But he had no idea what to do. "Can you forgive me?"

Again she nodded.

"Do you want me? Is that why you tried to seduce me?" This was a dangerous conversation.

"Yes," she whispered so quietly he almost didn't hear her.

"Do you have any idea how much I want you right now?"

"Yes."

"You do?"

A slow smile brought her lips upward. "Far more than you think I do. When you were in the throes of your fever, you also had a hallucination. A very erotic hallucination."

He cringed. "Did I say some things I shouldn't have in front of you?"

"You did far more than that."

"Well, you must tell me," he demanded.

"Very well. You reached for a certain hard part of your body and stroked yourself while imagining it was my mouth on you."

"Hell," he muttered. "Did I?"

"Yes, calling my name."

"Bloody hell." Her fingers skimmed up his back. God, when had she moved?

"So tell me, if I did that right now, would that be breaking your vow?"

She wanted to . . . Lord. "No," he said before even considering the question. He wanted her mouth on him so badly he would have said anything.

She wrapped her arms around his chest and softly kissed his neck. She slid her hands down his chest to the buttons on his trousers. He should stop her. But the idea of her fingers or her mouth on his cock almost made him come. Once she had his trousers unbuttoned, she moved off the bed to face him.

"Please take that gown off," he whispered. "I want to see all of you."

"Very well." She turned her back to him. "I will need some assistance."

He rose off the bed and then unbuttoned her dress and skimmed it down over her body. With shaking hands, he untied her stays until they dropped to the floor. He was never going to be able to do this.

Desire for her drummed through his body, making his shaft stiffen even more.

"Well?" she asked when he had paused. "Do you want me to take off my shift?"

"No," he rasped. He wanted to undress her completely. He wanted so much more than that, but there was only one way he could have her without breaking his vow.

He grasped the cotton fabric of her shift. Slowly, he lifted the fabric, revealing more of her pale skin to his gaze. As the fabric lifted over her rounded derrière, he wanted to stop and just stare at those mounds. Dear God, she hadn't even worn drawers at dinner. He continued to raise the undergarment up and over her head, leaving her in just her stockings and shoes.

Unable to resist, he kissed down her back over her derrière to the top of her stockings. He untied them both so they fell to her ankle. He skimmed his fingers down her trim legs, then lifted one foot, then the other, to remove her shoes and stockings. He kissed the length of her legs before slipping one finger into the crevice of her bottom.

She gasped as his finger slid over one hole before finding the moisture of her folds. She was so wet for him. The thought that she wanted him as badly as he wanted her almost made him throw her on the bed and delve deep inside her. Instead, his finger slipped inside her.

"Braden," she groaned as her hips undulated. "Oh, please."

"Not yet." He slipped his finger out to move it forward over her sensitive nub.

"Oh my, what are you doing?"

"Pleasuring you, sweetheart. Just enjoy the sensations. Let it happen." He could feel her trembling and knew she had to be getting close. He slipped a finger into her tight wetness as his other hand continued to rub her clitoris.

"Oh my God," she whispered as her climax rippled through her. She bent over to hold the chair in front of her as the spasms continued. "What was that?" she finally asked.

"The reason people do this," Braden said with a smile. Her face was flushed and her eyes large. With her leaning over the chair with her bottom in the air, all he wanted to do was rip off his trousers and sink into her. She was a virgin, he reminded himself. Her first time couldn't be from behind, holding a chair.

Damn.

He helped her to straighten up and then turned her in his arms. She slipped her arms around his neck and then kissed him. She was the most incredible woman he'd ever met. As her tongue played with his, he pressed her hips to his, reminding her of her intention. Slowly, she pulled away with a smile. Her full lips were swollen from their kisses.

"If I am to be naked, so are you, my lord." She grazed her hands up his chest and slipped the jacket off his shoulders. She then worked on the small buttons holding his shirt closed. Once they opened for her, she tugged the shirttail out of his trousers and whipped the garment over his head. He moaned softly as her fingers played with the soft matte of hair on his chest. Her lips replaced her fingers and hot kisses crossed his chest until she found a nipple. She flicked one with her tongue until he groaned.

"Do you like that?" she asked innocently.

"Yes." He was barely able to speak.

"Me too." Her lips continued downward until barred by his loose trousers. She pulled them down over his hips with his drawers at the same time. His cock sprang free from its confinement, bobbing in front of her. "I wondered what this looked like," she whispered, grazing her nails up the hard length of him.

"Tia," he groaned.

"I liked watching you when you were hallucinating," she admitted. "I wanted to pull the coverlet down so I could see everything, but I didn't."

Just the idea of her watching as he masturbated made him groan again. "Tia, you are driving me mad."

"Good," she said, before enveloping him in her warm mouth.

She slid him in and out until he was shaking with desire. "Tia." He was so close to the edge he had to stop her. "Stop, sweetheart, please."

Slowly, she slid him out and looked up at him. "Am I doing something wrong?"

"God no, far too right." He lifted her up and pressed her body to his. The feel of her skin on his was incredible. And felt more right than any other woman he'd been with. "I am making love to you now."

Tia's brows furrowed. "What about your vow? You rejected me earlier and now it is all right. Why?"

"Not now, Tia. We'll talk about that later."

Before she could utter another word, his lips were on hers. His tongue warred for dominance and she let him have it. The sensation of her breasts against his hard chest made them tingle. Moisture pooled between her legs in anticipation. She wanted to feel that hard shaft filling her completely.

Gently, he moved them both to the bed and lay on top of her. He trailed kisses down her throat until he reached one taut nipple aching for his touch. He plucked it with his mouth, finally drawing the tight bud into his mouth and suckling. Tia arched her back as if to get closer to something. She doubted she could feel a climax like the one she did a while ago. Certainly, that couldn't happen more than once in a night.

Her hips rubbed against his, trying to ease the pressure building inside her. He slipped his finger between her legs and rubbed that special spot again.

"Braden," she moaned as the pressure grew more intense.

"Shh, Tia, I'm here."

She felt his shaft at her opening, pressing forward, eager to get deep inside her.

"You're so tight, sweetheart. This is going to hurt," he mumbled against her neck. "I'm sorry." He plunged inside her.

"Oh God," she exclaimed, not expecting it to hurt that much.

"I'm sorry," he said. He kissed the tears that fell. "I'm sorry."

"I'm all right," she lied. Right now she felt as if she'd been ripped asunder. His thickness filled her, but the ache was still there.

"Shh, just give it some time." He kissed her softly. "Relax, the worst is over. Soon it will be nothing but pleasure."

How could that be possible? But as he kissed her lips and then down her neck, her body softened. Slowly, the ache eased. He reached between them and found her nub again. As he rubbed her there, she closed her eyes to the sensation. Moisture slickened her passage and as he moved slowly, she shivered.

"All right?" he whispered.

"Yes."

"I'm going as slowly as I can, but I'm so close, Tia."

"Please, keep rubbing me there."

"You do it," he moved her hand down to her clitoris.

Feeling through her wet folds, she found it and rubbed as he slowly slid out. Her body tightened. "Oh my," she moaned.

"That's it, sweetheart. Rub harder."

She did as he suggested, just as he glided back inside of her. The pressure came back and slammed into her, arching her back as she trembled from the feeling of her climax. "Braden," she exclaimed.

"Oh God," he moaned before thrusting twice more and then stilling over her body. "Tia, oh God, Tia."

Both spent the next few minutes trying to catch their breath and realizing what they had done. For Tia, it was a strange experience to have a man lounging on top of her as if it were the most natural thing in the world. Slowly, she felt his flaccid member start to slide out of her. For a brief moment, she felt empty inside. As if he was supposed to be inside of her forever.

He finally rolled off her and then brought her to rest her head against his chest. She could hear his strong heartbeat pounding in her ear. Something about that sound made her feel safe in the cradle of his arms. But another part of her felt guilt for making him break his vow.

"Braden," she whispered, looking up at his blue eyes.

"Yes?"

"I'm sorry."

"For what?" he asked with a frown.

"Making you break your vow."

He smiled slowly. "You did not make me break my vow. I vowed never to take another woman except my wife."

"Exactly. And I do not believe I am your wife."

"No yet," he said softly. "But you will be."

Chapter 15

Tia raised her head off his chest and stared down at him. "Have you gone completely insane? I am not about to become your wife."

He tilted his head and smiled. "Of course you are. You just haven't realized it yet."

She would have to pull out her research books on belladonna poisoning. Could it cause a form of madness that would make a viscount believe he should marry a wise woman because they had made love? She certainly hoped it was just an effect of the poison.

"Put your head down and stop thinking about it," he said quietly.

"How do you expect me to do such a thing?"

"I haven't officially proposed to you."

She sighed and put her head back down. Perhaps he was saying all this to lessen his guilt over his vow. It did put him in a tough spot. Somehow, he would have to justify to himself that he hadn't broken his vow when, in fact, he had. "I suppose you haven't."

He slowly caressed her arm. "Are you feeling all right?"

Was she? She hadn't expected that making love with a man would be so exciting. But it was odd at the same time. She had always said she wanted marriage before she indulged in the physical aspects of love. But she couldn't tell him that after his brief comment on marrying her. That would only reinforce his belief that they should marry, when that would be the worst thing for both of them. They would never suit. Attraction they had, love they did not.

"Tia?"

"I am all right."

"Indeed? Do you realize what a terrible liar you are?" He rolled her over to her back and then rolled on top of her. He kissed her softly with such tenderness it almost made her cry. "What is bothering you?"

She closed her eyes to keep his prying gazing from reading too much. "I didn't know what to expect, Braden. It was all a little much."

"Open your eyes, Tia," he demanded.

She didn't want to. Every time she stared into his light blue eyes, she was lost. How could she feel anything for him? He'd fully admitted that he was a rake. He'd said he done some dreadful things as an adolescent—most likely justified if his father had truly died, leaving them nothing.

"Tia."

She blinked her eyes open and stared into his eyes. She'd been told by so many people he was a rake. Why had he decided to reform before she met him? This would be so much easier if he just left the room and her life. Surely, the lust she'd felt for him would be satisfied now.

"Braden," she whispered.

Why did she have to see good in him? He was supposed to be a gambler, a rake, and possibly a killer. And yet, she knew how well he treated his servants and tenants. She knew how much he cared for his brother, even when Jonathon had made a mess of his life. Braden could have forced her to go back to the estate several times, but he hadn't.

"What is wrong?" he whispered and then kissed her jaw. "I don't want to see you sad."

She wrapped her arms around him. His comfort enveloped her, making her feel safe. "Please don't speak of marriage," she pleaded. "I cannot think about marrying you."

He sighed. "As you wish."

"Don't be angry."

He rolled off her and stared at the ceiling. "Why would I be angry?

I wait over six months to make love to a woman and instead of being pleased that I wish to marry her, she turns me out."

"The only reason you want to marry me is because of your vow. What exactly was your vow to your friends?"

"That the next woman I made love to would be my wife." He tossed off the coverlet and picked up his trousers. "So it was all for naught. I suppose I can go back to my corrupt ways now."

"Braden, please wait."

"Unless you are going to consent to be my wife, there is nothing left to stay for." He quickly grabbed the rest of his clothing off the floor and stormed from the room.

Tia stared at the door, unable to move. Finally, she lay back down and let her tears fall. Why would this bother him so much? They were opposites, weren't they? He enjoyed town life, while the more time she spent here, the more she missed her home and family.

There had to be more reasons they wouldn't suit. She frowned in thought.

They both want to save Jonathon. No, that was a commonality, not disharmony. He'd lived his life like a rake, except he didn't seem to be that any longer. Or at least he was trying not to be one. There had to be more that they did not have in common!

Perhaps the question for him was, Why did he want to marry her? And there was only one way to find out.

Braden lounged in a chair by the fireplace in the library. He sipped brandy, wondering how long it would take to convince Tia to marry him. When he'd had what he thought was a brilliant plan, he never imagined she would refuse him. Ever since he attained the title, women had thrown themselves at him in order to wring a proposal out of him. He'd just assumed Tia would consent.

He should have known better. Tia was unlike any other woman he'd ever met. Had he thought out the plan, instead of succumbing to it in a moment of weakness, he would have realized that she would never agree. She obviously still had feelings for his brother. Otherwise, she would have returned to the estate to check on her sister. Or accepted his proposal.

Still, the only way to complete his reformation was to entice her to accept him and his flaws. It might take time, but it would be worth it. Tia would make a good wife, albeit difficult at times. He could handle her . . . except when she ran off, his conscience reminded him. But would she make a good viscountess?

Probably not.

She was far too willing to speak her mind, do things her way even if she bucked convention. Maybe that wasn't a bad thing if she were to be married to him. Most would say he wasn't a good viscount. Which he wasn't. He didn't know anything about being one. A rake, a scoundrel, or a gambler—that he knew how to do.

But he promised his mother he would become a better person and take the opportunity in front of him. Then again, he also promised to look after his brother and that wasn't going so well, either.

Who would know if he didn't keep his vow?

He would.

So, there was no option here. He would find a way of marrying her. He sighed before taking a mouthful of brandy. The heady liquid danced across his tongue before warming his belly.

"I'm sorry."

Braden turned his head to see Tia standing at the threshold in her night rail with a shawl over her shoulders. "Come into the room by the fire before you catch cold."

Slowly, she walked into the room and sat in the wingback chair closest to the fire. He rose and poured her a brandy. Handing it to her, he said, "I assume you have recovered from your brandy intoxication and can drink it again."

A slight smile raised her lips. "Perhaps, but only one glass."

"I will make certain that is all you drink." He returned to his seat. "Now, what were you apologizing for?"

"Refusing your offer."

"Have you reconsidered?"

She shook her head. "No, I just thought I was rather rude about it. You deserve someone better."

Braden tilted his head back and laughed heartily.

"And what is so amusing about that?"

"You are one of only a very small handful of people who would ever say I deserve someone better. Most would say I never deserved the title, much less a beautiful, caring woman to share it with." He sipped his brandy before adding, "And they would be right."

"No," she said softly as she stared at her drink. "You are trying to reform yourself. A man who attempts such a thing should be looked upon with envy. There are very few people who can truly change."

But could he? After only six months, he'd broken his vow.

"What is wrong?" she asked.

He shrugged. "I don't think I'm doing a very good job of reforming if I can't last more than six months."

She went silent for a while. "I did deliberately entice you. And you did reject me the first time."

"I suppose I did. But the blame is solely on me. I should never have walked into your room."

"You were trying to make me feel better. There is nothing wrong with that." She gave him a half smile before sipping her brandy slowly. "Honestly, why would you want to marry *me*?"

Braden stared at her lovely, freckled face. When did he start to love freckles on a woman's face? She was beautiful, but that was not what she'd want to hear. "You are a very caring person, Tia. I would never tire of you."

Watching her face fall, he wondered if she needed platitudes of love. He didn't love her . . . did he? Of course not.

"So now what?" she asked.

He decided it was time to drop the idea of marriage. Obviously, getting her used to the idea would take time. "I'm not entirely certain."

"I suppose we go back to what we were doing and find Jonathon before he kills himself."

It always came back around to his brother. Braden did want to find him, but now wondered what would happen once he did. Would Tia run into his arms and profess her love? He couldn't think about that or he would never try to find Jonathon.

"Braden?"

He looked over at her and his heart pounded in his chest. "We find Jonathon."

"Of course we will. But not tomorrow. I want you in bed all day." Her cheeks reddened in embarrassment.

He raised an eyebrow at her.

"I meant, you must rest one more day before returning to your normal activities."

"I believe I proved an hour ago that I am up to any task."

She gave him a humorless look. "You shall rest one more day." Tia sipped the last of her brandy and rose. After placing the glass on the table, she said. "I shall go up now."

"Good night."

"You're not coming up?"

"I suppose if I don't, my wise woman will scold me." He rose slowly, feeling weaker than he wanted to admit to anyone. "Sleep in my room tonight. We made a mess of your bed."

"I couldn't do that," she said, walking toward the threshold.

"I shall be a perfect gentleman."

"And who would want that," she muttered so softly he almost didn't hear her.

Braden smiled. "Come along."

She hesitated when they reached the door to his room.

"Why are you stopping? You've been sleeping in my room for the past few nights."

"In a chair."

"Well, you can sleep in a chair tonight if you prefer it to a nice, soft bed." He brushed past her and opened the door. "I promised to behave tonight."

"Very well." She walked into the room and then into the bed-chamber. Quickly, she slipped off her shawl and crawled under the covers.

Braden tossed some coal on the fire before sitting on the edge of the bed. After removing his shirt, he unbuttoned his trousers and slid them off. For her modesty, he kept his drawers on. Once under the covers, he drew her near.

"I thought you were to be a gentleman tonight?"

"I am. I just want to hold you," he whispered, then kissed her head.

She released a long sigh. "Why did you make that vow to reform? You couldn't have been all that bad. I know you said you'd been with too many women, but that doesn't mean you have to be celibate like a priest."

"It wasn't just women. It was everything. Before my mother died, she made me promise that if I inherited the title, I would do better in life. Settle down and find a fine woman to marry. Stop gambling and chasing women."

"And have you done that for her?"

"I am trying, Tia. I really want to make the estate profitable again."

She pushed up on his chest and stared down at him. "The estate is not profitable?"

"It is not what an estate of that size should be making. I have money from the Red Door to invest in Middleton Hall. By making a few changes, things should improve. We're far from bankrupt, just not where I want the estate."

"And if things don't improve?"

"They will." *They must.* He was determined to give his children a better life than he'd had. Braden closed his eyes as he thought about his children. He had always been so careful with other women to be sure he didn't spill his seed inside them. The last thing he'd wanted was some bastard-born child or a woman attempting to coerce him into marriage. But with Tia, he hadn't even thought about it. She could be carrying his child right now.

The idea that she might be carrying his child warmed his heart and soul. With her caring nature, she would make a wonderful mother. But he also knew that unlike most women, wise women didn't care if they had children outside of marriage. So even if she were to become with child, there was no certainty that she would marry him.

She was without a doubt the most vexing woman he had ever met.

Chapter 16

Tia awoke the next morning with a heavy arm around her. Deep breathing from behind her forced the weariness from her eyes. She blinked and looked around slowly, remembering what had happened last night. She had given herself to Braden.

Willingly.

She'd told herself that it wouldn't matter. No one would care if she succumbed to his charms, but she'd been terribly wrong. She cared. In a way, she had broken her own vow.

She had done the one thing she'd criticized her own sister for too many times. God, what would Mia think of her now? Tia wondered if Mia had finally succumbed to the earl's charms as she had to Braden's. A wave of homesickness came over her. She missed her sister and even her mother. She wanted to walk the fields to see the tenants, tend their ills, and help them through this hard life they led. A tear fell over her nose to the pillow.

"Why are you crying?" Braden whispered in her ear before kissing the nape of her neck.

"I miss them," she whispered.

"Who?"

"Everyone. My mother, Mia, Selina, all the tenants, and the servants at the hall."

"Shh, sweetheart," he murmured. "Do you want me to have a carriage take you back to Middleton Hall?"

She shook her head. "Thank you, but no. We need to find Jonathon."

"All right. Unfortunately, this little poisoning has set us back again."

"Yes, it has. I need to leave before your valet comes in to dress you." Tia lifted his arm and slid under it to get out of the bed.

"You could stay here with me all day in bed," he said in a husky voice.

She glanced over her shoulder and her knees went weak. The coverlet was down to his hips, exposing his broad shoulders and bare chest. The urge to climb back into bed was overwhelming. But she couldn't do that. She had work to do today.

"Do you mind if I go to the park? With a maid, of course."

"That should be fine. Why are you going to the park?"

"I need to speak with Emily and I thought that might be neutral ground for the both of us."

"As you wish."

"Thank you, Braden." She gathered her shawl and raced to her room. She wrote a quick note to Emily and then rang for Mrs. Abbott. Before the housekeeper arrived, Tia had already pulled out a day gown, changed into a fresh shift, and was waiting for her.

"My goodness, you are a in a rush today," Mrs. Abbott said as she entered the room. She glanced over at the bed. "So, things went as you had hoped?"

"Yes," Tia said, handing Mrs. Abbott her stays. "Please help me dress. His lordship has allowed me to walk to the park as long as I have a maid to accompany me. Would you like to be my escort?"

Mrs. Abbott laughed. "I have far too much work to take a leisurely walk in the park. I need the maids, so you can have one of the footmen. It's safer that way."

Tia frowned. "Safer? What do you mean?"

"Someone attempted to kill his lordship. And possibly not for the first time. The past two viscounts died under suspicious circumstances. People already know you are his mistress. If someone is trying to kill him to inherit and they suspect you might be carrying his heir, you will be in danger."

Tia bit her lower lip. What Mrs. Abbott said made some sense. Still, as long as she didn't marry him, she could be no threat. "I will consider your words carefully. Do you have any ideas on who might be involved in this matter? All the rumors are that it was his lordship who murdered the previous viscounts in order to inherit."

Mrs. Abbott tightened Tia's stays. "Do you believe that? Because I certainly do not and neither does the rest of the staff."

"No, I don't believe he had anything to do with the deaths. But who, then?"

"I would have to wager Mr. Jonathon Tavers. No one has seen him. He came to town and didn't stay at his brother's house."

"I cannot believe Jonathon would try to kill his own brother," Tia remarked. "He loves his brother."

"Yes, but he might love the title and all that goes with it even more." Mrs. Abbott slipped the sage dress over Tia.

Jonathon? She couldn't imagine Jonathon trying to kill anyone, much less his brother. Did Braden suspect him? Perhaps that was the real reason Braden wanted to find him. She had to discover the truth.

"Thank you, Mrs. Abbott. I will be down for breakfast in a few minutes. I must speak with his lordship about something."

"Of course. I will let Mr. Nelson know you need to borrow a footman." Mrs. Abbott headed for the door.

"Mrs. Abbott, might I ask a favor of you?"

She stopped and nodded. "Of course."

"Would you take the linens off the bed? I should hate for anyone else to see them."

Mrs. Abbott's face softened. "Of course, my dear." She looked over at the bed and stared at the stained sheets. "So you really were a good girl. Did his lordship offer to make you a respectable woman?"

"Yes and no," she mumbled.

"I don't understand," Mrs. Abbott said as she removed the sheets.

"He said we should marry, but he never exactly proposed to me. Not that it matters. I could never marry a viscount. Could you ask a footman to deliver this for me?" Tia handed her the missive for Emily.

"Of course," Mrs. Abbott remarked. Once the sheets were removed, she left the room and Tia to her thoughts.

She had to ask him about Jonathon. Could he really suspect his brother of trying to harm him? Tia walked to Braden's room and knocked softly.

"Come in." His deep voice sent shivers down her back. It brought back memories of last night.

She opened the door and found him already dressed and sitting at the small table in his salon. "Why are you out of bed?"

He tilted his head and smiled at her. "Indeed? Back for more already? I should think you might be a tad sore."

"I need to speak with you about something and then you are to get back in bed. I told you that you need one more day of rest."

"Tia, I am not going to spend my day in bed . . . unless you are with me. I promise not to exert myself today. But I need to speak with a few people."

She put her hands on her hips. "You are not going out. Someone is trying to kill you."

"Exactly. And the last time it happened in this very house." His voice grew louder with every word. "Now, what do you need to talk about?"

"Do you suspect Jonathon?"

He sighed and looked up at the ceiling. "I don't know. In all honesty, yes, it has crossed my mind that he might be the one involved."

"How could you believe that?"

"I have no wish to believe my brother is embroiled in two murders and two attempts on my life." His shoulders sagged. "But who else could it be?"

"There has to be someone else."

"I know you want to believe the best of Jonathon, but he has changed in the past few years."

She finally sat down in the chair across from him. "Do you honestly think Jonathon could be caught up in this mess?"

"I don't want to believe that, Tia. I truly don't. But I don't know what to think anymore. I know I wasn't involved in the previous viscounts' deaths. Someone has taken a shot at me and then attempted to poison me. Who else could want the title enough to kill for it?"

Tia stared at his handsome face. He had shaved this morning, which gave him less of a dark look. His blue eyes shone with frustration. There had to be someone else involved. "What about your cousin . . . Alistair?"

"Alistair would have to get through four people to become viscount. The previous two viscounts, me, and then Jonathon. He would never survive the scandal. The suspicion would fall directly on him. He's a smart man. He knows if he befriends the current viscount, he can ask for whatever he needs."

"But why Jonathon?"

"If he inherits, the estate and my personal fortune fall to him, giving him the funds to continue his habits."

Tia blinked quickly to keep the tears at bay. It couldn't be Jonathon, but hearing Braden's logic made her wonder.

"I am sorry, Tia. I know how you feel about him."

He knew how she felt about Jonathon? *She* didn't even know how she felt about him. The only thing she was certain of was that she didn't love him. As least, she wasn't *in* love with him. She would always love him, but more like a brother. "Thank you. I believe I shall go for my walk now."

"With a maid," he commented.

"Actually, Mrs. Abbott needs all the maids, so she suggested I take a footman."

He smiled at her. "Even better."

What was it about his smile that made her heart skip a beat? "What are you going to do?"

"I need to speak with Mr. Brady, the runner I hired to find Jonathon. After that, I want to discover if Adams has seen Jonathon or heard any rumors about him."

"Very well, I shall see you at dinner then," Tia said and then walked to the door.

After a quick breakfast, she went to the park and sat on a bench overlooking the Serpentine. Thirty minutes passed with no sign of Emily, then an hour. She wasn't coming. Slowly, Tia rose from the bench and started to leave.

"Miss Featherstone!"

Tia turned at the sound of Emily's voice. "Oh, thank God!" She raced back to the bench and sat down next to Emily.

"We mustn't talk for long," Emily said, scanning the area. "I'm sorry, but I can't be seen with you. My husband would have my head."

"I understand. Have you heard any more of Jonathon?"

"Yes, my husband said Mr. Tavers was at the club last evening."

"Which club?"

"White's, of course," Emily said, as if Tia should know that fact.

"Oh." Tia certainly couldn't go there.

"And he then went to Lady Bunworth's soiree. I did not attend. I find myself very tired lately."

"That's to be expected," Tia said quickly. "It will get a little better in the next few weeks and by the end you will be tired again. Is everything else going all right?"

"Yes, I am well. My husband found a fine physician."

Tia shuddered, remembering her mother's story of the London physician whom she saw deliver a baby with filthy hands. The poor woman almost died and her mother blamed the physician. "Please tell him to wash his hands before coming near you."

Emily turned and looked at her strangely. "Very well. What are you going to do now?"

"I would like to pay a call on Lady Bunworth, but I do not expect she will see me."

"She will. Just tell her you are Middleton's betrothed. That will set her on her ear," Emily said with a laugh. "She'll hate the fact that he was able to find a bride with his reputation. And despise you for being that woman."

"Then why will she see me?"

Emily giggled again. "You have so much to learn! She will see you because you will soon outrank her."

Tia's head spun with all the nonsense of Society. It was enough to make a person mad. "The woman will see me because she believes that one day I shall outrank her?"

"Yes. Would you like me to accompany you? This could be interesting," Emily said with a grin.

"No, you go home and rest. How has your husband been toward you?"

Emily sobered. With a shrug, she said, "He has already found a new mistress and has told me that he won't visit my bedroom again until after the baby is born."

Tia sighed. "I'm so sorry, Emily."

"There is nothing I can do to stop him." Emily's lips tightened into a straight line.

Was it any wonder Tia had no desire to marry? Although, she knew not all men were like that. Her own father had been a wonderful husband for her mother . . . and a great father. If she could find a man of a similar nature, she would marry with no hesitation.

"Very well," Tia said. "I will pay a call to Lady Bunworth to see if she can give me any information on Mr. Tavers."

"Good luck." Emily scanned the area before giving her a quick hug. "I miss you."

"I miss you too."

"Perhaps we can meet in a few days." Emily stood and then said, "Send me a note."

"I will do just that." Tia watched as Emily left. She did miss being able to talk with another woman. Mrs. Abbott was a fine woman, but nearly twenty years her senior. She longed for a friend closer to her age.

She watched as Emily ambled toward the awaiting carriage. Tia needed to call on Lady Bunworth. There was just one issue, she had no idea where Lady Bunworth lived. Tia rose from the bench, ready to run toward Emily, only to see her carriage slowly pulling away. She would never be able to catch her.

Now what would she do?

As she strolled back toward Middleton's house, she wondered how he would feel about visiting his cousin. They didn't seem to get on terribly well. And she still wondered if Alistair had something to do with the poisoning. Mary had been in his employ for his sister Constance before coming to work for Middleton. Tia wondered why Constance hadn't brought her to Lord Bunworth's home.

Once Tia reached the house, she made her decision. She would ask him to accompany her. If he chose not to, she would go alone.

"How was your walk, miss?" Nelson asked, closing the door behind her.

"Very nice. It is a beautiful fall day." She removed her bonnet and handed it to him. "Thank you, Nelson. Is his lordship in the study?"

"Yes, miss, but he has company."

"Oh?"

Nelson smiled at her. "Mr. Cranborne and Mr. Adams."

Her curiosity piqued. What were both men doing in the study with Middleton with the door closed? Perhaps if she went to the library, she might hear something. "Nelson, I will wait in the library for his lordship to finish his meeting."

"Would you like tea?"

"Yes, please." She walked to the library and then stared at all the books. Unable to hear anything but mumbled voices from the room next door, she pulled out a book. The collection here was nowhere near as extensive as at the estate, but excellent just the same.

She opened the books of herbs and scanned. It appeared to be very old, but fine, resource. Finding a chapter on belladonna, she read through it again until sadness overwhelmed her. If only she'd had this book a year ago. It might have saved that little girl's life. She flipped a few pages and read the chapter on herbs that helped ease labor pains.

Braden waited for his friends to say something, but they seemed to be dumbstruck by his comment about Tia. Finally, Jack blinked and looked over at Adams, who only shrugged.

"He is obviously lying," Jack commented.

"I most certainly am not!" Braden exclaimed. "She rejected my proposal."

"You expect us to believe that a woman who has nothing refused to marry a wealthy, titled gentleman?" Adams folded his arms over his chest.

"Why would I lie about such a thing?" Braden's irritation grew.

"Because you want us to believe you didn't break your vow," Jack said. "A woman like Miss Featherstone would do anything to become your wife."

"Indeed?" Braden rang the bell for Nelson. "We shall see about that."

Nelson knocked before entering the room. "Do you need something, my lord?"

Jack sniggered. "I still cannot get used to people calling you 'my lord.' "

"Has Miss Featherstone returned from her walk?" Braden asked, ignoring his annoying friend.

"She has, and is in the library reading. Is there anything else?" Nelson asked quietly.

"No, and thank you, Nelson." Braden rose from his seat. "I believe we shall now set the record straight. Come along."

Both men followed him out of the study to the library. Braden paused for a moment and stared at her. Tia's windblown hair had fallen out of the coiffure, leaving red tendrils framing her face. She appeared so at peace here. He cleared his throat to gain her attention. "Miss Featherstone, my dearest friends have a rather personal question they would like to ask you. Please do not feel you have to answer them if you believe it too delicate."

She smiled as she turned her head at them. A devilish twinkle entered her eyes. "Well, my lord, it would depend on the nature of the question."

"It regards a certain proposal of marriage from me."

"Indeed? And what would the gentlemen like to know about that subject?"

Jack took a step into the room. "Did he propose marriage to you and then you rejected his offer?"

Braden stared at her for a long moment. She had such a twinkle in her eyes, he wondered if she would tell them the truth.

"If you call being told you would marry a person a 'proposal,' then I suppose he did. Personally, I did not feel that was a proper proposal. What do you think?"

Adams stifled a laugh. "She's starting to grow on me, Middleton." He turned his attention on Tia and said, "I would to agree with you, Miss Featherstone."

She smiled, revealing a slight dimple in her right cheek. "Not that it mattered."

"How so?" Jack asked.

"I would have rejected a proper proposal as quickly as I did an improper one." Tia's brow rose.

Jack laughed. "Come now," he said, walking to the chair across from her. "A wealthy man who happens to be a viscount makes an offer and you would refuse?"

"Yes, I would," Tia replied. "Why would a man like that want to marry a poor country woman? Now, if love were involved, then I might change my mind. But do you honestly believe a man like Middleton could fall in love with me?"

Adams looked between them both and slowly nodded. "It might be possible."

Braden stared at his friend. "Why do you sound so surprised?"

This time, Tia giggled. "With *your* reputation?"

"I am not the same man I was six months ago," Braden said in a defensive tone. "I have no wish to return to that lifestyle."

"It wasn't all that bad," Jack muttered.

"I have to agree with Jack," Adams said. "You didn't seem all that upset about your lifestyle until after—"

"I just didn't show it," Braden interrupted his friend. He had no desire for Tia to learn exactly who had been the impetus for him to change his life. "I could be a good husband."

"Perhaps," Adams drawled.

"Yes, but until Jonathon is found, nothing else matters," Tia spoke up. "And I was told he paid a call on Lady Bunworth last evening."

"He did what?" Braden asked. "Why didn't you tell me as soon as you returned from your walk?"

Tia put aside her book and rose. "You had callers."

"It's them," he said, waving his hands at his friends. "They already know that we are looking for my brother."

"Well, I believe we should pay a call on Lady Bunworth," Jack said with a grin.

"We cannot all go pounding on her door," Tia said. "His lordship and I will go. My friend also told me, Jonathon was at White's last night. So you two, go there."

"I can't go to White's," Jack replied. "I'm not a member."

"I am," Adams said with a shake of his head. "You can enter as my guest."

"And you," Tia said, looking over at Braden, "will introduce me as your betrothed."

"Will I?" he said, cocking an eyebrow at her. "I don't believe you have accepted my offer."

"No, I haven't. But your cousin is not aware of that fact. I am quite certain that she will not accept me into her home under any other circumstances."

"You are most likely correct on that mark. Very well," said, holding out his arm to her, "shall we go visit my cousin and set London on its ear?"

"How so?"

"You have just caught a viscount, my dear. The world will never be the same."

Chapter 17

Tia took Braden's arm as he helped her out of the carriage. Looking up at Lady Bunworth's house, a shiver of fear swept across her. She hadn't thought about the repercussions of being introduced as his betrothed. Her only thought had been to gain entrance into the home. But news of their engagement would spread like fire all over London. What would happen when the truth came out that they weren't to marry?

"Middleton, please wait," she said, before they walked up to the house.

"Come along, Miss Featherstone. Do not think of the future, only now." He forced her forward either deliberately to ignore her concerns or because he didn't want to be seen skulking in front of his cousin's home.

"But—"

"Not now. We will discuss this later." He knocked on the door and they waited in silence.

"My lord," the butler said with a bow. "Please come in."

They walked into the home and the butler showed them to a small salon. The house was much smaller than Middleton's house in town.

"Please tell Lady Bunworth that I am here with my betrothed," Middleton said.

"I shall see if Lady Bunworth is at home," the servant said stiffly.

The butler left and Tia couldn't help but giggle. "Surely he knows if she is at home."

Middleton stifled a smile. "True, but he doesn't know if she will accept us into her home."

Tia shook her head. She would never understand these people. "Why would she not? You are her cousin."

"True, but if she doesn't wish to speak with me, then the butler will say she is not at home. It is common courtesy."

Footsteps announced the return of the butler. "Lady Bunworth will be down presently, my lord. I have ordered tea."

"Thank you," Middleton said.

Once the butler walked away, Tia whispered, "What will happen once everyone finds out we are not engaged?"

"Not now, Tia."

Lady Bunworth appeared at the threshold. Her lips were pursed, her face drawn, and her eyes narrowed. "You had the nerve to bring that woman into my home, cousin?"

He rose and bowed. "You are speaking of my future wife, Constance."

Lady Bunworth inhaled and slowly released the breath. "Very well, Middleton. Welcome to the family, Miss Featherstone."

"Thank you, my lady."

"You may call her Constance," Middleton said with a smile.

His cousin eyed him critically. "You are looking well, Middleton."

"Thank you, Constance."

"Where is the tea?" Constance turned and shouted down the hall.

"Coming, my lady," a voice called from down the hall.

Constance walked to the sofa and sat down. A footman rushed into the room and placed the tea service on the table between them, before leaving the room with all haste. She poured the tea and handed a cup to each of them.

"So," she drawled. "Other than to announce you have decided to make Miss Featherstone an almost respectable woman, why are you here?"

"Ah, Constance," Middleton said. "Always straight to the point."

He sipped his tea as if to make her wait for an answer. Finally, he set his cup down and looked over at her. "I heard a rumor that my brother paid you a visit last evening. Is that true?"

Her face went pallid. "Yes, he called on my husband. Why?"

"I haven't seen him since I returned to town. I would like to speak with him."

Tia watched the expressions running through her face.

"You haven't seen him at all?" Constance sounded truly surprised. "I spoke with him briefly before Harold came downstairs. Jonathon said he had seen you only two days ago."

Middleton's shoulders sagged. "No, he has not paid a call on me."

"How odd," Constance said with a shrug.

"Is Bunworth home that I might speak to him about this?" Middleton asked.

"No, he is at his club. Was that the only reason you stopped by?"

"Yes," Middleton said.

"No," Tia said.

Middleton turned and stared at her. "It is not?"

"No," Tia said again. "Why did you not take your maid with you when you married?"

"Mary?" Constance shrugged. "She and I had a falling out over a certain hairstyle I wanted. She thought it was inappropriate for a soon-to-be-married woman. So I insisted Bunworth hire a new maid before I married him. Why?"

"Do you have any idea where she is?" Tia asked.

"Alistair told me she was in your home, Middleton." She quirked a brow and looked over at Tia. "For her."

"She was, but she left suddenly and with no notice. It was quite odd," he replied.

"Hmm, no, I have not seen her." Constance rose from her seat. "I really must ask that you take your leave now. I have to call on my mother."

"Of course," Middleton said as he rose. He gave her a quick bow. "Good day, madam."

"Good day."

Constance said nothing to Tia as she walked past. Tia stopped and said, "Good day, Lady Bunworth."

"Good day, Miss Featherstone. And good luck getting that one to put a ring on your finger."

Tia trailed behind Middleton, who seemed to be in a big hurry to leave his cousin's home. Not that she could blame him. The woman was a witch. Tia scrambled into the carriage while Middleton followed her. "Well, that was fruitless."

"Not at all. We know Jonathon was there last night and was lying to Constance about seeing me. We also know that Adams and Cranborne are both at White's right now. They know we were speaking with Constance, so they will strike up a conversation with Bunworth."

"Do you believe what she said about Mary?" Tia asked.

Middleton released a sigh. "Honestly, I don't know. It doesn't take much to get a maid sacked. Perhaps Alistair felt Mary wasn't in the wrong, so he kept her on. I don't know."

"Something just doesn't feel right," she whispered.

"On that we can agree."

She looked up to his handsome face and smiled. "Now what?"

"We go home and rest until Adams and Cranborne return."

"I agree that you should rest, but is there nothing else we can do?" There had to be something. "Perhaps we could go to White's—"

His loud laughter caught her off. "Sweetheart, we could never go to White's."

"And why exactly not?"

"Because you are a woman and White's is strictly for men."

"Oh." She supposed she should have known that. But there weren't any men's clubs in the Midlands of which she was aware.

He squeezed her hand. "You wouldn't have known that. I apologize."

"How do people learn all this?" she asked quietly. Back home, she always felt quite intelligent. But here? She was completely ignorant of some of the most basic of information. She didn't belong here. Perhaps it was time to accept that fact and return home.

"It's no different than how you were raised."

"What do you mean?"

"You were raised by a woman who made you read books on herbs, taught you how to set a bone, birth a baby, and help an elderly person pass comfortably to the afterlife. The women here are made to read

Debrett's to learn every peer's name, how to converse about the weather, and other unimportant things so as not to look too intelligent in front of a prospective husband. Personally, I would rather have a conversation with you than any of the women of Society."

"You would?"

He stared down at her with a smile. "Of course."

Sneaking a look up at him, she sighed. If she returned to the estate, she would miss him terribly. How was it possible that she would miss him? But she would. That was the most ridiculous thought ever. She barely knew him.

But she was discovering that he wasn't the man she'd assumed he was from all the rumors. He certainly wasn't heartless. She had a terrible feeling that she was falling in love with him.

"What is wrong?" he asked. "You have gone quite pale."

"N—nothing," she muttered.

"Tia . . ."

Thankfully, the carriage slowed to a stop in front of his home. As soon as she could, she scrambled down with his help and rushed into the house. "Good afternoon, Nelson," she said and continued up the stairs to her room.

She ripped off her bonnet and gloves, tossing them on a nearby chair. Then she paced. And paced. She couldn't be in love with him, she told herself. That just wasn't possible. She wasn't that naïve. She knew nothing could come of it. His offer of marriage was only to ease his guilt for breaking his vow. Nothing more!

A knock halted her stride. Assuming it was Mrs. Abbott, she said, "Come in."

She turned away from the door and continued her pacing. It took a few seconds to realize just how quiet Mrs. Abbot was this afternoon. Tia turned and found Middleton with his back against the door and his arms folded over his chest.

"What are you doing in my room unannounced?"

"You told me to come in," he said with a smirk.

"I thought you were Mrs. Abbott." God, why wouldn't he leave? The longer he stood there sending her those smoldering looks, the more her thoughts turned sensual. And she shouldn't—no, *wouldn't*— let her mind go there.

"There are usually only two reasons women pace in their bed-chambers." He tilted his head slightly.

"Oh? Only two? I can think of many reasons a woman might wish to pace in her room," Tia retorted. Perhaps if she could summon her anger at him, then she wouldn't think about stripping off his jacket and shirt so she could run her fingernails down his chest.

"The first is that she is not telling her lover something important."

"You are not my lover," she countered.

"Then it must be the obvious." He stepped away from the door, slowly stalking her. His blue eyes shimmered.

She took a step back for each he went forward. "What is obvious?"

He continued to pursue her until she felt the wall behind her. He smiled at her predicament. "The only other reason for a woman to wear a carpet so thin is frustration."

"What frustration?" He couldn't possibly know her thoughts.

"Frustration of a carnal nature," he whispered near her ear.

She shivered when his lips plucked little kisses around her ear. "I believe you might be wrong about that."

"Am I?" He trailed kisses down her jaw.

"What about your vow?" she whispered hoarsely. She couldn't want this again. Well, she *shouldn't* want this again.

"We have already discussed that." He kissed just both corners of her mouth before bringing his hard lips down on hers.

Resist him, her conscience screamed at her. But she didn't want to resist him. Slowly, she opened her mouth for him, letting his tongue find hers. The heat of his mouth on hers made her melt against him.

He broke the kiss and stared down at her with those penetrating eyes. "Do you have any idea how much I want you right now?"

Emboldened by the desire she would see in his eyes, she placed her hand on his trouser-covered cock and stroked him. "I believe I do."

"Tia," he groaned as he ripped off his jacket. "If you weren't so inexperienced I would take you against the wall right now."

"Against the wall?" The image that came to her mind excited her, sending moisture to her folds. "How?"

"God, I love your curiosity." He backed her against the wall again and then lifted her up. "Put your legs around my hips."

She wrapped her legs around him. Feeling the pressure of his bulge against her, she whispered, "Oh, yes, please, Braden. Like this."

Braden groaned. He couldn't do this to her yet, no matter how much his body wanted him to sink into her wetness right this second. "You're so new at this, Tia. It might be too much."

"Now," she said as she rubbed herself against him.

"No," he said. He wrapped his arms around her back and carried her to the bed. "I am going to make love to you . . . properly."

A slight look of disappointment crossed her eyes. "You don't have to be such a gentleman with me."

He tore at his clothing until he was naked. Slowly, he knelt over her. "You make me want to be a gentleman for a change."

She blinked her eyes quickly, as if attempting to hold back tears. "You shouldn't say such things," she whispered.

He stretched out over her and kissed her sensually. When he broke away from her, he stared into her brown eyes. "I will never be good enough for you, Tia. But I'm going to spend a lifetime trying to be."

Before she could utter a sound, he kissed her hard, demanding a response to his passion. Feeling her soft tongue scrape against his sent desire flaring through his body. Her soft moans encouraged him. Skimming his hand down her throat to her bodice, he realized his mistake. With a slight laugh, he pulled away.

"What is wrong?" she panted.

"We are doing this all wrong," he said, rolling off her.

"We are?"

Braden rose from the bed and pulled her up with him. "We both really should be naked. Now turn around."

She did as he requested and he had her stripped out of her clothing in just a few moments. Standing before him in just her stocking and garters, she shivered from either desire or the room temperature.

"Sit on the bed so I can remove your stockings."

"I can do it." She reached for the garter, but he pushed her hand away.

"I will do that."

"As you wish." She sat down on the edge of the bed and waited.

He quickly untied the first garter and slowly skimmed it down her leg. She released a staggered breath. After undoing the second, he brought his lips down to the soft skin of her thigh. Kissing his way down her leg, he removed the other offending stocking.

Once the stocking was off, he trailed kisses back up the long length of her leg. When he reached the apex of her thighs, he drew a finger along the crease. Feeling her quiver brought a smile to him. He moved his head between her legs and let his tongue follow the path of his finger.

"Braden," she exclaimed. "What are you doing?"

"Enjoying the taste of you."

"Oh," she said with a sigh.

Tia lay back against the bed as his tongue slid between her folds. This couldn't be right. But it felt so good. Her body tingled from the sensations. She felt a finger probe her entrance before sliding into her. Her heart pounded in her chest as he continued bringing her closer to the edge. As he stroked her harder, his finger sliding inside and out of her, her every nerve drew taut.

"Braden," she screamed as release finally washed over her. Her entire body shook from the powerful climax. "Oh, my God," she whispered.

He crawled back on the bed and kissed her softly, the taste of her still on his lips. Slowly, he kissed her neck, drawing gooseflesh to her arms. When he reached her breasts, he stared down at them for a long moment before plucking a tight nipple into his mouth. Instantly, her body reacted and readied for more.

She moaned as his mouth moved to the other nipple, eager for his attention. She reached for his hard cock and stroked it softly until he groaned.

"You are driving me mad," he whispered, staring down at her.

"Good," she replied with a slight smile.

He moved away from her reach and settled between her legs. Feeling his manhood at her entrance, she tried to relax. She knew it wouldn't hurt like the first time, still, she had no idea what to expect.

He entered her slickness gradually, as if testing her comfort level. Her body eased him inside, stretching to accommodate his size. The feeling of fullness was overwhelming.

"Are you all right?" he asked as he filled her completely.

"Yes," she replied with a shiver. "You feel so good inside me."

He groaned slightly. "You feel so good around me. You're so tight and wet. I just want to stay here all night."

"It's still afternoon," she said with giggle.

"Exactly."

Then he moved slightly and her laughter stopped. Just that minor movement was enough to make her realize how close to the brink she was from his being inside her. This time he slid out of her and then back in. She looked up into his eyes and was lost. She was his in body and spirit. She loved the man.

Watching his face tighten as he fought off the passion trying to take over his body made her love him more. She lifted her legs and wrapped them around his hips, bringing him deeper inside her. Her body was on fire. Climbing higher with every stroke, she never wanted this to end. But soon, she was at the top with no place to go but over.

"Yes," she whispered as she tightened her inner muscles around him.

"Tia," he moaned.

An explosion of color burst upon her. "Braden, oh Braden," she said, shaking with the emotion and passion sweeping over her body.

"Tia." He stroked her twice more before closing his eyes to his own climax.

He collapsed down on her, his breathing ragged. She wrapped her arms around him, enveloping him in her love. "I love you," she whispered.

Chapter 18

Braden stilled. His breathing all but stopped with her words. She didn't mean them, of course. Far too many women had spoken words of love in the heat of the moment, only to retract them once morning came and they fully realized whom they had fucked. He would let it go for now. He couldn't speak words of love to her. Not when he wasn't certain what he felt for her was anything but six months of pent-up lust.

He didn't like red hair and freckles on a woman.

Did he?

"Braden?"

Oh God, she was going to want to talk about this. He supposed he could pretend to have fallen asleep.

"I know you're awake."

"How could you know such a thing when I'm on top of you?"

She laughed softly. "Your breathing is much too erratic for a sleeping man."

Damn her and her wise woman skills. "Well, you have me there." He rolled off her and brought her close. *Please don't bring up words of love right now.*

"Is it always that good?"

Oh, thank God, she wanted to speak of sexual intercourse. "No. Sometimes it's even better. Were you sore?"

"No." She wrapped an arm around his chest. "When can we do that again?" she whispered.

"After I rest."

She looked up at him with worry on her face. "Did this exhaust you? I knew we shouldn't do such a thing until you were completely healed from the poison. I should let you get some—"

"Sweetheart, I am well. After making love, it takes some time before a man is ready to do that again."

"It does?"

He smiled at her innocence. "Yes."

"I am learning quite a bit about the male anatomy." She put her head back down on his shoulder.

"What did you do if someone asked you a question about such things?"

"I referred them to my mother."

He chuckled. "I think I'd prefer you to your mother when discussing such things. She is . . ." His voice trailed off so as not to insult her mother.

"A termagant?"

"Now, I wouldn't have called your mother that," he said in an innocent tone.

This time she laughed. "I would. Sometimes I think she scares her patients as well." She sobered. "Honestly, her patients respect her completely."

"I have heard she is excellent at what she does."

"Yes," she said faintly. "Definitely better than me."

Braden closed his eyes. He was certain she was thinking back to her patient that died of the belladonna poisoning. If only there was some way of helping her get over her guilt. He rolled her over onto her back and stared down at her. "Have you ever asked your mother if she suffered something similar to what you are going through with that child?"

She shook her head. "No. How could I? She is the one who told me to let it go and learn from it."

He cupped her cheek with his hand. "Sweetheart, you did learn from it. I'm living proof of that."

"I know. And you might not be here if I didn't take my mother's advice, but letting that little girl's death go is impossible."

He couldn't imagine the anguish she suffered over this child's death. He wanted to take away all her pain. Slowly, he brought his head down and kissed her softly. Kissing her warmed his heart in a very unexpected way. He pulled back and stared down at her again. Oh dear God, he loved her.

The shock was almost too much to bear. He hadn't loved someone since. . . . Thankfully, a knock on the bedchamber door interrupted his insane thought process.

"My lord, Mr. Adams and Mr. Cranborne are here to see you."

"I shall be down in a few minutes. Pour them some brandy or tea."

"Of course, my lord."

Braden kissed the tip of her nose. "I must go. If you would like to join us in the library that would be fine."

"Thank you," she said, before wrapping her arms around his neck and kissing him sweetly.

"Do that again and I will forgo my friends in lieu of your tempting body."

She smiled up at him. "Go speak with them. Let your poor body rest a while longer."

She had no idea that his body was nearly ready to go again. "As you wish."

Braden dressed quickly and joined his friends in the library. Walking into the room, he said, "Good afternoon. What did you find out?"

He walked to the corner cabinet and poured a brandy for himself. Both of his friends were already sipping their drinks.

"Breaking your vow again?" Jack asked before putting his glass on the table.

"We had this discussion earlier," Braden reminded him. "We will marry." Now more than ever he wanted to marry her.

"Bunworth was at White's. He told us that Jonathon paid him a visit last night. He said Jonathon attempted to extort some money out of him."

Braden scowled. "Did he say why?"

"No. Nor did he say if he gave Jonathon the money," Adams replied.

Braden shook his head. His brother was in a far worse state than he imagined. Why was he trying to extort money from Constance's husband? Maybe Bunworth was keeping a mistress and Jonathon was trying to protect Constance. "Anything else?"

"Yes, Bunworth said he was supposed to deliver the money tonight at the Edmondsons' ball."

"Did he now? Hmm, I believe we are all going to a ball tonight," Braden said.

Jack shrugged. "Nothing better to do tonight. Are you bringing her along?"

"No, she would only be a distraction." And Braden didn't want her to see how low Jonathon had sunk.

"A very lovely distraction," Adams commented.

"Yes, but a distraction I don't need when trying to find Jonathon."

"She won't take it well," Jack added.

"She is not to know where I am going. I will tell her that it is a club and women are not invited." And he hoped she would believe his lie.

Tia sat in the library reading while Braden investigated another potential sighting of Jonathon at another club. She glanced up from her reading and wondered just how many clubs there were in London. Not that it mattered. As a woman, she wouldn't be allowed entrance to any of them.

She could hear a slight commotion at the front door, but assumed Nelson would handle the issue. What could she do? She had no authority in this house. Footsteps sounded in the hall.

"Miss Featherstone, you have a caller," Nelson announced as he stepped into the room.

"At this hour?" It was nearly eight.

"Yes, miss. It is Lady Eldridge."

Emily was here! At this hour! Something must be dreadfully wrong. "Where is she?"

"In the salon."

Tia rushed past Nelson and ran down the hall to the salon. "Emily, what is wrong?"

Emily sat on the edge of the sofa, wearing a beautiful russet silk gown. "It is just as I thought. You and his lordship haven't heard the news."

"Middleton is not at home. What is the news?"

"Mr. Tavers is supposed to be at the Edmondsons' ball tonight."

Tia tilted her head up toward the ceiling. Of all the nights that Braden had to leave her alone. "What are we going to do?"

"You are going upstairs right now to dress for a ball." Emily rose and then yanked on Tia's arm. "We don't have much time. The ball has already started and I don't know how long he will be in attendance."

"Very well. Help me dress. Mrs. Abbott has the night off." They both hurried upstairs to Tia's room. She opened the linen press and stared at her meager gowns. She reached for the blue silk, but Emily brushed her hand away and pulled out the red silk.

"I can't wear that outside the house," Tia protested.

"Yes, you can and you will. The Edmondsons' will allow you entrance because they tend to like to have their balls talked about for a few days. You showing up alone and wearing this dress will shock several people."

"Emily, I don't need more people gossiping about me."

"Shh," Emily reprimanded. "You will be the viscountess some day and everyone will be horrified that they spread such rumors about you."

Tia highly doubted that, but tonight she wasn't going to think about it. She would find Jonathon and bring him home. Together, she and Braden would find an excellent place for him to overcome his opium issues. "Very well," she finally said to Emily. "You win."

"I always do," Emily muttered.

Within an hour, she was dressed and ready to go. "How am I going to leave with Nelson at the door?"

"Leave that to me. Just be ready and when I get him in the library, walk outside. My carriage is right in front."

She hated sneaking out like this. Braden would be furious if he returned home before she did. Hopefully, Jonathon would be easy to find for once. If she could bring Jonathon home, Braden's anger would not be an issue.

"We need to leave now. Stay at the top of the stairs until I get Nelson in the library." Emily opened the door and then ambled down the stairs.

Tia released a long-held breath before following her to the top of the staircase. From her vantage point, she could hear Emily.

"I just need to get my gloves, Nelson. I left them in the library."

"I will get them for you, my lady," Nelson replied.

As his footsteps faded away, Emily slowly opened the front door and then waved her down. "Hurry!"

Tia raced down the stairs and out the door before Nelson returned. Amazed that the footman at Emily's coach just opened the door for her, she scrambled inside before the front door opened. Safely ensconced in her friend's carriage, she caught her breath while waiting for Emily. She peered out and noticed her friend walking toward her.

Once Emily was inside, Tia asked, "Was Nelson suspicious?"

"Not at all. I told him you had decided to retire."

Tia leaned back against the velvet squab and sighed. Then she giggled. "I don't think I've ever done anything like that before."

"I should hope not," Emily replied. She smiled over at Tia. "But we were quite good at it, weren't we?"

"Yes, we were."

"So who are the Edmondsons'?" Tia asked.

"A younger couple who run with a very fast set. Their parties are known for gossip, especially who sneaked off with whom."

"What do you mean?"

Emily laughed. "You're not that innocent, Tia. Different couples will pair off, find a room, and have sexual congress."

"At the party?"

"It happens all the time. Just at most parties it is much more secretive. At Society balls, a woman would be subject to scandal, which is why the fast set stays in London. Those Society matrons are all out at their country estates, haranguing the girls out there."

"So as Middleton's mistress, it wouldn't amiss to attend this party?"

"Not at all. I'd be surprised if Middleton wasn't invited."

Tia nodded. She wondered how many times he had taken a woman to a room at one of the Edmondsons' parties. Based on what he'd told her, it most likely happened a lot. She refused to think upon that any longer. He had changed.

"We're here," Emily said with a note of excitement.

Tia followed Emily out of the carriage and up the few steps to the house. Before the door even opened, the raucous sound of jovial voices emanated from the home. This definitely was not a sedate Society ball. A tremor of fear came out of nowhere and sliced through her.

The door opened and they entered arm in arm. To say the party was a crush would be an understatement. They could barely move through the corridor to the salon. The sound of music came from a back room. Tia silently wished Braden could have been here to dance with her. She'd so enjoyed that at Lady Whitfield's ball. What was she thinking? Braden would be furious with her, not wanting to dance.

"How are we supposed to find Jonathon with all these people?" Tia asked

"Just do the best you can," Emily said, close to her ear. "The crowd will thin in the next hour or two."

Hour or two? By then Braden might have returned home. "I can't stay that long."

"Stop worrying. Middleton is not your master. If you wish to go to a ball, you can do that."

Tia scanned the room, but didn't see Jonathon. Another man with dark blond hair caught her eye. Emily's husband had his arms wrapped around a petite brunette with a full figure. Tia's mouth almost gaped when she noticed his thumb rub the woman's breast in public. "Emily, I don't see him here. We should check another room."

"As you wish," Emily replied coldly.

Tia looked over to see her friend staring at her husband. "Come on."

"I cannot believe he was doing that in front of everyone."

"I know."

"I hate him," Emily muttered. "If I could leave him I would."

"But we all know you cannot. So, you will have to either determine a way to get him back into your bedroom, or learn to live your life alone." Tia had no idea where her vehemence on that topic came from.

They entered the next room, only to find the same thing. There were so many people that trying to pick Jonathon from all the rest was nearly impossible. Feeling as if this was a lost cause, Tia said, "I don't see him here. Perhaps this is a waste of our time."

"We must keep looking," Emily insisted. "The gaming is set up in the library. We should check in there."

Tia followed along as best she could, afraid if she lost sight of Emily she might never get out of this place. Thankfully, the gaming room had few people, which only made it easier to check. She scanned the room quickly, but her gaze stopped on a man she knew. "Oh dear God," she whispered. "We have to get out of this room immediately."

Emily wasted no time in exiting the room. "Who was that?"

"Mr. Cranborne. He was supposed to go to the club with Middleton. If Cranborne is here, then they must have left the club and Middleton might be home by now!"

"Stop worrying. He probably had a few drinks and will retire."

If only she could believe that. But Tia doubted he would retire without checking in on her.

"I told Nelson you were very tired. I am certain he will relay that information to Middleton. Just enjoy yourself." Emily grabbed two glasses of wine from a footman and gave one to her.

"Only one for you," Tia warned her.

"Of course."

Tia sipped her wine, now on the lookout for Mr. Cranborne. No matter what Emily said, Tia couldn't relax, knowing Braden could be at the house right now. Her hand shook as she brought the glass to her mouth. The fruity essence warmed her body and on an empty stomach, quickly went to her head.

"I see Lady Bunworth down the hall. I shall ask her if she has seen Jonathon yet," Emily said, handing Tia her half-full glass of wine.

Tia finished her wine and then drank Emily's while she waited. An older man with graying temples walked over to her.

"Aren't you a fetching thing," he said, staring at her breasts. "Would you like to find a room and talk?"

"I am quite certain anything we need to talk about can be said right here," she retorted coldly.

"Who do you belong to?" he asked.

"No one," she said and walked away.

"Well, you might just be wrong about that." Shock washed over her as her arm was held in a viselike grip. Before she could utter a sound, he forced her upstairs. He knocked on the door, before hurling it open and pushing her inside.

"What the bloody hell are you doing here?" Braden demanded.

Chapter 19

Braden couldn't remember the last time he felt this furious with another person. He folded his arms over his chest and stared at her. Did she have no sense at all? This was the type of party that could end up with her raped.

"What am I doing here?" Tia shouted. "What are you doing here? This doesn't look like a men's club to me."

"Where I go is no one's business."

"And where I go is no one's business either," she retorted. Her brown eyes flashed as her chest rose and fell, quickly displaying her anger.

He couldn't seem to take his eyes off those full white globes. Dammit, he felt like an adolescent around her. Already his cock was thickening. And why the bloody hell not? That red silk gown was made for one thing only.

"Where you go is my business," he finally said. He grabbed her arm and pulled her up against his chest. "As long as you are in my house, you are under my care. Do you understand?"

"Then perhaps I should leave," she said with a shrug of her shoulders.

He walked her back against the door, blocking her exit with his body. Her words from earlier rang in his ears. She had all but begged him to take her against the wall. Well, she was about to have her fantasy fulfilled.

"You are going nowhere," he whispered harshly in her ear. "You are mine." Before she could argue, he kissed her roughly. Part of him wanted to punish her for putting herself at risk. Another part just wanted her. He pushed up her skirts with his hand and split her drawers. Already her folds were moist.

She struggled slightly beneath him, her movements only urging him on. He knew she wanted this as badly as he wanted it. He moved his hand away from her addicting heat, only to unbutton his breeches. He slid his breeches down his hips just enough to free his shaft. Her hand reached for him, but he slapped it away. Nothing was going stop him now.

He picked her up and brought her warmth down on him. She moved her legs to straddle his hips.

"Oh, God," she said as he lowered her completely.

"You are mine," he whispered, sliding in and out of her sweetness. "No one will ever do this to you. No one."

"Yes," she cried. "I don't want anyone else—only you."

Braden was losing his mind with desire for her. Everything about her made him insane, from her freckles to her sweet warmth. He couldn't imagine spending a day without her. He bent his head to kiss her hard, reminding her that she would always be his. Oh, God, he would always be hers.

"Braden, yes," she whispered. "Yes."

He felt her inner muscles clenching down on him as her orgasm tore through her. She clutched his shoulders as if unable to stand the overwhelming sensations.

"Braden!"

God, he couldn't take any more. He thrust into her once more and let go to the driving passion. Spilling his seed into her, he could only whisper, "Tia, my Tia."

Neither moved for a few moments as spent passion had exhausted them both. Braden nuzzled her neck, inhaling the sweet aroma of her lavender soap. "Do you have an idea how I felt when I saw you here being propositioned by that lech downstairs?"

"I think I have an idea now," she whispered back.

"Never go out without me. You don't know these people as I do. Most of them are the most degenerate people you will ever meet. They don't care who they f—make love to, whether married or not, innocent or as wanton as they are. Some don't even care if you are willing or not."

He felt a tear drop from her face to his.

"I'm sorry. I had no idea."

"I know," he whispered. "I don't want to see you hurt. It would kill me if something happened to you."

"Emily told me she'd heard that Jonathon was supposed to be here tonight. You had only told me you were going to a men's club. You never told me which one. I had no way of getting a message to you."

"It's not your fault. I lied to you."

She pulled back until her head hit the door. "Why did you lie to me?"

With aching arms, he helped her off him. After putting himself back to together, he looked at her watery eyes. "I always intended to come here. I knew it wasn't the type of party you should attend. So I lied and told you I was going to a club."

"Because I wouldn't be able to go to a club with you." She pressed her lips together.

"Sweetheart, you have already had one man proposition you."

"And another one take me against a door in a stranger's bedroom."

"True, but at least I wasn't a stranger," he said with a slight grin.

"I am not certain about that," she retorted.

"Tia, I may not be the best man in London, but I'm far from the worst." He straightened out her skirts and adjusted her bodice. "I'm afraid I've made a mess of your hair."

"Let me see." She pushed away from him and went to the mirror. "Bring the hairpins that fell to the floor." She quickly put the pins back into place and looked almost respectable ... except for that gown. No woman could look respectable in that dress.

"Oh dear!" she exclaimed as she turned around. "I left Emily downstairs alone!"

Just what he needed: Emily being assaulted by some rake. "Let's find her and get out of here."

"What about Jonathon?"

"Just before I saw you, I was told that he had already arrived and departed."

Her face sank. "We missed him again. How it that possible?"

"He is deliberately avoiding me. By now, he has to know I am searching for him. Yet, he still hasn't had the decency to pay a call at my home."

She walked over and wrapped him in a warm hug. "I am sorry, Braden. I suppose I'm not helping matters when I run off without telling you." Before he could get used to her heat, she pulled away. "But I promise that I won't do it again."

She cupped his cheeks and kissed him gently. He accepted her comfort, savoring her warmth. He was doing exactly what he said he wouldn't . . . falling in love.

"We need to find Emily now," she said after pulling away slightly.

"I suppose we do. Maybe her husband will find her and take her to a bedroom," Braden said, waggling his eyebrows.

"I doubt it. Eldridge has a new mistress with him tonight."

"Here?"

She nodded sadly. "And Emily saw him with her."

"Bastard."

"I couldn't agree more. I swear he saw her too and he didn't make a move to protect her from all the others here."

Braden took her hand. "Let's go find her before something untoward happens."

They walked hand in hand toward the steps. A door closed behind them and Braden glanced back, only to see Emily straightening her skirts as she walked. Even from this distance, he knew what she'd been up to . . . but with whom? Damn. There was only one person she would risk being with.

As they reached the last step, Braden said, "I shall look in the salon. Why don't you check the gaming room?"

"Alone?"

"I'm right here. No one will get past me."

"All right." She walked down the hall just as Emily reached the last stair. Braden grabbed her arm and took her aside. "What the bloody hell are you doing?"

"I was looking for Tia," she said innocently.

"We both know who you are looking for," he said roughly. "Is he upstairs?"

"I don't know what you mean," she replied in a hushed tone.

"Yes, you do. Were you upstairs with Jonathon?"

"How could you think I would do such a thing to my husband?" She pulled her arm out of his grip.

"Because I know exactly the type of woman you are, Emily. My darling Emily," he sneered.

She looked visibly shaken. "Please don't tell Tia about us. She is the only friend I have in town."

"Where's Jonathon?"

"The last door on the left. But I don't know if he's still there."

"No one has else has come down those stairs."

She nodded. "I realize that, but the servant staircase is right next to that room."

"Dammit. Find Tia and tell her I went back upstairs for a moment. And do not let her leave without me."

"Of course. Where is she?" Emily asked as he reached the middle step.

"The gaming room."

Braden raced up the stairs and then ran down the corridor. When he reached the last door on the left, he threw open the door so hard it bounced against the linen press. As the door sprung back, he hit it with his fist. "Dammit!"

The room was completely empty. Once again, Jonathon had managed to evade him. He returned downstairs via the servants' staircase, but as he expected, there was no sign of his brother. He found his way back to the hall, where Tia and Emily waited for him.

"Look who I found," Tia said. "What were you looking for upstairs?"

"I thought I had dropped something in the bedchamber we . . . searched."

"Did you find what you were looking for?" Emily asked in an innocent tone.

Braden only shook his head. "No. I was mistaken."

He was tired of chasing him. Tired of trying to make Jonathon understand how important it was to be responsible. Feeling defeated, he sighed. "Lady Eldridge, may we share a ride with you? I came with my friends, but they are not ready to leave just yet."

"Of course, my lord."

By the time they returned home, it was after midnight and Tia was exhausted. The difficulties of trying to find Jonathon had worn them both out. Braden walked to her room and then stopped.

Dark circles lined his eyes. She reached up and cupped his cheek. "You need your rest."

"Stay with me tonight," he murmured. "I know you are tired. So am I. I just . . . I just need you with me tonight."

Tia blinked back tears. "Let me get my night rail."

She grabbed her night rail before following him to his bedchamber. "Can you help me?" she asked, turning her back to him.

Braden quickly helped her out of her dress and stays. "How much do you know about Lady Eldridge's relationship with Jonathon?"

She shrugged before putting on her night rail. "Emily didn't speak much about it, except to say she wasn't sure if he was the father of her baby or her husband. There was only a week between the last time she saw Jonathon and her wedding. Why?"

He climbed into bed. "She's hiding something from you, Tia."

"What do you mean?" Tia slipped under the covers and then snuggled up against him. She inhaled the scent of his soap with a sigh.

"I didn't dare speak of this before now, but as we left the bedchamber at the party, I glanced back and noticed Emily adjusting her skirts as she left a room too."

Shock knifed through her. "You think she and Jonathon were in a bedroom together . . . making love?" That could not be true.

"She told me he was upstairs, but not until I forced it out of her."

Tia went still. Her only friend in London was cuckolding her husband and lying about her knowledge of Jonathon's whereabouts. Braden's arms tightened around her, enveloping her in his strength. "How could she do such a thing?"

"Lord Eldridge is far from a perfect husband. I am not defending what she did, but it cannot be easy to see your husband openly dallying with his mistress at a party. I would just like to know why she didn't tell either one of us that Jonathon was at the party. Why is he staying away from both of us?"

"I wish I knew," she said softly. *Why would Jonathon refuse to pay a call on Braden?*

"Every time you have received word or rumor of Jonathon it's been from Lady Eldridge. How is it she tends to hear of his whereabouts when no one else knows?"

Tia's mind spun. How had she not thought to question Emily about that? "I don't know. I never thought about it until now. I suppose I assumed she was hearing something from the gossips or the servants."

"I have had two runners looking for him. One is not known to be with Bow Street and is a member of Society. Not even he has heard a rumor of Jonathon."

"You think he has contacted her, don't you?"

"I cannot think of any other way that she could know where he is, when no one else does," Braden replied.

Tia didn't know what to believe any longer. A sense of betrayal crept over her. "I need to find out if she knows where he is."

He reached over and caressed her cheek. "She may just lie to you in order to keep him safe."

"But if she knows something, I have to convince her to tell me." There was only one way to do that. "I will tell her about his opium eating. If she truly loves him, she will want him to get help."

He shook his head. "Or she will deny that he has a problem. Many people in love will only see the good in the other person, not their faults."

"Then what do you suggest?" she asked, frustration lining her voice. A part of her wondered if his words were a warning about his own faults. Was she seeing only what she wanted in him?

"Perhaps we should return to the estate," he said softly.

Tia propped herself up and looked down at him. "You can't mean that."

"I think I do." He looked away from her, but she still saw the pain in his eyes. "There is nothing I can do, Tia. He doesn't want my assistance."

"Give it just a few more days. If we still haven't been able to speak with him, then we shall return to the estate."

He looked back at her. "Then what?"

"What do you mean?"

"Do we return as man and wife? As an engaged couple on the brink of marriage? Or will you continue to be my mistress out there where everyone will know?"

She bit down on her lower lip. The idea of their future hadn't penetrated her mind. "I don't know," she whispered.

"I could give you anything," he said, caressing her face with his hand.

Anything but love. Every time she remembered how she told him she loved him, only to get no response, a small piece of her died. She refused to live in a loveless marriage. "I can't give you an answer right now."

"When?"

"Before we return."

"So by the end of the week," he said.

"Yes. At the latest." Now she had four days to determine the best way to tell him that when they returned to the estate, their relationship was over. Her heart ached with the thought. She didn't want to end the closeness she felt with him. She wanted to fall asleep every night to the sound of his heartbeat in her ear and his arms wrapped around her.

She put her head back down on his chest and attempted to keep the tears at bay. How would she be able to endure knowing he was so near, but unable to touch him, kiss him, or soothe his worries? It would be impossible. She would give in to her yearning for him.

Listening, she heard his steady breathing and realized he had fallen asleep. She let her tears fall. Crying didn't help, but she couldn't seem to stop. Why would he press her to marry him when he didn't love her? Was he frightened someone was trying to kill him, so he wanted to be married with an heir on the way? It seemed the only answer that made any sense to her, except there were many women in Society who would fall at his feet for the chance to become a viscountess.

She tossed and turned all night, barely sleeping at all. Finally, at seven, she slipped out of the bed and headed to her room. Her head ached from lack of sleep and worrying. Perhaps lying down in her bed would help. She reached for the door handle and then stopped when she heard a commotion down in the hall.

"Where are they?" a woman demanded.

Tia froze. She knew that voice all too well. She couldn't possibly be here. That would mean she knew about Tia's relationship with Braden.

"My lord, is she with you?" Nelson said calmly.

"Yes, Nelson. This is my wife. She is looking for her sister, Miss Featherstone."

Chapter 20

Braden woke to Tia slamming the bedroom door and shouting at him. He rubbed his eyes before opening them to see her standing near the foot of the bed with wide eyes and looking frantic. She was speaking so quickly, he had no idea what she was saying. "Tia, slow down and tell me what is wrong," he demanded.

"They are here," she said. "Both of them. Oh my God, he told Nelson she was his wife! That cannot be true!"

"Who is here?"

"My sister and her husband! He sounded just like the Earl of Hartsfield. But she wouldn't marry him. No matter how much he loved her, she would never feel comfortable marrying an earl."

Hart was here? In London? He rolled over and looked at the clock. "Why are they here at this hour?"

"I have no idea! You must get up!" She came around and pulled his arm. "Maybe I should hide. Just tell my sister you never found me."

"Sweetheart, if your sister is here, she has already heard the rumor that you are my mistress."

She covered her mouth with her hand. "No," she mumbled.

"Why does it matter if your sister knows that we are lovers? She had relations with two men before Hart. I doubt she will condemn you for doing the same." Slowly, he slid out of bed and rang for his valet.

"Of course she will admonish me. I told her that I would never do such a thing. I said dreadful things to her when she took up with that second man."

He drew her into his arms and hugged her. "It will be all right. I shall be there with you."

She nodded her head slowly against his chest. "I would still prefer to hide here."

He chuckled softly. "I have never seen you so skittish. Just calm yourself and we will face them together."

"Very well, but be warned, she was born five minutes before me, so she believes she is my big sister and can tell me how to live my life."

"Duly warned. Now go call for a maid to help you dress. We are not going to meet them like this."

She finally giggled. "I do believe seeing you dressed—or should I say, undressed as you are—she might understand why I am with you."

Braden laughed. "So you are only with me for my body?"

Finally, her adorable coquettish manner recovered as she leveled him a seductive grin. "That is the best part of you."

"Go," he said with a laugh.

She rushed to the connecting door and turned the handle, but the door didn't move. "Why is this locked?"

"Because you haven't unlocked it from your room," Braden said with a chuckle.

"Oh!"

He laughed as she ran out of the room to her bedchamber. Hearing her rustling about in her room, he rang for Wilson, but when his valet entered the room, so did Nelson.

"Good morning, my lord," Nelson said as Wilson said the same. "You have a caller at this odd hour and one of them seems most upset."

"Ah, the Earl and Countess of Hartsfield," Braden said and then smiled at Nelson's gaped mouth.

"How did you know that?" he asked.

"Miss Featherstone heard them in the hall. She informed me of their arrival and her sister's state of angst."

Nelson leaned in closer. "She is far from angst. The woman is livid, my lord. I have sent in tea and biscuits, but that won't hold her for long. I'm quite surprised she hasn't stormed upstairs."

"I'm sure Hart would prevent that as best he could."

"I do hope so, my lord."

He would love to get Hart alone before meeting Tia's sister, but Nelson was most likely correct that she would storm upstairs. "Tell them we will both be down presently."

"Very good, my lord," Nelson replied before turning and leaving the room.

Braden dressed quickly and then knocked on Tia's door. Hearing her admit him, Braden slipped into the room and waited as Mrs. Abbott dressed her hair.

"We are almost done, Middleton," she said. "I don't suppose they have decided to leave."

He chuckled. "No, we will have to face them."

"Stop fretting, Miss Featherstone," Mrs. Abbott reprimanded. "We all have to pay the piper for our actions."

"You are not helping, Mrs. Abbott," Tia said.

"I know," the housekeeper replied with a wink to Braden. "You are dressed. Now go face your sister."

"Come along, Miss Featherstone," Braden said, holding out his arm to her.

She took it slowly. Looking up at him with her big brown eyes, he felt a pang of pity for what she must be going through.

"Thank you for going in with me," she whispered.

"Stop fretting. It will be all right." He squeezed her hand.

They walked down stairs to the salon. Entering the room, Tia halted at the threshold for a long moment and stared at her sister. She broke away from him and ran into her sister's arms.

"Oh, Mia!" she cried. "I really am so happy to see you." She pulled back and stared at her sister. "I sent you a letter a week ago. Did you get it?"

"We were in Suffolk," she said slowly. "Now, what exactly is going on here? Mother instructed Middleton to bring you back as soon as he'd found you. He left six weeks ago."

"Yes, but he didn't find me for—" Tia glanced back at him—"was it a fortnight?"

"Yes." Braden finally moved to Hart and shook his hand. "Good to see you and congratulations, Hart."

"Thank you."

Hart moved closer. "This may get nasty before they are through."

"I realize that. What should we do?"

"Stand by and be ready to separate them if necessary."

"Wonderful," Braden muttered. He grabbed a cup of tea and sat down to watch the performance.

"Why did it take him two weeks to find you? Mother gave him the address." Mia eyed him with suspicion.

"Amy and her husband had been evicted. They had left no forwarding address, so I was staying at an inn in Whitechapel." Tia moved to a sofa and sat. "At least I was, until Middleton found me."

"Whitechapel?" Hart commented. "That is not a very good section of town."

"I had no choice. I had very limited funds," Tia said, taking a cup of tea from her sister's hands.

"So why didn't you just return once he found you?" Mia asked and then added, "That was weeks ago."

"She didn't stay long at my house," Braden added.

"I don't understand." Mia sipped her tea.

Although they were twins, Tia's sister looked far different from her. Mia had sable hair, no freckles, and was slightly taller than her sister. But they both had the same wide, brown eyes that dominated their faces.

Braden sipped his tea before replying. "I succumbed to a slight accident that first night. After she patched me up, she gave me laudanum. So the next morning, I slept much later than my usual. When I awoke, I discovered that she had left."

"You left him!" Mia exclaimed, glancing at her sister.

"You were not there, Mia." Tia put her teacup down and glared over at him. "I went for a walk in the park and met a lovely lady who wanted to help me. She offered to let me stay with her. So I did so for a fortnight until Middleton found me yet again."

"Why would you stay with someone you had only just met?" Mia asked.

"Because I was not ready to be forcibly escorted back to the estate," Tia retorted. "And then there was the poisoning."

"The what?" both Mia and Hart asked at the same time.

Braden watched the reactions as Tia explained the poisoning to her sister. Mia's brown eyes grew large as she glanced back and forth between Tia and Braden. Concern lined Mia's face and he was certain the worry wasn't for him.

"Someone is trying to kill you?" Hart asked. "Why didn't you send a note? I could have helped."

"I believe you were busy with your own business," Braden said with a nod toward Mia.

"True," Hart admitted. "But I am here now."

"There is still something that has not been explained," Mia interrupted them. "There has still been several days of them living together with no poisoning and no mishaps. Rumor has it that you are his mistress. Is that true?"

"Miss—excuse me, my lady, I do not believe that is anyone's business except Miss Featherstone's and mine," Braden said stiffly.

"She is my sister so it is my business too," Mia retorted, crossing her arms over her chest. "How dare you suggest it is not."

"Indeed. Then one has to assume you are blameless. For why else would you be the one to cast the proverbial first stone?"

Mia's cheeks reddened as she stared at her feet.

"Middleton, that is enough," Hart warned.

"I agree. The subject is to be put to rest. Miss Featherstone has been proposed to, so it is up to her if she decides to become a viscountess or a woman of scandal." Braden rose. "Hart, I need to speak with you privately."

Hart glanced at everyone in the room before nodding. "Very well."

Tia couldn't look at her sister, the earl, or even Braden as the men left the room. Her cheeks felt as if they were on fire with embarrassment. Now that she and her sister were alone, Mia would attack her for her mistakes.

"I am sorry, Tia," Mia said softly. "I suppose I am the last person who can scold you for your behavior with a man."

"Thank you for understanding."

"Honestly, I don't understand. Middleton has a dreadful reputation as a rake and some say he may have been involved in the deaths of the previous viscount and his son. How could you be with such a man?"

Tia stared at her sister with a raised brow. "Indeed? And the last man you were with before Hart beat you. Middleton has only treated me with love and respect." Perhaps not love, but there had been some respect. "And he had nothing to do with those deaths. Since he has returned, someone has tried to kill him."

"Are you going to marry him?"

"I haven't decided yet."

"Why?"

She wasn't sure how much to tell her sister just yet. While they had been close growing up, since she moved to Middleton's estate, they had grown apart. Mia's dalliances with men hadn't helped the situation. But Tia needed someone to speak with and since Emily's friendship was now in question, it must be her sister. "When I told him I loved him, he didn't say a word, Mia. Not a word."

"Oh," Mia whispered. "I am so sorry, Tia."

"How can I marry a man who doesn't truly love me? I don't want that. I want what Mother and Papa had. They were so happy together."

"Yes, they were," Mia said. "I want that too."

"Are you happy?" Tia hoped her sister hadn't married Hart for the wrong reasons. The man had loved her for years, but Mia had never seemed to notice. A dreamy look entered her sister's eyes.

"Very happy, Tia. Did you know he loved me?"

"I think everyone knew but you."

"I still cannot believe I never noticed," Mia said softly.

"Do you love him?" Tia asked hesitantly.

"So much, Tia. That's why I was so upset when I found out you were Middleton's mistress. I don't want that for you. You deserve a man who loves you as much as you love him."

Tia pondered her sister's words carefully. Mia was right. How could she marry Braden if he didn't love her? It would not be the right thing to do. Emily was a perfect example. Tia refused to live her life as Emily did, watching her husband take mistresses right in front of her. Or sneaking behind her husband's back to meet with a man. Tia would not settle for a life like that just to become a viscountess, not when that wasn't even important to her. The dresses were lovely, but beyond that, there was such a stiffness to the people in Society. She didn't want that.

"You are right, Mia. I do deserve love. And I won't settle for anything less." Which meant in a few days, her time with Braden would be over.

"Are you certain he doesn't love you?"

Tia blinked and then stared at her sister. "How can you ask such a thing? You were the one who wanted me to come straight home."

Mia played with the folds of her dress. "I know that. But seeing how much you love him, it softens my feeling toward him. If you feel so strongly about him, he can't be as terrible as I thought."

"He's not. He actually was for a long time, but when he became the viscount, he made a decision to reform."

Mia smiled. "That speaks highly of him." She frowned for a moment. "I thought you were in love with Jonathon? And where is he in all of this?"

Tia explained what had happened with Jonathon over the past few weeks. And Braden's decision to return to the estate at week's end. The only thing she left out was how Emily fit in to this dreadful mess.

"So if you weren't in love with Jonathon, why did you run after him?" Mia asked.

"He's eating opium, Mia. When he was at the estate, he admitted to me what he'd been doing and that he hadn't touched it in over three months. After he returned to London, I assumed it was because the craving for it had come back. I wanted to help him."

Mia covered her mouth. "That is part of why we are here."

"Because of Jonathon?"

"No, Hart's brother, Charlie, is having the same issue. We brought him to Dr. Simmons for treatment."

"That is what I had hoped to do for Jonathon. But we cannot seem to find him." Tia sighed. "Was Charlie receptive to the idea of treatment?"

"Not at first," Mia replied, explaining all that had happened at Hart's estate. "Once he saw what had happened to me, he was repentant."

"I do hope the physician can help him."

"I hope you can find Jonathon. Poor Charlie had become almost mad with the addiction."

Tia worried her lower lip. Jonathon's actions of the past few weeks were definitely showing the signs of a man with an opium issue. If only she could have seen him last night. She could have questioned him about his symptoms. Perhaps once she'd pointed out all that she noticed, Jonathon would see reason.

Tia shook her head. Anyone who had gone down such a horrible path rarely saw their opium use as an issue. They always had control of the problem, or so they said. She highly doubted Jonathon would be any different.

And if he didn't want to be found, he would hide out until Braden returned to the Midlands.

Chapter 21

"Glad to see everything worked out so well for you, Hart," Braden said, leaning back against a chair in the library.

"Well, it took long enough," Hart replied with a laugh. He sobered quickly. "Seriously, I want to help you out any way I can."

"There is a lot I didn't say in the salon." Braden wished it was a little later in the day. A little brandy might make telling Hart this easier. "Emily is with child."

"Yours?"

"No, things never progressed to that point with us. She's not sure if it's Jonathon's or Eldridge's child. But I know she was with Jonathon last night at the Edmondsons' party. I saw her leaving a bedchamber. She admitted afterward that Jonathon had been upstairs."

"And I take it by the time you went upstairs, he was gone."

"Exactly," Braden said. "He took a risk to see her there, knowing I might be in attendance. It makes no sense."

Hart laughed. "Of course it does. The boy is in love with her. You should be able to understand that. You barely took your eyes off Miss Featherstone while we were in the salon."

"Perhaps, but Miss Featherstone is not married to an earl."

"The former Miss Featherstone is," Hart said with a chuckle. "I apologize. I'm still a little thrilled that she is finally my wife." Hart

looked over at him. "If Eldridge discovers what happened, he may call out Jonathon."

Braden tilted his head back. He hadn't even thought of that possibility. "You are right about that. Mistress or not, Eldridge will not want anyone to know he was being cuckolded."

"Have you confronted Lady Eldridge on where Jonathon is staying?"

"No."

"I believe the both of us should pay a call on her today," Hart said.

Nelson knocked and then entered the library. "We have set out a lovely breakfast for you and your callers, my lord."

"Thank you, Nelson." Braden rose and turned to Hart. "Shall we go discover if the sisters have killed each other yet?"

"I haven't even heard any shouting." Hart stood. "Which, as I think about it, is probably not a good sign. They may be planning some way to get into trouble."

"Mia too?"

"I will tell you all about that over drinks one night. I have a feeling we can commiserate with each other."

Braden shook his head. "If she is anything like her sister, I do feel sorry for you already. I had to literally drag her out of Whitechapel."

Hart laughed as they headed out of the library to the breakfast room. "We are both in for a wild marriage."

"Assuming I can even get Tia to the altar," Braden added.

Hart laughed. "I told Mia it was for her own safety."

Braden stopped walking and scowled. "Tia might be safer alone than with me right now."

"You seriously think that maid tried to poison you?"

"Do you have any other ideas on how that belladonna got in my brandy? Tia told me it had come from her bag. Then Mary disappears."

Hart shrugged. "Poisoning is a woman's method of killing. But you didn't know her, so who hired her to do it? I doubt she just decided to join your household staff and murder you."

"That's what I want to know, but no one has seen her. I spoke with Alistair and he seemed genuinely upset by everything. I just don't think it was him." Or maybe Braden was losing his touch at knowing when a person was lying to him.

"Well, he should be upset if it wasn't him. After you and Jonathon, he's next in line."

"True, indeed."

"What is so important about this title that has people killing over it?" Hart asked. "It makes no sense to me. Was it well-off?"

"The estate is slightly profitable, but scarcely worth killing over. But we can finish this discussion later." He nodded to the ladies walking out of the salon.

Tia had a large smile on her face that warmed him. He was glad her reunion with her sister went better than she'd expected. But he did wonder what they had been plotting.

Once they were all seated, the footmen served them a fine breakfast of ham, eggs, sausage, bacon, kippers, rolls, coffee, and tea. Braden's stomach rumbled as he smelled the aromas in the room. "Thank Mrs. Abbott and Cook for arranging this on such short notice."

Mr. Nelson nodded.

"So I am assuming you two would like to spend the day together," Braden said to Tia and her sister.

"You don't mind, do you?" Tia said with a smile. "It has been weeks since we've had any time together."

"Of course not." Braden felt a rush of relief through his body. Now, she wouldn't insist on going with him to Emily's. "Hart and I are going to search an area of town for Jonathon. It is not a good area, so I would prefer you stayed with the countess."

"The countess?" Mia said with a laugh. "You are going to be my brother-in-law. Please call me Mia."

"Thank you, Mia," Braden said before staring at Tia. "But am I to be your brother-in-law? I have not heard anything to be certain."

"Give her time, Middleton," Mia replied with a smile.

As breakfast finished, Braden ordered a coach, allowing the women to use Hart's if they wanted to go out. Before leaving, he did ask them to take an armed footman should they decide to go anywhere.

Hart and Braden arrived at Emily's home just past eleven. It was early for morning calls, but Braden didn't care. He would prefer no one discovered he and Hart were here. By now, hopefully Eldridge would be at the club or riding through Hyde Park.

Hart gave his card to the butler at the door and they were welcomed into a small salon. It took Emily twenty minutes before she finally arrived at the threshold of the salon and then she stopped.

"Middleton, I was not told you were here," she muttered.

"You know why I am here," he replied.

"Yes, but not why the earl is with you. And congratulations on your marriage, my lord. I would love to meet your wife."

"Thank you. You have already met her sister. In fact, you know her quite well," Hart said with a slight grin.

"I have?" She entered the room hesitantly, choosing the chair closest to the door.

"Yes. Miss Featherstone is my wife's twin sister. Though, they look nothing alike," Hart added.

Emily's face went pale. "Tia is your wife's sister?"

"Yes, she is." Braden said no more as a footman brought in tea. Once he left, Braden continued, "But we are not here about the women. I want to know where Jonathon is, Emily."

Emily stared at her hands as color blotched her cheeks. "He doesn't want to see you yet."

"What do you mean by *yet*?" Braden demanded.

"He said he can't see you until he figures something out." She looked up at him. "I swear I am telling you the truth. He wouldn't tell me why."

"Emily, my brother has a problem. He needs help. That is the only reason I am trying to find him."

Emily pressed her lips together as if mulling that over. Finally, she said, "He told me about the opium. He also told me he hasn't had any in months. But he believes you are trying to lock him in Bedlam."

"No. I want to speak with him. If he needs help we will get it for him, but I would never lock him in Bedlam."

"I will let him know that," Emily said.

"How are you meeting him?" Braden asked softly so no servants would hear.

"He writes coded letters to me, claiming to be my ill aunt. Eldridge has even read them and believes they are from a woman."

Braden sighed. If she were telling the truth, then once more they had clues to follow. "You are taking quite a risk to see him. If Eldridge discovers you are cuckolding him, you put my brother's life in jeopardy."

Emily stared at him with cold blue eyes. "My husband is not about to discover anything. Most of the time he is too busy with his latest mistress to care what I am about. And you will not tell him because if you do, Tia will find out about us. I'm assuming you haven't told her, have you?"

Heat scorched his cheeks. "No, I have not."

Hart shook his head. "What a mess you two have made."

Braden still didn't understand one thing. "Before we go, I have one question, Emily. Why did you send me the note regarding Lady Whitfield's ball? You could only have meant for me to find Miss Featherstone."

A slow smile lifted her lips. "Because I knew that while I was not the right woman for a man like you, Middleton, Tia certainly is that woman. I just never expected you to scandalize her by kissing her on the dance floor."

"You did what?" Hart asked

"He ruined her," Emily asserted. "He truly should marry the girl."

"I have asked her!" Braden said with another shot of frustration. "She is the one who hasn't agreed to marry me yet."

"Perhaps she doesn't believe that you love her," Emily said with a tilt of her head.

Braden looked away from her prying gaze. The two women to whom he'd spoken words of love had rejected him. It was foolish to think Tia was any different, but a part of him wanted that more than anything in the world. Tia had told him that she loved him, but he had put that off to their lovemaking. Women always wanted to be in love when they let a man have them.

"My lady, Lady Bunworth and Miss Tavers are here," the butler announced. "Shall I escort them in?"

"We should take our leave now," Hart said as he stood. "Good day, Lady Eldridge."

"Good day, my lord."

Braden rose just as his cousins entered the room. Lady Bunworth released a slight gasp while Miss Tavers smiled at them both. "Good day, Lady Eldridge." He gave a quick bow. "Good day, cousins."

Constance glanced between them both with a puzzled look upon her face. "Good day, my lords." She turned her attention on Hart. "Lord Hartsfield, how fortunate to see you here. I was . . . was hoping I could speak to you about an urgent matter in private. Middleton, I shall see that Hart is returned to his home."

How odd that Constance would *need* to speak with Hart when he so rarely went to town and had only arrived yesterday.

"That is fine, Lady Bunworth." Hart turned to him. "I shall just walk home once we are finished here. Can you make sure Mia returns home safely?"

"Of course," Braden said with a bow to the ladies. "Good day, ladies."

Braden left the house, still bewildered by what Constance would need to talk with Hart about. He walked to the carriage, only to find his driver gone.

"Sorry, milord, I'm coming," a voice called from behind him.

"Where have you been?"

"I saw a man I knew from my last position. We were catching each other up on things."

"Very good," Braden said with a smile. "I would like to return home now."

"Will the earl be joining you?"

"No." Braden climbed up into the carriage. As they drove down the street, he resolved to have Emily Eldridge followed by a runner. If she met Jonathon again, the runner would intervene and bring his brother home. That settled in his mind, he sat slight forward, eager to return to the house. It was time to court the woman living under his roof.

But as the carriage hit a rut, Braden heard a loud crack and braced himself for the accident. The wheel broke loose from the coach, tipping the coach to the right before crashing to the ground. He felt his head hit the side and then everything went black.

"Mia! Get down here this instant!" Hart's voice boomed through the hall as he held Middleton's limp body in his arms.

"What is going on?" Tia said, jumping to her feet. She ran out of the salon and stopped in disbelief. "No!"

Mia pushed passed her sister. "What is wrong—Simon, bring him up to his lordship's room. Nelson, get the housekeeper to boil water. Tia, where is your bag?"

Tia barely heard her sister. She could only stare at Braden's body. He looked limp and blood dripped from his head.

"Tia!" Mia shouted.

She blinked and looked at her sister. "Not again. I can't go through this again."

"Where is your bag?"

"In my room," she answered.

"Where is your room?" Mia yelled.

"Upstairs, of course."

"God help me." Mia grabbed her arm and yanked her toward the staircase. "I don't know this house—show me."

Tia followed her sister in a daze. She couldn't lose him. She couldn't.

"Which room?" Mia asked as they reached the top step.

"Here." Tia opened the door to her bedchamber.

Mia seized the satchel and raced out of the room. "Where is Middleton's room?"

"In here, Mia," Hart's voice shouted from Middleton's room.

"I was going to show you," Tia said softly. She followed her sister into Braden's bedchamber. The love of her life lay lifeless on the bed. She couldn't comprehend what was happening.

"What is wrong with your sister?"

"Shock," Mia replied.

"What can I do to help?" Hart asked.

"Get her a brandy and a seat before I have a second patient to attend to and this one is enough."

Hart poured a brandy and forced Tia to sit on the chair. "Sit, Miss Featherstone. Middleton will be all right."

She wanted to believe that, but couldn't. Hart pressed a brandy into her hands. Without a thought, she drank it. Nelson and Mrs. Abbott raced into the room.

"What is going on?" Mrs. Abbott demanded.

"Take care of Miss Featherstone," Hart replied. "My wife is helping his lordship."

"But Miss Featherstone should be helping him. She is the wise woman," Mrs. Abbott said with her arms on her hips. "She saved him twice since she's been here."

"It is my turn now, Mrs. Abbott," Mia said in a stern tone. "I am Tia's sister and also a wise woman. My sister is in shock. Please get her a blanket or shawl and cover her. Make her drink that brandy."

Tia watched Mrs. Abbott's head nod up and down. She felt as if she was in a dream, watching the scene unfold before her from a great distance. The housekeeper sat next to her, then forced the glass of brandy to Tia's lips. She sipped a little down, savoring the warmth it created in her belly. Mrs. Abbott then removed the glass from Tia's hand and slapped her across the cheek.

Tia's head hit the back of the chair. "What the bloody hell are you doing?"

"Forcing you out of your daze," Mrs. Abbott said. "I trust you with his lordship. I don't know if your sister is a good wise woman, but I know you are. Now get over there and take care of him."

Feeling like she'd been scolded by her mother, Tia hung her head as she walked to the bed.

Mia smiled over at her. "I actually didn't suggest that, but I am quite happy she did it."

"Do be quiet." Tia examined his head, putting aside her feelings for him as she scrutinized his injury.

"The cut isn't terrible, but could probably use two stitches. Do you want me to do sew him up?" Mia asked.

"No," Tia replied. "If he's going to have a scar on his head, it will be from me."

Hart chuckled in the background. "Other than the cut to his hard head, how is he?"

"He will be all right," Mia said to her husband. "If he survived boxing with you, he has to have a hard head."

"He boxed with Hart?" Tia asked as she readied her needle. She hated sewing head injuries, but thankfully her sister was right that the cut was not large. "Hold him down."

Hart approached the bed and then held onto Braden's head as Tia sewed the wound. "I don't know how you ladies do this," he said, looking away from the blood.

"You get used to it," Tia replied. "All done."

"You don't always get used to it," Mia said. "I do it because I have no choice."

"You still get queasy from the blood?" Tia asked her sister.

"Sometimes. With head injuries, always because there is so much blood. I hate it." Mia took the needle from Tia and set it in some brandy to clean it. "Another reason I was quite pleased that Mrs. Abbott forced you out of your shock. You are far better at this than I."

"Thank you." Tia washed the blood out of his hair, then put a patch of linen over the wound to keep it clean. "Now we just have to wait for him to awaken."

"I am awake. I think," he said groggily. "What happened? And why does my head hurt like hell?"

Tia took his hand and squeezed it. "You were in a carriage accident."

"In town?" he mumbled. "Doesn't make sense."

Hart sat in a chair near the bed. "He's right. It doesn't make sense. There was no extra swaying on the trip to the Eldridges' home this morning. The carriage was in good order. No sign that a wheel was going to break."

Tia turned her head to Hart. "Why were you at Lady Eldridge's home this morning? Middleton said you were going to a section of town that was inappropriate for women."

Braden squeezed her hand. "Sweetheart, I needed to ask her if she knew where Jonathon was staying. That is all."

"Did she?"

"She swears he only sends her coded messages," Braden said. "But why did the carriage lose a wheel? We did hit a rut, but not a deep one. Bring Mr. Sanders up to me."

"Braden, you need to rest," Tia insisted.

"I've taken worse than this," he replied. "Mrs. Abbott, tell Mr. Nelson I want Sanders up here."

"Of course, my lord," she said and quickly left the room.

After a few minutes, Mr. Sanders entered the room with his head bowed down. "I am dreadfully sorry, my lord. I cannot possibly imagine what happened. The carriage was checked before you called for it. I personally inspected the carriage this morning."

"And the wheels were all right?" Braden asked.

"Absolutely, my lord. Not a one was loose."

"Could a rut have caused the accident?" Hart spoke up.

Mr. Sanders looked over at Hart. "In the country, I would say yes because they can grow so deep. But in town? I find it highly unlikely. People fill them in as soon as they see them. The chance that a rut just formed and then you hit it would be unusual, to say the least."

"That seems to be my life lately . . . unusual," Braden muttered softly. "What about the driver?"

"Townsend has been with us for over a year, my lord. I've never had an issue with him."

"Was he injured in the fall?"

"No, my lord. He managed to jump down as the carriage tipped. He was very lucky indeed."

Braden was glad to hear his driver survived without a scratch, unlike him. "Thank you, Mr. Sanders. Please see that the carriage is fixed."

Mr. Sanders bowed and left the room. Tia inhaled a sharp breath. "I cannot take this any longer. You need to get back to the estate."

"It will be all right, Tia," Braden cooed.

"No, it will not! Someone is trying to kill you! It is time you took this seriously." Tia pulled away from him to pace the room. "I cannot do this any longer."

"Perhaps we should take our leave now," Hart suggested to Mia.

"Of course." Mia moved to her sister. "If you need me, send a footman and I will be here quickly."

"Thank you."

"Hart, before you leave, fill in one blank for me," Braden said. "How did you come to bring me home? I thought you were detained by Lady Bunworth."

"It was odd indeed, Middleton. She offered me her congratulations on my marriage and wanted to know if she could pay a call on Mia. By the time I left the house, you were only a block away. I saw the carriage tip."

"And why couldn't she say that to you in front of me?" Braden asked.

Hart shrugged. "She said she didn't want to insult you, because she is not comfortable calling on Tia."

Tia didn't doubt that answer. Personally, she didn't care if Constance ever called upon her. Once her sister left with Hart, Tia sat on the bed next to Braden and stared down at his handsome face. All her emotions bubbled to the surface. "I thought I was going to lose you," she said to him. "Can we please leave for the estate? You will be safe there."

"One condition," he whispered.

"What is it?"

"That you marry me before we leave."

Chapter 22

Braden's heart stopped as he waited for an answer from her. If he was going to return to the estate, he wanted her on his arm as his wife. She was something worth living for and he wanted to do this properly. No more of his adolescent and rakish ways. He wanted a wife and family. He wanted to prove that he could be a good viscount and provide for his family, tenants, and servants.

She stared at him for what seemed like hours before whispering, "I cannot marry a man who doesn't love me."

He didn't know what to say. Telling her he loved her right now would make her think he was only saying those words to get her acceptance. But what choice did he have? "Tia, I never wanted to fall in love. I have done it twice and each time it ended in heartache." He reached up and touched her cheek. "But I couldn't seem to help myself with you. You made me mad. Insanely mad and totally in love with you."

She blinked and looked away from him. "How do I know you aren't just saying that to get me to marry you?"

"Why should I want to marry you, if not love? You are not an heiress and even if you were, I don't need the money. You are not from an important family. And I don't need those connections either.

There is only one thing you have to offer me . . . love. And that is all I want from you."

Her lips trembled. "I do love you, Braden."

"I know you do. And I understand why you're hesitant." He smiled up at her. "Marry me anyway, Tia," he whispered. "Be my viscountess, the mother of my children, my lover."

"How do I know you won't have a mistress like Emily's husband?"

He tilted his head and stared at her. "I am done with other women, Tia. I have had my share and several other men's shares as well. Those encounters meant nothing to me. I want you. Only you."

He watched the conflicting emotions on her face. He wanted to soothe her worry, but only time would prove to her that he was speaking the truth.

Finally, she whispered, "I will marry you."

He sat up and kissed her softly. "I promise to make you happy." He broke away as his head started to pound. He put a hand to his temple as if that would make the pain stop.

"Are you all right?"

"I will be. It's just a headache. Why don't you rest with me for a while?"

She smiled down at him. "Only if you promise it will be rest."

"Agreed."

She slipped under the covers with him and rested her head on his shoulder. Just having her this close was wreaking havoc with his body. He no longer wanted to rest. Other than a headache, he felt fine. And she felt far too good up against his body.

"What happened when you were young?" she asked softly.

So much for what he had in mind. "What do you mean?" he asked, hoping he would be able to change the topic of conversation.

"After your father died. How did you survive?"

Braden closed his eyes against the memories. If not for meeting Hart, there was no telling how his life might have ended. If she were to be his wife, she should know the truth, no matter how ugly. "After my father died, I had to find work or we would have been evicted. My mother took in sewing, but that didn't bring in enough. Unfortunately, the only kind of work I could find was far from legal."

"Why didn't your mother contact the viscount?" she asked.

"She was too proud. No one in my father's family was happy to see him marry my mother. She was a woman of no means and not much family. She was the daughter of a baker."

"He must have loved her very much if he chose to marry her."

"No," he said harshly. "He didn't love her at all. She was with child."

"Oh," she whispered. "How sad."

"My father's family was certain she was attempting to wring an offer out of him. Most didn't believe she was having his child."

Tia pushed against him to look down at him. "Well, that is hardly fair."

"Was it? Look at me, Tia. Do I look like Jonathon? Do I look like any of the previous viscounts?"

She glanced away. "Your coloring could have come from some ancient relative," she said softly.

"Or it came from my real father."

"Did she ever speak of it?"

Braden shook his head. "No. I think she wanted to believe I was my father's son. I wanted to believe it too," he admitted, more to himself than to her.

"I'm sorry. Do you have any idea who he might be?"

"None at all. At this point, it doesn't matter, except that I feel horrible for inheriting over Jonathon when he is likely the true heir." He had never told a soul what he just admitted to her.

"But there is nothing you can do about it." She reached out to caress his check. He snatched her hand and kissed the palm. "This was your parents' decision."

"I know that, which is in part why I decided I had to change myself. I could no longer be the self-absorbed man who only cared about his own pleasure. If I was going to inherit, I promised my mother I would be a good viscount. An example to all those born into a title who do everything they can to ruin themselves and their titles."

She smiled down at him. "I'm sure she would have been very proud of you. But how did you learn to box?"

He tilted his head back and laughed. "That would be all Hart's fault. I met him when I was seventeen. We didn't agree on a few things and got into a fight. I have never taken a beating as he gave me that day. So I asked him to show me how to fight."

"What did you argue over?"

Braden rolled his eyes at her. "A woman, of course."

"Of course," she said with a laugh. "I shouldn't have expected anything different from you."

"Exactly. After that we became friends." He rolled her over on her back. "Now, I have had enough talking about my past. I am feeling very well rested."

She giggled softly. "Are you now? As your wise woman, I should tell you to rest more."

"As my betrothed, you should be welcoming my advances," he replied.

"I do welcome them," she said with a sigh when he kissed her neck.

Tia woke a few hours later to find Braden's arm wrapped around her waist, holding her against his hard chest. She savored the sensation of his warmth. But she wondered if she'd made the right decision. Marrying him would be difficult, only because of their very public relationship. Everyone would know that she'd been his mistress.

Did that matter?

The more time she spent in London, the less she liked the majority of the people she met. Out in the country, most people wouldn't know what happened in town. They would be happy that their wise woman had decided to marry and have children. And then there was the idea of children.

She had always wanted children. Now her children would be proper ladies and gentlemen. They would go to good schools or have excellent tutors to learn far more than she had been taught by her father. Her son would be viscount one day. Hopefully, not for a very long time, though.

It was the right thing to do, she decided.

"Stop fretting," Braden whispered in her ear before kissing her lobe. "Everything will be fine."

She turned in his arms to face him. "Now why would you think I'm fretting?"

He smiled. "You bite down on your lower lip. It's very adorable."

"I do not do that," she said with a laugh.

"Trust me, you do."

"How are you feeling?" she asked, looking at the bandages.

"Head still hurts a bit, but it's better."

Tia bit her lower lip. "Who do you think is doing this?"

He touched her lip as if to remind her to stop biting down on it. "Honestly, I can only think of two people with a motive."

"Jonathon and Alistair," she said softly. It made no sense to her. She knew Jonathon and had met Alistair twice. Jonathon was no killer. He was far too kindhearted for that. And he never seemed interested in the title when they had talked at the estate. He'd even told her what a burden it was on his brother.

Alistair, while he needed money, also didn't seem the type to kill over a title. He couldn't possibly imagine that he would ever have a chance to inherit. And all suspicion would be on him if he did.

"What do you think?" he asked, caressing her lip with his thumb.

"I can't imagine either of them doing such a thing."

Braden nodded. "I can't either. Of course, if Jonathon is still eating opium, then he might be a little mad from it. A madman who needs money is a dangerous thing."

"True." Tia went silent in thought for a moment. "Who inherits after Alistair?"

"I have no idea. We would have to go back deep into the family history to determine that. My understanding is our grandfather was the only surviving male in the family. We would have to go back to his father."

"Well, I want you to rest, so why don't we do that in bed? You tell me what books to get and I'll go find them." Excitement gripped her. At least they had something to occupy their minds so they wouldn't go mad.

"I'm afraid most of the books are at Middleton Hall. You could try to find a family Bible in the library."

Slightly deflated, she sighed. "Of course the books on the family would be at the estate. I should have realized that. It's another reason for us to get back there as soon as possible."

He leaned back and chuckled. "I thought you didn't want to return to the estate. People will expect that you will take up your wise woman duties again."

She leaned over him and kissed him softly. "I understand. My holiday if over. I'm looking forward to returning to my duties there. I've missed them all more than I thought possible before I left. Besides, I'm rather tired of only nursing you."

"Oh?"

"Yes, you are a dreadful patient. I tell you to rest and you make love to me," she said with a giggle. "You need to learn to listen to your wise woman."

"I shall do my best."

"You stay here. I'll look for some books. Do you want to dine up here tonight?"

"That sounds lovely."

She dressed quickly and bounded down the stairs. She informed Nelson of Braden's progress and their desire to dine in his bedchamber. Her cheeks heated with embarrassment, but Nelson only nodded. Walking down to the hall, she wondered what the butler must think of her. And why was it bothering her now? She'd been here for over a fortnight.

She strolled into the library and then stopped. There were hundreds of book here. How would she find what she was looking for without assistance? "Nelson, do you have a minute?" she called out.

"Of course, miss."

Once he entered the room, she said, "I am trying to help out his lordship with some books about his family. Do you know of anything regarding the prior generations of his family?"

Nelson's white brows furrowed. "Hmm, there is at least one family Bible here." He scanned the shelves before pulling two books down. "Here are two of them. Be very careful with the second one, it must be at least two hundred years old."

"Thank you."

"Wait, here is a family history written by one of his grandmothers." Nelson stood on the ladder and reached up to the highest shelf for it.

"How did you know where all these books were?"

"I catalogued the library for the previous viscount. He was fastidious regarding his library. The estate has some wonderful books on the family history."

"Excellent. I am quite sure his lordship will be pleased to hear it." Tia slipped back upstairs to find Braden dressed and sitting on the bed. "Why are you dressed? You have nowhere to go."

"I would like to be decent when they bring up the food. I'm famished."

"Well, that is always a good sign." She placed the books on the beds. "Did you know that Nelson catalogued the library here? He said we should be happy to find more books on your family history when we arrive home." Home? That beautiful old house would soon be her home.

"I was not aware Mr. Nelson took care of the books too. I need to know more about the house and the estate. Since he has been here for thirty years, I should utilize his knowledge more."

"I agree."

They each took a book and started to leaf through it. Tia stared at all the names and wondered what his relatives would think of him marrying her. They would probably all be horrified to learn he was marrying the estate's wise woman. And yet, staring over at him, she no longer cared what anyone thought of her, save Braden.

"This one only goes back to my grandfather," he said, closing the book. "Anything in yours?"

Tia went back to her book. "It goes back much further, but I'm confused about one thing."

"What is it?" He leaned in closer and stared down at the same page.

"Right here," she said, pointing to a page. "It says Lady Violet Tavers, Viscountess Middleton in her own right, married Randolph Haverty, who took her name."

"That makes no sense. Why would she have inherited the title?"

"I have no idea. Shouldn't that be in the letter of patent?"

"Yes, but that is most likely at the estate. Perhaps there was a special reason that enabled her to inherit. It's just so uncommon." He sat back against the pillows and picked up the last book on family history.

A knock sounded, announcing food had finally arrived. A footman entered the room and stopped when he saw them both lounging on the bed with books in their hands. "Where would you like this, my lord?"

"Right here on the bed."

Tia almost laughed at the gaped expression on the poor boy's face. They must have scandalized him.

The footman carefully placed the tray on the bed. "Is there anything else, my lord?"

"No, that will be all. Thank you."

As soon as the door closed behind him, they both broke out into laughter.

"I believe we may have horrified that young man," Braden said, still laughing. "We will be the talk of the servant hall tonight."

"I am quite sure it isn't the first time."

"And won't be the last time either," he said, pulling the tray closer. "Chicken. How did she know I wanted chicken tonight?"

"Are they not paid to read your mind?" she teased. "I am quite sure Mrs. Abbott knows that chicken is your favorite dish, so she asked cook to prepare it."

"I do believe my servants need a raise."

"They probably do," Tia agreed.

They back sat back against the headboard and pulled their plates onto their laps. Tia had never eaten in bed unless she was ill. It seemed quite decadent to her. "I could get used to this," she admitted after a bite of chicken.

"Which, the chicken or eating in bed?" he asked. He reached for his wine and sipped it slowly.

"Both."

They chatted more about the family history they had discovered so far. All too quickly, they had finished their meal. Tia rose and moved the tray off the bed so they could continue reading through the books.

"My lord, I must speak to you immediately," Mr. Nelson said from the hall frantically.

"Come in, Nelson," Braden answered.

"My lord, I am dreadfully sorry to disturb you, but this is very important."

"Well, what is it, Nelson?" Braden asked.

"It's your brother, my lord."

"Jonathon?"

A sense of dread came over Tia. Nelson's manner was too extreme for it to be good news.

"Yes, my lord. Your brother is in the salon."

Chapter 23

Braden's heart pounded in his chest. He glanced over at Tia's wide-eyed face and smiled. "I will be down in a minute, Nelson. Find out if he wants something to eat."

"Yes, my lord."

He jumped out of bed and looked in the mirror. Other than the lack of a cravat and a bandage on his head, he was respectable enough to meet his brother. Tia scampered off the bed and straightened her skirt.

"I need you to stay upstairs," he said quietly, knowing she would put up a fight.

"I will not!" she exclaimed.

"Yes, Tia, you will. I need to speak with Jonathon alone for a few minutes. If he is still eating opium, he might not be sane. I will not put your life at risk."

She tilted her head. "But you will put your own life at risk. No, I will go with you."

She was, without a doubt, the most vexing woman he had ever met. "I will lock you in this room if you try."

"I dare you to try," she taunted.

Braden ran for the door, grabbed the key, and left the room before she had barely moved. He locked the door and pocketed the key. "I will let you out when I know it is safe to do so."

"Do you realize how many ways I could kill you and no one would know it was me?" she shouted.

He laughed. "I will remember that, Tia."

"I could make you suffer in so many ways."

"I have no doubt about that either," he said with a chuckle as he walked toward the steps.

She pounded on the door for good measure, but to no avail.

Once he reached the bottom step, he stopped and glanced back. "Nelson, if Miss Featherstone should find a way out of a locked room, please make certain she does not interrupt my conversation with my brother."

"Of course, my lord. Am I to assume she was not happy about being locked up?"

Braden laughed again. "Not in the least."

Nelson attempted to stifle a grin, but Braden saw it.

With a bit of trepidation, Braden walked to the salon. He stood at the threshold, staring at his brother, who hadn't noticed his appearance just yet. Jonathon stood to the side of a window, peeking outside. His blond hair was longer than usual and his clothing disheveled. He appeared different from the man who had stayed with him at the estate most of the summer.

"Jonathon?"

"Thank God, you're all right," Jonathan said before striding across the room and embracing him.

"What is going on?" Braden asked. "Wait, let us move to my study for some privacy."

"As you wish."

They both walked out of the salon only to hear a loud bang on a door upstairs. Braden rolled his eyes and Nelson grinned.

"I take it you have company?" Jonathon asked.

"Don't ask," he muttered, shaking his head. He wasn't certain how his brother would take his relationship with Tia. That was one reason he insisted she stay upstairs. Another was his own insecurity about how she truly felt about Jonathon. Would she fall back in love with him the moment she saw him? He refused to think about that.

"Brandy?" Braden asked as he entered the study.

"Yes, please." Jonathon took a seat in a chair by the fireplace while Braden poured the brandy.

"I have been searching for you for weeks. I know you were aware of my arrival in town, so why haven't your paid a call until now?" Braden handed Jonathon a snifter.

Jonathon sipped the brandy and sighed. "I had forgotten just how wonderful a good brandy could be to the soul."

Braden clenched his snifter in frustration. "Jonathon."

"Oh, very well, I couldn't see you." He took a long sip and then said, "I was afraid putting the two of us in a room together for any length of time would be a danger to our health."

"What nonsense are you speaking of? I would never hurt you." Braden stared at him. His brown eyes looked clear, not bloodshot from the drug.

"Someone is trying to kill us both. That carriage accident proves they are after you too."

"Are you saying someone has made an attempt on your life?"

"Yes. It wasn't until my mind started to clear at the estate that I was able to put it all together. I was encouraged to start on opium by an acquaintance. Why would someone I scarcely know care what I did? But he told me this would solve all my problems."

"What does this have to do with someone trying to kill you?" Braden wondered if there were some lasting effects of the opium, even if Jonathon had stopped using it. He would have to speak with Tia regarding that matter.

"I was getting to that," Jonathon said. "Before I came out to the estate, someone took a shot at me as I was leaving the Red Door. Considering how much I had lost, I knew it couldn't have been someone trying to steal my winnings. Once I was at Middleton Hall, I remembered the rumors of your involvement in the late viscount's death and his son's death as well. I was certain you wouldn't have done such a thing. That's when I concluded that someone had tried to kill me."

He wondered if his brother was grasping to make a connection here. "Jonathon, just because someone encouraged you to start eating opium and a random shot almost hit you, it doesn't necessarily mean someone was trying to kill you."

"Indeed. But I was determined to find out. That is why I returned to London."

"And that was the only reason? Emily had nothing to do with your desire to return?" Braden asked before picking up his snifter for a sip of brandy.

"Perhaps," his brother admitted with a shrug. "But I also wanted to see if anything happened to me here."

"And has it?"

"I was robbed and beaten not a fortnight after I returned." Jonathon stared at a red scar on his hand. He rubbed his finger across the mark. "Thankfully, a friend found me. And more importantly, thankfully this friend listened and did not give me laudanum. It's been four months, Braden. I feel so much better than I have in a very long time."

Braden smiled at him. "That is good news indeed." Not that his brother's words would stop him from worrying. "Has anything else happened?"

"The place I was staying at burned to the ground. Luckily, no one was at home when it happened." Jonathon drained his brandy. "Has anything else happened to you?"

He scowled. "You haven't heard?"

"No." Jonathon's eyes narrowed. "But I take it there was something else that happened."

"Yes, I was shot at and poisoned." He still wasn't ready to tell Jonathon about Tia being here. Since his brother hadn't mentioned her, Braden assumed Emily hadn't told him.

Jonathon frowned. "I see. You need to leave, Braden."

"I planned on leaving in a few days. But now that I know your life might be in danger too, I feel I must stay on. We need to figure out who is trying to kill us, Jonathon. Alistair makes the most sense, but I just cannot see him killing someone." This mess was driving him insane.

"It's not Alistair."

Braden looked over at his brother. "How can you be certain? He has the most to gain from both of us being killed."

"True, but I know for a fact that he was out of town this week. Yet, you still had a carriage accident."

"That matters not. He could have hired someone," Braden said slowly. "How did you find out about that and not the other attempts?"

Jonathon's cheeks reddened. "I was waiting for a chance to speak with Emily. She was supposed to go to the park. Then I noticed you and Hart pay a call and then Constance."

"Where were you?"

"Across the street, hiding behind a carriage. I didn't have a great view, but I could see the door."

Braden tapped his fingers on the arm of the chair. He'd been wondering most of the day if someone might have tampered with the carriage while he and Hart were inside. "You didn't notice anyone near my carriage, did you?"

Jonathon shook his head. "I saw your driver get down and walk around the corner to speak with someone. But if someone had come up on the other side of the carriage, I might not have noticed them."

Braden released a long breath. "I don't suppose you are on good terms with Constance?"

"Is anyone? I don't think even Alistair likes his sister," Jonathon said with a laugh. "Why?"

"Well, she paid a call on Emily and I thought she might have noticed someone nearby the carriage. Unfortunately, she seems rather displeased with me, although I'm not certain why." Braden assumed it was due to Tia, but he wasn't about to say that to Jonathon.

"I could try to call on her tomorrow," Jonathon said. "She might also have some insight on Alistair."

"Be careful around her." Braden had no idea what made him say that. Constance had never done anything that would deem her dangerous. Her biggest fault was her attitude and gossiping. Not much different from most of the ladies in the *ton*.

"You don't suspect her, do you?"

Braden shook his head. "No. But if she discovers that you are possibly the father of Emily's child, she will take great delight in sharing that with everyone."

"Emily's child?" Jonathon muttered. "Emily is with child?"

Damn! "I apologize, Jonathon. I thought you must know."

"But I didn't know." His brother's face grew white. "I had no idea," he said slowly. He raked his hands through his hair. "My child?"

"I am dreadfully sorry."

"I need to see her." He rose. "I will speak to you tomorrow. We have to come up with a plan for catching whoever is trying to kill us both."

"All right." He walked his brother to the door. Upstairs, another bang of the door sounded.

"I do believe whoever is up there would like your attention," Jonathon said.

"Yes." Unfortunately, Braden doubted it was his attention Tia wanted right now. She would be furious when she discovered Jonathon had already left.

Once his brother departed, Braden contemplated leaving her locked up for a while longer. Maybe she would fall asleep. Knowing her, she would stay awake to spite him. He walked slowly up the stairs with a grimace on his face.

"What has taken you so long?" Tia demanded the moment the door opened. She slipped passed him and raced for the stair, eager to see him again.

"He has already departed," he said, walking into the room.

She stormed back to the bedchamber and slammed the door. "What do you mean, he already departed? I wanted to see him too! I wanted to see for myself if he needed medical assistance with his opium eating."

"He had to speak with Emily." Braden removed his jacket and flopped on the bed. "He didn't know about the baby. I mentioned it, assuming she had told him."

Tia covered her mouth with her hand. He must be so upset. If that child was really his, he or she would legally be Eldridge's child and possibly his heir. "I'm sorry. I had no idea either. I would have made the same assumption after last evening. She is starting to show slightly. I'm surprised Jonathon didn't notice."

"So am I," Braden admitted. "Perhaps he didn't want to acknowledge the possibility."

"Other than the issue with Emily, how was he?" Tia asked before sitting on the bed. A part of her wanted to lay down with him, but another part of her still held some anger for his stubbornness.

"He looked well. He has put on a little more weight and he showed no signs of the opium. He told me he hasn't touched it since before he came out to the estate in early summer."

"Thank God," she mumbled. But she still had so many questions to ask him. "Why did he suddenly decide to pay you a visit?"

Braden glanced away from her and frowned. She couldn't but wonder if he was formulating a falsehood to tell her.

"I would like the truth, Braden."

"Very well." Braden went on to explain all that his brother had told him. "I just do not understand who would want to kill us both."

Tia went silent for a few minutes. If it wasn't Jonathon or Braden, obviously, it had to be Alistair. While he had been downstairs with his brother, she had been researching the few books on the family history. Nothing obvious had come to her. There were no other male relatives that she could see. "I do not know either, Braden. Perhaps your cousin hired someone to kill you both so he could inherit. We do know that Mary had been in his employ."

"I know," he whispered. "I just cannot believe it was him."

"Was he having any financial difficulties?" she asked him softly. Seeing the pain on his face, she leaned over and caressed his cheek.

"Yes, but he didn't act as if it was all that dreadful. He just needed to be relieved of a few servants. I asked around and no one had heard anything different." He clasped her wrist and moved her hand to his mouth, where he kissed it sweetly. "So if it is truly Alistair, how do we prove it?"

That was a very good question and one for which Tia had no answer. "Perhaps you have your runner watch Alistair? Not that the runner would be able to catch Alistair if he was meeting someone he had hired."

"Exactly."

"And if someone he hired attempted—" Tia paused, not wanting to complete the sentence, but knew she must. "—to kill you or your brother, even if you captured the person, he might not give up Alistair's name."

"Right again," he said, still clutching her wrist. "Jonathon wants me to return to the estate."

"I think he's right." Finally, she moved to lie next to him. "I want you safe, Braden," she whispered.

"I know, sweetheart." He turned to face her on the bed. "I want you safe too. That is why I believe we should return the day after to-morrow. I will get the special license tomorrow and we'll marry before leaving on Friday."

"Very well," she said. "Only if you are certain."

"Certain of what? Marrying you? Absolutely. Leaving to keep you safe? Again, yes. You are the most important thing in my life." His pale blue eyes stared into her soul. "I will do everything in my power to keep you safe."

"And I will do everything in my power to keep you safe and healthy."

Chapter 24

The next morning, Braden rolled over to curve his body against Tia's. He had barely slept last night, imagining all the things that could go wrong until he had her safely ensconced at Middleton Hall. He wrapped his arm around her and brought her sleeping form next to him. How had he fallen this deeply in love with a woman he had only known for a few months? And until a few weeks ago, they had barely spoken with each other.

Now, he could imagine waking up next to her every morning. He wanted his ring on her finger now, not tomorrow. His hand rubbed her belly. Could his child be in there right now? For once, he hoped there was a baby on the way. With other women, he'd been so careful not to spill his seed, but with her, it hadn't occurred to him. Perhaps he'd wanted her with child so she would marry him.

Braden inhaled her sweet scent. If he could only figure out who was behind the attempts on his life, then his life would be perfect. He had a woman many men could only dream of, he had wealth from his notorious past, an estate that was bringing in a small income and with improvements would earn more, and he had an illustrious title.

And someone trying to kill him.

"Stop worrying," Tia's groggy voice whispered.

"Now why would you think I'm worrying over something?"

"Because when I worry, I bite my lower lip, as you so kindly pointed out. You, on the other hand, tap your thumb. It's been hammering my belly since you curled yourself around me. Would you like to talk about it?"

"No," he immediately said, then regretted it. "I apologize. It's a habit not to speak of things with my . . ."

"Lovers?" she supplied.

"Yes." He kissed her neck. "I just want this man found," he admitted. "I want our life to start without worrying about who might be after us." He was surprised at how lovely it felt to speak of his feelings with someone other than his male friends.

"Will we be safer at the estate?"

"I believe so."

"But you are still concerned," she added.

"Yes. I am going to meet with the runner I hired and tell him what I know about Jonathon and what has happened to him. Then I shall get the special license and we will marry in the morning before we leave. Send a note to Hart and your sister so they can witness the event."

"I will."

He tightened his arm around her as he nuzzled her neck. "Please don't leave the house today. I couldn't bear it if something happened to you."

She nodded. "Please be careful today." She rolled over and stared at him. "I couldn't bear it if anything happened to you either."

He wanted to make love to her right then, but he had far too many things to settle before leaving for the estate. "I need to get out of bed."

"So soon?" she said, tracing a finger down his jaw.

He groaned. "Yes. I really must." He clasped her hand and kissed it. "This we will do later."

"Good."

He quickly dressed and went downstairs for some coffee and food. As he ate, he pondered what he could do to find the person responsible for trying to kill him. A knock at the front door brought him back to reality.

"My lord, Mr. Alistair Tavers is here to see you and says it is of the utmost importance."

"Show him to my study, Nelson."

Braden wondered why Alistair would be here so early in the morning. It was only nine. With a shrug, he walked to the study, where he found Alistair pacing the room. "Alistair, what is wrong?"

"Thank God, you are all right," he said. Relief filled his face. "When it happened, I could only assume someone must have gotten to you and Jonathon."

"Sit down and tell me what has you in such a state."

Alistair took a deep breath and sat in a chair. "Last night, I was arriving home and as I left the carriage, someone took a shot at me. It just missed me."

"What does that have to do with me?" Braden asked. "I certainly had nothing to do with it."

"Of course you didn't," Alistair said vehemently. "I thought if someone was trying to kill me that you and Jonathon must already be dead."

"I see." Braden stared at his cousin. Nothing in his attitude today looked as if it was a performance. Alistair seemed genuine. "And if I were dead and Jonathon too, you would be the next viscount."

"I don't want that responsibility," he said with a wave of his hand. "I wouldn't mind the money, but I also know most of what you have is from your gaming interests and not the estate. It would only be a burden to me."

"Good point. I spoke with Jonathon yesterday and he also believes someone is making an attempt on his life."

"Good God! What the bloody hell is happening?" Alistair rose and started pacing again. "Why would anyone want to kill us all? Is there some kind of curse on the title?"

Braden almost laughed at the idea of a curse on them. "Do you have any idea who would inherit if you had the title and died?"

Alistair halted his pace. "I have no idea. It never occurred to me to check, because I assumed the chance of inheriting was too slim. After Constance and Louisa, there are no other close relatives and they obviously cannot inherit."

A very strange plan came to Braden's mind. "Why don't we find out?"

"What do you mean?"

"What would happen if all three of us should happen to die in an accident?"

"Dear God, don't think of such a thing."

Braden laughed. "I meant, what if everyone thought we had died?"

"Oh," Alistair said with a slight grin as he realized Braden's plan. "Then whoever believes he is the next in line to inherit will appear to claim the title." He sat back down. "But Middleton, that could take weeks. I don't want my sisters to believe me dead all that time."

"It might take that long," he drawled. "Or it might not. If this person is so eager to inherit that he would attempt to kill five people, I doubt he will wait a long time to claim the title." Even the idea of someone attempting to kill so many for a title seemed mad at best. "No one would believe the man had nothing to do with our deaths."

"But where will we go?"

"Good question." Braden rubbed his chin. "I believe we need to speak with Jonathon and make sure he is willing to be a part of this plan." Which brought up another question: How did he contact his brother when he had no idea where he was staying?

"Once you get word to your brother, let me know. I shall be at my home until this is settled."

"Very good. I will let you know as soon as I hear from him."

Alistair bowed and left the room. Now Braden was left with trying to determine a way to contact Jonathon and there was only one person who could assist him. He left the house, still wondering what he would say should Eldridge be at home. What excuse could he have for paying a call on Emily?

There was only one he could think of.

When he arrived at the earl's home, he knocked on the door. He handed his card to the butler and waited to be admitted.

"Lord Eldridge is not at home, my lord," the stiff butler replied.

Which was just a way of telling him that Eldridge did not want Braden to enter his home. "I am here to see Lady Eldridge. It is concerning her dear friend Miss Featherstone."

"Miss Featherstone?" The butler frowned before opening the door fully to him. "Wait in the salon, my lord. I shall let Lady Eldridge know you are here."

Feeling as restless as Alistair must have, Braden paced the room. Finally, delicate footsteps sounded from the hall. He stopped and turned to see Emily standing at the threshold with a look of worry upon her face.

"Middleton, what happened to Tia?"

"Lady Eldridge, please sit down with me on the sofa so we can talk."

"Oh, God, she's dead, isn't she?" Emily covered her mouth as tears formed in her eyes.

"No. She is not dead." He sat on the sofa and patted the place next to him. "I must speak with you privately."

She tilted her head and then nodded. After sitting, she asked, "What is wrong with Tia?"

"Nothing," he said softly. "I must get a message to Jonathon. He came to my home last night, but wouldn't tell me where he was staying."

"I honestly don't know where he is staying," she whispered. "I leave a missive for him."

"Where?"

"At Hyde Park. If you go in at Grosvenor Gate, there is a small group of trees on the right. One of them is forked and at the fork, there is a cut in the tree just large enough for a folded piece of paper. That is where we have been leaving the notes."

"Thank you, Lady Eldridge."

"What exactly are you thanking my wife for, Middleton?"

Braden looked over to see Eldridge standing at the threshold with his arms folded over his chest. "Miss Featherstone is missing. I thought Lady Eldridge might have heard from her."

"And has she?" he asked.

"No." Braden rose from the sofa. "I must take my leave now. Thank you for your time, Lady Eldridge."

"Of course, my lord. I wish you only the best in finding her."

"Thank you." Braden bowed toward Eldridge. "My lord," he muttered. Once out of the house, he returned home only long enough to write a note to Jonathon. He rode out to Hyde Park and prayed he found the right tree before he left the missive. Now, he needed to get the special license and a note to the runner.

After he arrived home, he found Tia in the library, reading another book on family history. "Sweetheart, are you still trying to figure out this mess?"

"Yes, I am. It is also quite interesting to learn of your family history."

Since Braden wasn't certain that this truly was *his* family history, he only shrugged. "I must speak to you in private." He closed the door and sat across from her. "I spoke with Alistair this morning and he believes someone is trying to kill him too. I believe our only choice is for all three of us to die in an accident."

She sat up straight. "What exactly are you talking about?"

"We need to stage our deaths. That way, whoever is trying to kill us will come forward. Until he does, we don't know who it may be."

"That is a mad idea! You have no way of knowing if that person is the one trying to kill you."

Braden sighed. "Who else could it be?"

"I don't know!"

"Don't be angry with me, sweetheart. I just want this over."

Tia shook her head. "I am not angry," she admitted. "I too want this over. I only worry that you might not have the right person."

"What do you mean?"

"You have no way of knowing if Jonathon and Alistair are telling the truth. If the three of you go together someplace, one of them might kill you."

He hadn't thought of that possibility. She might be right and if she was, he was only giving the killer the opportunity to kill without being caught. But if nothing else, he now understood how prepared he needed to be if they went with this plan.

"Braden?"

"I'm sorry. I was woolgathering. There is always the chance that you are right. But at this point, I believe we may not have any other options. I want this settled, Tia. Now."

"I understand, but there is another issue."

"What?" he asked, assuming she was only trying to stop him.

"How exactly will you make people believe all three of you died in an accident?"

Braden shrugged. "We shall stage a carriage accident. Perhaps outside of London, where there are some dreadful roads and hills. Let the word get out that the three of us are going to the hunting lodge."

Tia rolled her eyes. "A carriage accident will never do. A coroner will need to verify the bodies."

Braden swore softly. That had never crossed his mind. Now what would he do? "There has to be a way."

"You will need three dead bodies," she whispered. "And a fire."

"You are starting to scare me," he said with a smile. "I must remember to never get you too angry with me."

She giggled. "The fire must be hot enough to destroy the bodies and make them unrecognizable. And they need to be very close in size to you all. It might help if it looks like you all were drinking heavily before the fire started, which would explain why you didn't get out."

"Thank you," he said, before kissing her quickly.

"My lord," Nelson said from the other side of the closed door. "Mr. Brady is here to see you."

"Thank you, Nelson. Show him to my study." He looked over at Tia. "That is the runner I hired. I must speak with him."

"Of course."

He rose and then looked down at her with a grin. "I have the special license, so you will be married in the morning and possibly a widow by afternoon."

"Do not jest about such a thing!"

"Tia, everything will work out. I promise."

Tia read for over an hour as Braden spoke with the runner. She looked up from her book several times to wonder how she could convince him that the plan to stage his own death was far too mad of an idea to consider. Perhaps if she could see Jonathon, he could talk some sense into his brother. Of course, that was assuming Braden didn't lock her in his bedchamber if Jonathon arrived.

There had to be some way of stopping him. She smiled. Perhaps she should lock Braden in the bedchamber, with her. That would keep him from leaving and be quite enjoyable in the process.

Realizing it might be quite a while before he came out of his study, she went upstairs to find another book she'd left in her room. When she arrived, she found Mrs. Abbott packing her clothes.

"Am I leaving, then?"

Mrs. Abbott started. "Dear girl, you gave me such a fright. His lordship asked that you be packed and ready to leave after the ceremony tomorrow. I have time now, so I thought I would get a start on it."

"Thank you." She placed the book next to the valise and trunk. "It is still difficult to imagine that as of tomorrow I shall be a viscountess."

"I would think so," the housekeeper replied as she folded a chemise.

Tia sat down on the bed with a sigh. "Do you think he is making the right decision, Mrs. Abbott?"

"About marrying you?" she asked, turning her head to look over at the bed.

"Of course, about marrying me. I am truly nobody."

Mrs. Abbott stopped her packing and walked over to the bed. "I think he must love you very deeply to have decided to marry you. The question is, do you love him in return?"

Tia bit down on her lower lip and shook her head. "I do love him, Mrs. Abbott."

"Then you have nothing to fear, miss. With love, you both can conquer anything. And you will be a viscountess."

Then why did she feel such a nagging sense of doubt about her upcoming nuptials? She didn't question her feelings. Of that, she was confident. And she did believe he loved her. So why did she have any doubts?

"So why am I nervous?" she finally asked.

Mrs. Abbott sat next to her and took her hand. "I suppose it is very natural for a woman to be nervous before her wedding. After all, this is a lifetime commitment. There is no getting out of a marriage, or at least the few options are very limited. Since I cannot see his lordship abusing you, there will be no divorce."

"I am not worried about that, Mrs. Abbott." She looked over at the older woman and grinned. "His lordship knows that I have too much of a knowledge of herbs and poisons. He would never hurt me in that manner."

"Only possibly in matters of the heart," she whispered.

Tia nodded. "I know marrying him is a risk. He was a horrible rake, but he tells me he wants to be a better person. I should believe that, shouldn't I?"

Mrs. Abbott squeezed her hand. "Yes, I think you should. After all, since he has been here, the most immoral thing I have seen him do is drag you into his house."

Tia giggled. "That was rather wicked of him."

"I hear the front door, so Mr. Brady must be leaving. Go down and talk him about your concerns. I am certain he will set your feelings to right."

"Thank you, Mrs. Abbott. I am going to miss you when we return to the estate."

"The next time you come to town, you will be her ladyship. I shall have to be all proper with you."

Tia squeezed the housekeeper's hand. "Do you really believe I shall ever be a proper viscountess? I do believe I will need your assistance quite often."

"Miss Featherstone, I cannot believe I am saying this after how I treated you the first day I met you, but I do wish you nothing but happiness."

Tia forgot about classes and propriety and hugged the housekeeper. "Thank you, Mrs. Abbott."

The housekeeper pulled away. "Now, go down and speak with your future husband while I pack these things for you."

Tia smiled as she walked out of the room. Loud voices boomed from Braden's study. Odd, Mrs. Abbott had thought the runner must have left. Perhaps someone else had arrived.

She walked closer to the room with trepidation. The voices became clearer to her.

"How could you bring her into my home like this?" Braden shouted. "This is utter madness. He will kill you."

"I don't care. I had to protect her."

Tia inched closer. That voice sounded like Jonathon. Who had he brought with him that had Braden so upset?

"Why are you so upset?" Jonathon asked. "He will not come after you."

The sound of a glass breaking split the air. "Have you completely lost your mind? Of course he will blame me just as much as he will you. She is a married woman. She belongs with him, not you."

"Look at her. I cannot bring her back to that bastard," Jonathon's voice boomed. "She needs medical assistance. I heard Hart married Mia. I will have Mia come over to help her."

There was no need for anyone to call Mia while she was here. She opened the door and gasped at the sight of Emily's battered face.

"Tia?" Jonathon stared at her in disbelief. "Oh, this is just too much." He turned back to face Braden. "Now I understand why you don't want Emily here. It makes perfect sense. Tia was the woman in your bedchamber making such a din. You never told her about Emily, did you? Or was this just to get back at me for stealing Emily away from you?"

"What?" Tia uttered. Braden and Emily had been what? Lovers? Courting? "What are you talking about, Jonathon?"

"Tia, it was nothing," Braden said slowly, approaching her.

"Do not tell me something is nothing when I can see it on all of your faces." Tia crossed her arms over her chest. "Why would Jonathon say you were trying to get vengeance for him stealing Emily from you?"

Jonathon shook his head with a scowl. "He had been courting Emily. But the first time I saw her, I fell in love with her. My brother was terribly jealous. He knows that you and I formed an attachment, so what better way to get even than to make you his mistress. You haven't changed a bit, Braden."

"That is not true," Braden said roughly. His face was dark with a murderous rage.

"I can't hear any more of this," Tia cried. She ran from the room, knowing she had to leave him forever.

Chapter 25

Braden collapsed into a chair as he watched Tia leave. He steeled himself against the emotions screaming at him to follow her. He couldn't bear her believing this story. *Tell her the truth*, he said to himself, but he could not do that. He rose to chase after her until his brother stood to stop him.

"Do not go after her," Jonathon warned. "We have to wait and make sure she leaves." Jonathon returned to his seat next to Emily on the sofa.

"That was the hardest thing I have ever done," Braden admitted slowly. He walked to the window and stared outside as if to catch a glimpse of her one last time. He doubted it was the best decision, but Jonathon convinced him that he could not marry her until after this mess was settled. Braden wondered if she would ever forgive him for the deception.

"I know, Braden," Jonathon said. "After what you and Emily told me, I am sure we can convince her that this was purely for her safety. If she was married to you, the next viscount could not make a claim for the title until after it was determined she was not carrying your child, and that could take months."

"We could have told her that. She would have understood my reason for not marrying her tomorrow."

"No," Jonathon said vehemently. "She needs to be away for her own safety."

"I understand, but it does not make the matter easier to swallow." He glanced away from them. "I fear she will never forgive me."

"Of course she will," Jonathon said. "I can explain it to her."

"No," he said harshly. "I will make this right with her. No one else."

"He is right, Jonathon," Emily finally spoke up.

"I will send for Mia at once," Braden said. He walked to the hall to speak with Nelson. "Has Miss Featherstone left yet?"

"She stormed out of here a few moments ago, my lord. Is everything all right?" Nelson looked down. "Please excuse my impertinence, my lord."

"She and I had a slight disagreement."

"She took her valise with her," Nelson added.

Good. So far their plan was working. "I see," he said. "Please send a note to Lady Hartsfield. Inform her that we need her medical experience, but it is not for her sister. I wouldn't wish her to worry."

"Very good, my lord." Nelson gave him a strange look before turning away to write the letter.

He walked with leaden feet back to the study. What were they going to do with Emily? "I sent for Mia."

"Thank you," Emily whispered.

"What do we do now?" Jonathon asked. "I can't let her go back to him."

"I won't go back to him," Emily said resolutely. "I will divorce him now."

"Divorce is extremely difficult," Braden said. "Very few women ever achieve it. I know Eldridge has been unfaithful and now this. But I need to understand what drove him to beat you."

Emily blinked her tears away. "Your visit this morning. I believe he heard more than I had imagined. He demanded to know if I was meeting Jonathon. And how I was doing it."

"Did you tell him?" Jonathon asked.

"No, of course not. Then he thought he could beat it out of me. If my maid had not come in, I don't know what might have happened."

Guilt spread throughout his body. She had been injured purely due to his visit. He should have known Eldridge would suspect her of harboring Jonathon. "Perhaps she can stay with Mia and Hart."

Jonathon went silent for a long moment before shaking his head. "That makes sense, but will Hart allow it?"

"Yes," he said without a thought. Hart had a soft spot for women. And knowing his past, he would want to assist Emily.

Within a few minutes, Mia and Hart arrived. Mia blustered into the room much like her mother would have done.

"What is wrong? Where is Tia?" She scanned the room. Seeing Emily, she went to her. "Who did this to you?"

Emily stared at her hands without saying a word.

"Can someone please tell me what is going on and where my sister is?"

"Lady Hartsfield, this is Emily, Lady Eldridge," Braden said. "I don't know if you have met my brother, Mr. Jonathon Tavers."

"Yes, I met him over the summer at the estate," she muttered. "Now that we all know who we are, I will ask again—where is my sister?"

Braden cringed. "Quite possibly on her way back to the estate."

"And why would she be doing that when you and she are to be married tomorrow?" Mia asked in an all-too quiet voice.

"There will not be a wedding tomorrow."

She glared back at him with eyes the same color as Tia's. "Why not?"

Braden sat down with a sigh. "I cannot tell you the specifics, but right now she does not want to marry me. Before you say anything, I will tell you that once this little mess is done, she will forgive me and marry me."

"I would not be so certain if I were you, my lord," Mia said, fishing some items out of her small valise.

"Why not?"

"We Featherstone women have long memories and don't always forgive so easily."

It was probably a good thing she did not see her husband shaking his head and mouthing the words *not true* to Braden. "I will take your words under careful consideration, Mia."

"You had best do that," Mia replied, wiping the dried blood off Emily's face. "How long ago did this happen?"

"Two hours ago," Jonathon said as he watched the wise woman.

"Why was I not called sooner?"

"There were other, more important issues that needed to be attended to, Mia," Braden said sharply. Hart leveled a deep scowl at him. "I apologize for my behavior."

"Did he hit you anywhere else? Are your ribs all right?" Mia turned her attention on Emily again.

"No, just my face," she finally admitted.

"And how far along are you?"

Emily's face went pallid. "How did you know?"

Mia gave her a look far wiser than her twenty-four years. "I knew the moment I saw you that you were carrying. So why would your husband have done this to you?"

"How do you know it was him?" Emily whispered.

"Just a feeling. Mr. Tavers is watching my every movement around you like a mother hen. So it isn't terribly difficult to assume what happened." Mia finished cleaning Emily's face. "You shall be bruised for a few days, but it's not that bad."

"Not that bad?" Jonathon shouted.

Mia turned her glare on him. "No, it wasn't all that bad, Mr. Tavers."

"How can you say that?" Jonathon said. "You have no idea what it is like to have a man beat you like this."

"Oh, you might need to intercede, Hart," Braden said with a cringe.

"My wife can fight her own battles, Middleton. I made certain of that."

Mia rose and placed her hands on her hips. "Indeed? Mr. Tavers, I should warn you to tread very carefully here. I spent weeks recovering at Hart's home because a man abused me. I am not saying what happened to her should be dismissed. But she will not need to stay in bed while her entire body attempts to recover."

Jonathon looked abashed. "I apologize, my lady. I had no idea."

"Now," Mia said, looking at all the men in the room. "What are we to do with Lady Eldridge? She cannot stay here. Nor can she stay with Mr. Tavers. And I will not allow her to return to her husband."

"I was hoping she could stay with you," Braden said in a gentle tone.

Mia rolled her eyes before glancing over at Hart. He shrugged. "It is all right with me. However, if her husband comes to my home to retrieve her, we have no option but to turn her over to him."

"You will do no such thing!" Mia exclaimed.

"It is the law, Mia," Hart said. "He has the legal right to bring her back to his home."

"It's not right," she retorted.

"I can't agree more."

Seeing Emily's white face, Braden said, "If it is settled, we need to get her out of here before Eldridge pays me a visit."

Mia and Hart departed with Emily as Jonathon watched from the window. Braden wrote a note to Alistair asking him to join them. Braden wondered where Tia was right now. He needed to speak with Mrs. Abbott.

"Nelson, ask Mrs. Abbott to come see me in my study."

"Of course, my lord."

Mrs. Abbott's hasty footsteps soon rang out from the hall. "Yes, my lord?"

Braden had hated asking for Mrs. Abbott's assistance, but it had been the only way Tia would return to the estate safely. "How did it go with her?"

"She took the money you gave me and told me she was heading back to her mother's house."

"Thank you, Mrs. Abbott."

"My lord—" Mrs. Abbott started and then stopped.

"Speak your mind," he said gently.

"Do you think it was for the best to send her away now? Begging your pardon, my lord, but what if she is carrying your child? She will need the security of your name."

"And she will have exactly that as soon as this mess is finished. Please don't say a word to any of the other servants. Only you and Nelson are aware of the situation."

"Of course, my lord." With a quick bow, she left the room.

Braden had turned in some favors from his gambling days to

make sure this would all go off without incident. As long as the servants kept quiet, everyone was would play their part. Alistair arrived at four, still looking apprehensive, but willing to agree to the plan as long as Jonathon was involved.

They discussed the plan in detail over dinner until each of them knew their part. The carriage was pulled around as if they were going for a normal outing. Alistair balked at the driver knowing where they were going, but it was necessary that someone could place them at the house. There was no other way this plan would work.

They drove toward the Red Door. Turning up an alley, they left the carriage and hurried with quite a bit of noise. Each of them carried a bottle of whiskey in their hands. They passed a few people who must have thought they were already foxed. A small, deserted home Adams owned sat away from the others. They entered the room and discovered Braden's favors had been turned in when they saw the bodies at the table. Playing cards were spread out as if the dead men had been playing before they keeled over and died. Adams would admit they had all been playing cards before he had been called back to the Red Door due to an issue there.

Jonathon lit the fire in the fireplace as Braden and Alistair spilled whiskey all over the bodies. Adams had supplied enough whisky that the small house should be up in flames in no time. They spread the alcohol all over the area of the room where the dead bodies were propped over the table. Braden lit the room and raced out the back door and down the street where Adams left the back door to the gaming hell open.

They were hurried up to the third floor. Braden went to the window and watched as the fire quickly engulfed the house. He felt a twinge of guilt for those poor dead men, but he'd been assured no one had come to claim them. So for now, all they could do was wait until Nelson reported back to Adams that the new viscount had arrived. And in Braden's case, wait and worry over Tia's safety.

Tia finally arrived back in the Midlands a few days after the incident in the study. She would be forever grateful to Mrs. Abbott for lending her the money to take the postal coach. She'd felt sorry for the passengers who had to endure her endless tears the entire drive.

After a few days, she now felt as if she had no more tears to shed. A certain numbness had come over her that she could not shake. Honestly, she preferred the numbness to the agony of heartache.

She walked slowly toward her mother's cottage, wondering what her mother would say to her. Knowing her, Mother would tell her to return to Middleton Hall as the wise woman there. When she finally reached the door, she didn't know what to do. Should she knock? Should she just go inside?

She decided to knock and open the door. "Mother? Are you home?"

"Mia, is that you?" a voice called from the bedroom.

"No, Mama," she said with a catch in her voice. "It's Tia."

Her mother ran from the room and brought her into a warm embrace. "Oh, my darling, where have you been?"

The dam burst and her tears spilled over. "Oh, Mama," she cried.

"Hush, it can't be as bad as that."

"It is so much worse," Tia mumbled. The heat of her mother's arm warmed her numb body.

"Come on, we shall sit and have some tea and you can tell me all about your travels. I can't imagine where you've been. I even sent Middleton to London to find you. I suppose I shall have to write him and tell him you have returned." She led Tia to the sofa by the fireplace.

"Please don't write him."

Her mother looked down at her. "Why would I not?"

"I do not want him to know I am here." Although, she supposed it would be the second place he checked, the first being Mia's home in London. If he even cared to look for her at all. At this point, she doubted he would.

"Oh my." Her mother sat next to her on the sofa. "I believe I had better hear this before making tea."

She didn't know where to start. How did you explain to your mother that you became a man's mistress?

"I take it he found you?" her mother asked.

"Yes." Slowly, she found the words to explain what had happened over the past few weeks. The tale sounded incredibly sordid.

"Oh my," Mother said again. "So you do love him?"

Did she? She thought she had been in love with him, but after hearing about how he was using her to get vengeance on Jonathon, she wasn't sure any longer. "I do not know."

"I know," her mother commented. "I can see how much you love him in your eyes and your tears. It wouldn't hurt this much if you didn't love him."

She couldn't deny that. It felt like someone had stabbed her in the heart and continued to turn the knife. "I do love him," she whispered. "But I don't want to."

"I don't know," Mother said. "I haven't known the man for long, but he never seemed the kind of man who would use another person to get vengeance. I think he could have thought of another manner of revenge on Mr. Tavers."

"Then why else would Jonathon have said that?"

"I am not sure. But it does seem as if something odd is going on in London these days." Her mother went to the fire to heat some water for tea. "Does he honestly believe that staging his own death will make the culprit come forward?"

"Yes, he does."

"Hmm . . . again, seems quite odd to me." Her mother turned away from the fire and stared at Tia for a long moment. "Are you with child?"

"I won't know for a week." Oh God, the last thing she had ever wanted was a child outside of marriage. She wanted the life her mother and father had, with a home full of love. Her lip trembled.

"Either way, we shall make things work out," her mother said, returning to the sofa with the tea. "Drink. Tea has a way of making everything seem fine."

Tia doubted a cup of tea would help her today. But like an obedient child, she sipped her tea and then put her head on her mother's shoulder. "Thank you, Mama."

"For what?"

"Understanding and not criticizing."

"I could never throw that first stone after what I did even younger than yourself."

Tia lifted her head and stared at her mother's red face. "And what exactly did you do?"

A slight smile lifted her mother's lips upward. "Shall we just say that even for twins, you and your sister were very premature."

For the first time in days, Tia smiled.

Tia spent the next fortnight at her mother's cottage, moping about. So far, her mother hadn't said a word to her about returning to her cottage at Middleton Hall. She hadn't said a word about her even helping out here. But after two weeks, she was ready to do something. Staying inside the cottage was making her feel too isolated. Today, she would return to her ways as a wise woman.

She hadn't heard a word from Braden and expected she never would. At least, she had one less worry as her monthlies had arrived like clockwork. Even if she had felt the bite of disappointment that first day, it was for the best not to be carrying his child.

"Mother, I need to get back to work," she announced as they ate a meager breakfast of toast and tea.

"I agree. With the colder weather setting in soon, I will need the assistance. If you do not feel comfortable going to Middleton Hall, I would understand it. I will not force you to return there and take the chance of seeing his lordship."

"Thank you. I doubt he has returned yet. And I think getting out and seeing people will help me."

"I couldn't agree more. It is far better to surround yourself with people who love you than to stay away from them all. There is not a soul on this estate or even Middleton's who wouldn't support you."

With her mother's boost of confidence, Tia set out to visit the tenants at Middleton Hall. And as her mother had said, they all welcomed her into their homes. If they had heard any rumors of her involvement with Braden, they remained silent about it. After six hours, she strolled back to her mother's cottage. The October air was getting much cooler now and it refreshed her weary soul.

She opened the door to find her mother and a man sitting at the table, deep in conversation.

"Tia, this is Mr. Andover. You need to sit down."

"Mr. Andover," Tia said with a bow. "How can I help you?"

"I'm afraid there has been an accident involving Lord Middleton."

Tia did her best to look surprised. As angry as she still felt over

Braden's deception, she would not give up his charade. Until he discovered the truth, his life was in danger and she could not let him die. "An accident? Is he all right?" Dear God, she hoped he had the sense to listen to her about the fire.

He shook his head. "I am sorry to say we believe he died in a fire."

"Oh, God." She covered her face with her hands. Where were all those tears when she needed them? She blinked furiously in an attempt to bring one to the surface. "Are you his solicitor, then?"

"No, miss. I represent the heir to the title."

"Mr. Jonathon Tavers, then?" she asked in an innocent tone.

"No, miss. I am afraid the fire claimed the life of Mr. Tavers and his cousin, Mr. Alistair Tavers too. The person I represent would like to remain anonymous until all the legal challenges are cleared."

"I don't understand, sir." She pulled her hands back and pretended to wipe away a tear.

"I understand his lordship requested a special license so you and he could marry. I need to know if that marriage occurred."

"No, sir. I needed to return unexpectedly to the estate to assist my mother. We were supposed to marry the day after I left."

The man blew out a relieved breath and then smiled. "So you are not legally married. Thank you for your time, Miss Featherstone. I need to return to London."

As the door shut behind him, she looked at her mother. "That was quite peculiar, don't you think?"

Her mother shrugged. "Not really. If you were his wife, the heir could not inherit until after it was determined that you weren't with child. You should be happy you were not a part of this or you might have been at risk."

Tia's eyes widened and her heart pounded against her chest. Braden hadn't just staged his own death. He had feigned that argument to force her to return home where she'd be safe. That devious bastard. She should hate him for not trusting her . . . but he knew she would have refused to leave because she loved him. "Oh, my God," Tia said. "That is why he did it."

"Did what?"

"Don't you see? He wasn't out for vengeance with Jonathon. He must have made Jonathon say that so I would believe them and leave. Because if we had married, the new heir wouldn't try to make a claim and my life might be at risk."

"What are you going to do now?" her mother asked.

Tia's shoulders sagged in defeat. "There is nothing I can do because I have no idea where Braden is right now."

"Well, he must be hiding someplace where he can trust people who either own the building or live in it."

She bit her lower lip in thought. Where would Braden feel safest? Why hadn't she thought of it before? The Red Door. But she couldn't just storm into the place, demanding to see a dead man. She wasn't certain they would even let her inside the gaming hell. "I'm going to lie down for a short while."

She walked into her old bedroom that she'd shared with Mia and looked at the book on the bureau. Mrs. Abbott had accidently packed the family history book Tia had been reading. She had meant to stop by the house and give it to one of the servants, but forgot it this morning. Not terribly tired, she picked up the book and started to read it again.

Enthralled by the long history of the family, she found an interesting passage that she needed to have Braden read. He would be very interested to learn that every few generations, a dark Tavers was born. This child was born with black hair and blue eyes. To date, the children had been either females or younger sons. She smiled, knowing how pleased he would be to learn this information.

After a quick break for dinner, she continued reading until she found something that made her rub her eyes and read again. *This cannot be possible.* Oh, dear God, if this was true, then she knew the heir to the title.

Chapter 26

After almost three weeks of being locked away in a room in the Red Door, Braden was about to go mad. The third floor had at one time been a high-end brothel, which they had removed when they bought the place. They were in the gaming business, not the whoring business. So Jonathon, Alistair, and Braden all had private rooms and took one room for conversation. Needless to say, Braden should be happy the accommodations were so fine, but not knowing what was going on in the world made him feel like a prisoner.

His biggest worry was Tia. Had she arrived back at the estate safely? Did she truly hate him? Would she ever forgive him? He would not know the answer to any of those questions until the bastard trying to kill them came forward. How much longer would this take?

It mattered not. He was done waiting for this to happen. He had to find out if Tia was safe or not. Nothing else mattered. He rose from his seat, gulped the rest of his watered-down brandy, and walked toward the door.

"Are you retiring?" Adams said, entering the room. "I thought we might share some of the good stuff. It's very quiet downstairs tonight."

"No, I'm leaving."

Adams put his arm across the doorway, blocking Braden's exit. "No, you are not."

"Bloody hell, man. I need to know if she is safe."

"If you leave now, you will ruin this for everyone. You will put your life at risk and for what?"

"For the woman I love," Braden said harshly. "I cannot stand here and do nothing. What if someone tried to hurt her when she left town?"

"Then I believe her sister would have heard something by now. Hart would have sent a note to me."

Braden knew his friend was right, but hated feeling helpless. "Very well, what do I do now?"

"Unfortunately, you wait." Adams poured two snifters of brandy and handed one to Braden. "Whoever is heir is taking their time. I heard a solicitor was asking questions of Nelson."

"To what end?"

Adams sipped his brandy. "About the night of your supposed death. Was it normal for the three of you to go play cards outside of the house, etc."

Braden returned to his seat and sipped the brandy. This was the stuff they served to the high-end clients who could afford it.

"If this man has to prove his legal right to inherit, it might take even longer." Braden lowered his voice so Jonathon and Alistair would not hear them from their bedrooms.

Adams dropped into a chair. "I wish there was something I could do for you."

"Just letting us stay here is enough. I cannot thank you enough for that."

A knock hammered the door at the top of the stairs. "Mr. Adams," a booming voice sounded. "We need you downstairs immediately. There is a woman attempting to gain entrance. She said she will not go away until she speaks to you."

"Damned women. When will a mistress learn she has no right to a man's time unless he decides to give it," Adams grumbled. "I will be right down to speak with her."

"Bring up more of the good brandy when you return," Braden said. "I think it might be the only way I am going to sleep tonight."

Adams laughed. "I will. And I might just join you in a glass or two."

"Please do. I am rather tired of the company I have to keep right now." At least all this time together had proved to him that Jonathon was no longer eating opium.

Adams walked away chuckling.

Braden went back to his worrying. A few minutes later, a commotion near the stairs forced him to look up. A flash of red entered the hall.

"This way," Adams said in an angry tone. "Do you have any idea of the danger you put yourself in, not to mention him?"

"He is here, isn't he?"

Braden's heart melted hearing her voice. She was safe. "Tia?" he shouted, not caring if he woke his brother and cousin.

The flash of red raced into the room and threw herself in his arms. "Braden," she exclaimed.

"What are you doing here? And how did you figure out I was here?" A million questions entered his mind, but those were the first out of his mouth.

She pulled away and cupped his cheeks before kissing him passionately. Her tongue brushed against his, sending desire spiraling through his body. Slowly, she broke away with a shy smile. "I know who it is."

"How can you possibly know? Did the man pay you a visit?"

"No, her solicitor did."

"Her? That makes no sense, Tia."

Her smile widened, showing her small white teeth. She yanked a book out of the valise she'd been carrying. "Yes, it does, if you read this."

"Go get some more brandy, Adams."

"I'll bring it up, but do not start this story until I return." Adams ran down the stairs.

Braden looked down at Tia. "I believe you must have figured out my deception. Were you terribly angry with me?"

"Yes," she admitted. "Until a solicitor paid us a visit and I realized exactly why you had staged that argument over Emily."

"It wasn't entirely staged, Tia." He hated having to tell her this because of how it made him look, but he had no choice. Keeping secrets between them was no way to start a marriage.

"What do you mean?" She took a step out of his arms.

"I had been courting Emily." Braden blew out a breath. "It was right after I inherited the title and decided to reform. I didn't want to fall in love again after Penelope, so I was purely looking for a woman who would be a good wife. No trouble. I thought Emily was that woman."

She pressed her lips together.

"Then she met Jonathon. I had come to love Emily in a sweet way. There was no real passion between us. But I guess there was passion with her and Jonathon. At first, I thought he had deliberately tried to entice her away from me. I was actually pleased when she married Eldridge. Now that I've seen them together, I realize they weren't thinking of me at all."

"Are you in love with her?" she whispered, trying to keep her tears at bay.

"No, sweetheart. I am in love with you."

Adams entered the room again and just stared at them. "You didn't tell him yet, did you?"

"No, we were waiting for you," Braden said, suddenly content. He could stay in this room forever as long as she was with him.

They all sat down before Adams asked, "Should we wake your brother and cousin?"

"Let them sleep. I want to hear why my betrothed seems to believe a woman is at fault here."

"Because she is," Tia said with a grin. "As I read through this book, I discovered two things of importance. First, you are most likely a real Tavers. Apparently, every couple of generations, a black-haired, blue-eyed child is born. To date, none have been firstborn males, so you may be the first. Secondly, when the letter of patent was written, the first Viscount Middleton begged for a codicil to be added, allowing a female to inherit should no male family members be alive."

"And that was allowed?" Braden asked.

"Yes," Tia continued. "The first viscount had only daughters and no other male members of his family were alive. The codicil was added on the condition that the man she married took the Tavers name. So far, there has only been one Viscountess Middleton in her own right."

Braden sipped his brandy in thought. There was only one female he could think of who would do all this. "Constance."

"Yes, I have checked the lineage and she is the next in line to inherit."

"Well, certain things are starting to make sense now," Braden said. "Mary used to be her maid. I wondered why she didn't go with Constance."

"Once you and Jonathon were out of the way, Mary could have poisoned Alistair," Tia said.

"Of course, but Constance must have been frustrated by my inability to die for her. She saw the opportunity to have Mary act as your maid, thus getting her into my house. And having easy access to the poison with your bag of herbs."

"Exactly. I would not be surprised to learn she wanted me blamed for your poisoning." Tia finally took a sip of her brandy.

Braden shook his head. "And she must have somehow learned that I was visiting Emily the day of the carriage accident."

Tia's eyes widened. "I had forgotten about that! She even asked Hart to stay so she could speak with him. That little bitch!"

"But why?" Adams asked. "Why would she care about becoming a viscountess? Isn't she married to a baron?"

"Yes," Braden replied. "So why would she care about becoming a viscountess?"

"I do not know," Tia admitted. "But she is the heiress apparent with you three dead."

Braden stood ready to leave. "I will go speak with her."

"And say what?" Tia asked. " 'I believe you tried to kill me, but here I am, not truly dead'? You cannot do that. We must come up with a plan."

"She is right, Middleton," Adams added before refilling his glass.

"And Miss Featherstone is the only one who can speak with Constance."

"Bloody hell, no!"

"Until we have proof that she is involved, you are to remain dead," Adams said as Tia nodded.

Braden shook his head. He was outnumbered, but the idea of letting Tia confront a possible killer sent pain straight to his heart.

Tia sat in the chair, tapping her finger against the glass in her hand. What Adams said made sense. She could pay a call of condolence on Constance for the loss of Alistair. It was just a matter of the lady letting her inside the house. But then what would she do?

"She has to do it, Middleton," Adams insisted. "Who else can?"

"Hart," Braden said.

"No," Tia finally spoke up. "She would never admit anything in front of Hart. But she might slip in anger toward me."

"No, I will not allow it," Braden said roughly. "Anything could happen to you."

"True, but I have to try. What good is pretending to be dead if she doesn't admit anything? I might be able to make her slip."

"I will be there too," Adams said. "I have business with Bunworth. There is no need for anyone to know that Miss Featherstone and I are acquainted with each other, but we will arrive near the same time. She will only be there a few minutes before I get there. Bunworth's study backs to the main salon where she has visitors."

"No," Braden said again. "I will not put your life at risk."

"My life is at risk until she is caught, because I am not leaving your side," Tia retorted. "Mr. Adams has an excellent plan and we will proceed with it. Would one be a good time?"

"A very good time," Adams replied.

"I have no say in this?" Braden asked sullenly.

"No," Adams and Tia said together.

"Miss Featherstone, do you have another dress?" Adams asked bashfully. "I do not think Lady Bunworth will receive you in that gown."

"Could you send a note to Mrs. Abbott? She will provide you with a more appropriate dress for paying calls," Tia said to Adams.

"Of course," Adams said. "I believe I shall leave you two and re-tire. Middleton, I do believe there is more brandy, but I doubt you'll need it now."

Tia glanced between them, not understanding their conversation. "What are you speaking of?"

"He will tell you, Miss Featherstone—or rather, he will show you." Adams chuckled as he left the room. "Good night," he managed to get out once he reached the door at the top of the stairs.

"What was that about?" Tia asked.

"I told him the only way I would sleep tonight is with some brandy." Braden rose and held out his hand for her. "But I believe I have found a far more pleasant way to sleep."

"Oh?" she asked in an overly innocent tone.

"Naked, sated, and with you next to me."

By noon the next day, Tia's nerves were drawn taut. With no maid to help her dress, Braden did his best to assist her with her stays, buttons, and pins. Her hair was another issue. Tia had no talent at dressing hair. She doubted Braden would do any better. Once she was dressed, she put her hair into a simple twist at the back of her neck.

"I should be wearing black, shouldn't I?" she asked, looking down at the blue muslin.

"Well, you don't have any black gowns here. Just tell Constance that you can't afford a new dress."

"I am sure she would believe that." She looked in the mirror and swallowed back her fear. "I need to bring the book with me."

"Why?"

"Because she won't believe me without it."

Braden reached over and handed her the book. "Please be careful. I hate the idea of you going out there and doing what I should be doing."

"You cannot without exposing what you did. Once she confesses, then we can explain that you did it for your personal safety. Or we shall lie and say the three of you had gone to your hunting lodge, not that house to play cards." She leaned over and kissed him softly. "Try not to worry."

"That is surely an impossible task," he whispered.

A knock hammered the door. "Are you ready, Miss Feather-stone?"

"Yes." She walked out of the room and noticed both Jonathon and Alistair standing in the hall.

"Be careful, Tia," Jonathon said solemnly.

"Yes, please have a care, Miss Featherstone," Alistair added.

"Thank you, gentlemen." Tia felt dreadful for them all. It could not be easy to see a woman trying to coerce a confession out of someone. Her hands shook as she grabbed her reticule from the hall table.

Adams took her arm. "You will go first. I will have my driver park a block away, so if by chance anyone sees you it will appear that you had walked to her home. I will arrive soon after by carriage."

"What if one of them is not at home?"

"I have a boy watching the house. If either leaves, he will give a sign as we drive by. If they are not both home, we shall do this an-other day." He showed her around to the back door so no one would see them leave together.

"Thank you for all your assistance, Mr. Adams. You are a good friend to Middleton."

Adams acknowledged the compliment with a nod.

They drove through Mayfair in silence, each trying to formulate their upcoming conversations. As the carriage rolled past the Bun-worth home, Adams glanced out the window. Tia tried to see what he looked at, but the man's body blocked her sight. He sat back and pounded once on the roof of the carriage.

Before she had a chance to ask, the carriage slowed to a stop. "Am I to assume they are at home, then?"

"Yes." He waited in the carriage as the driver helped her out. "Do not take any chances, Miss Featherstone. Middleton will kill me if some any harm befalls you."

"Thank you," she said softly. Her nerves were tight while she walked down the street. She had to get Constance to confess. Tia just had no idea how she would even get the woman to speak with her.

She approached the door with trepidation. She lifted the brass knocker and let it fall from her hand. The door opened and the butler stood at attention.

"Miss Featherstone to see Lady Bunworth."

"I shall see if she is at home. Please wait here."

Tia was certain he only let her in so she could get out of the light rain that had just started to fall. The butler whispered to a footman and then returned to his post. Tia waited for close to five minutes before the footman returned.

"Lady Bunworth will be down presently." He gestured to the salon. "Please wait here."

Tia walked into the salon and prayed this was the one that backed to Bunworth's study. She had no way of knowing if it did. This was the same room in which Constance had entertained her and Braden.

"Well, this is a surprise indeed," Constance's voice sounded from the hall. "Why would Middleton's mistress pay a call on me?" She entered the room with a bluster of black bombazine. "I could only think of one reason and the answer is no."

Tia rose and gave her a quick curtsey. "I have no idea to what you are referring, Lady Bunworth. I only came to give you my condolences on the loss of your brother."

Her face softened slightly, almost making Tia think she had the wrong person. "Thank you, Miss Featherstone."

The front door opened and Tia heard Adams's voice.

"Now who is it?" Constance asked in an annoyed tone.

The butler walked past the door. "It's a Mr. Adams to see Lord Bunworth."

Constance's eyes widened as if in panic. "Mr. Adams?"

"Yes, my lady." The butler continued on with Adams following on his heels.

"Are you all right, Lady Bunworth? You look quite peaked." Tia felt a pang of concern for the woman.

"Do you know of Mr. Adams?"

"No, is he someone of importance?" Tia asked, wondering how the lady knew of him. There was only one way that made sense. And that changed her tactics.

She shook her head. "No, he is not important at all." She sat in the chair across from Tia. "Why exactly are you here, Miss Featherstone? I doubt you came all this way just to give me your condolences when a simple note would have sufficed. I suppose you came here to beg me for money?"

Tia smiled at the bitter woman. "Why would I have a need for that? Oh, I am dreadfully sorry. You must not have heard that Middleton changed his will. Since I was to be his wife, I am the sole beneficiary to his fortune. Of course, the estate will go to the next heir, but Middleton confessed to me that the estate was doing poorly."

"I beg your pardon?" Constance rose from her seat and glared down at her. "He left his fortune to you, not the next viscount?"

"Yes, Lady Bunworth. Apparently, we both received what we wanted. Me, the money. And you, the title. That was what you were after, wasn't it?"

Chapter 27

Tia wondered how long it would take to get a reaction from the woman. She had barely counted to ten before Constance's ire exploded.

"How dare you enter my home and treat me so disrespectfully!"

Tia tapped her lip with her finger. "Oh my, did I get that wrong? Were you after his money too?"

"Get out of my home."

"Do calm down, my lady. I only speak the truth. I would hazard a bet that if I searched this home, I would even find a certain maid still in your employ. It was truly brilliant to keep Mary at your brother's house, should you need her to use a poison on him."

Constance raised a brow at her. "And yet you saved Middleton from poisoning. Why?"

Ah, curiosity. It might just be the lady's downfall. "I had no choice. We were not betrothed yet. I needed him to commit to marriage to get him to change his will. But saving his life did bring us closer . . . much closer."

Constance sat back in her seat. "I never expected you to be so ruthless, Miss Featherstone. But I had no part in the fire. That was all God's doing. Unless you had some part in it?"

"No, my lady. I was visiting with my mother in the Midlands."

"That's not to say you couldn't hire someone to start a fire."

Tia leaned forward with a smile. "Is that what you did?"

"I have no idea what you are talking about, Miss Featherstone," she said with a slight laugh.

The woman was evil. Tia had no way of finding out if she truly had been trying to kill them. "I did feel bad about Mr. Jonathon Tavers and your brother being with Middleton. I hadn't expected that."

"But how did you realize I was next in line?"

Tia smiled again as she pulled the book out. "This book. I had started to read it one day to ease the stifling boredom of Middleton's attentions. It has several interesting facts."

"I read the book and that is how I determined I was in line for the title."

"And you wanted the title, didn't you?"

Constance leaned forward. "Wouldn't you? I'll bet you would have married the bastard for it. Just like your sister married for one."

"No, my lady. It was purely the money."

"Hah! You loved being in Society until Middleton turned you into his mistress."

"But now that I have his money, I can do whatever I want. Once the war is over, I can leave the country and start a new life as a wealthy heiress, while you are stuck with a title and an estate that was poorly managed." Tia knew she was getting under the woman's skin.

"What do you really want?"

"I just want to hear you admit it." She shrugged. "I would even be willing to pay for the privilege."

Constance looked out toward the hall as her husband's voice boomed from the study. "How much?"

"How much do you need to settle what you owe Mr. Adams?"

She blinked and stared at Tia with her gaped, bow-shaped mouth. "I thought you didn't know who he was?"

Tia tilted her head with a smile. "My late betrothed was a partner at the Red Door. Yes, I know Mr. Adams. And seeing your reaction to his appearance here, I can only assume you like to gamble."

"Whore," she whispered.

"Bitch," Tia retorted. "How much, Lady Bunworth?"

"Five hundred pounds."

Tia couldn't imagine anyone wagering that kind of money. "Done."

"Yes, I hired someone to kill Middleton, my brother, and Mr. Tavers." She leveled Tia a smug grin. "And you would be right that Mary is upstairs brushing out my gown for tonight's soirée. But the fire was nothing to do with me."

"Thank you, Lady Bunworth. That was worth every pound." Tia rose. Noting Adams and Bunworth in the hall, she inched to the side so Constance wouldn't see them. "Tell me, did you not wonder why I wasn't wearing black?"

Constance shrugged. "I assumed you were already looking for your next keeper."

"No, my lady. I have no need to grieve for a man who is still alive."

Her eyes widened. "What are you talking about?" she demanded.

The front door opened and the gentlemen walked inside. Alistair glared at his sister. "Will you not welcome me back from the dead, sister dear?"

Braden and Hart walked back into the salon, where Tia and her sister sat drinking tea. It had been a very long day, but he was so happy to be home again. Soon he and Tia would refurbish some of the rooms and make this truly their house.

"So what will happen to Lady Bunworth?" Mia asked. "Will she hang?"

"My, what a bloodthirsty wife you have, Hart," Braden said with a laugh. He sobered, remembering poor Bunworth's face. "No, she will not hang. Bunworth is having her sent to Bedlam, which may be worse."

"Oh my," Mia said with a shiver. "That is a horrid place."

"But at least now, you and Jonathon and Alistair will be safe," Tia said. "That woman needs whatever help Bedlam might be able to provide her. I have never seen such an evil look in a person's eyes before today."

"How is Alistair?" Hart asked. "It can't be easy to live with the fact that your own sister tried to have you killed."

Braden nodded. "Louisa is with him. We will check on him before we leave on Wednesday."

"How is Jonathon doing?"

"Not well," Braden admitted. "Hearing that Eldridge forced Emily back to his home sent him over the edge this afternoon. He went to see Dr. Simmons. Jonathon is afraid he might be tempted to go back to the opium."

"Very wise choice," Hart said. "That is where we took Charlie for his opium problem. We visited him yesterday and he is doing so much better."

"It's only been a few weeks, but already Charlie looks clearer in the eyes and mind," Mia added. "I hope they both do well there."

They went silent when they heard a knock on the door. Nelson said, "Your Graces, I am certain they will see you in the salon."

Selina raced into the room just as Tia stood to greet her. Selina threw herself into Tia's arms and jumped up and down.

"The Duke and Duchess of Northrop, my lords," Nelson said, suppressing a smile.

"Not the most proper greeting, my dear," North said with a laugh.

"Do be quiet, dear. These are my dearest friends and we are in their home alone, so no one cares what I do. I might even take off my shoes." Selina pulled back from Tia's embrace. "I am so happy for you."

"Thank you, Selina," Tia said happily. "Now that you are in town, you can come tomorrow for the wedding!"

"Once I heard from your mother all that was going on, I insisted Colin take me to London." Selina giggled. "Don't I sound like a proper duchess . . . insisting people do what I request."

Braden turned to North. "Are we really supposed to let these women out in Society next spring?"

"Not mine," he said with a grin. "She will be far too big with child for the Season. I would suggest you and Hart get busy. If we keep them with child, we might never have to face the scandal these three will produce in town."

Braden sat back and sipped his brandy with a smile. "I think we should let them create the biggest scandal in town. They most likely will, anyway."

After a long day and an evening full of friendship and love, Braden and Tia finally retired for the night.

"Should I sleep in my room tonight?" she asked shyly.

"No, your room is now in here," he said, opening the door to his room. "This is our room. I don't believe a man and his wife should sleep apart. That is what leads men to mistresses and I have no intention of ever having anyone but you in my bed."

She turned in his arms and kissed him. "Are you happy? Are you concerned about marrying a poor wise woman who might be off delivering a baby when you want to make love?"

"Not at all. I will be the one accompanying you."

"Forever?" she asked with a smile.

"Forever," he said, before kissing her again. "I love you, Tia. More than I have ever loved any woman. And I will never forsake you for another. You are my love, my life."

Don't miss Selina's and Mia's stories!

Bewitching the Duke

ONLY HER DESIRE ...

After losing his wife in childbirth, Colin Barrett, Duke of Northrop, does not trust healers. So when he discovers Selina White cleansing his home, he is livid. As duke, Colin is accustomed to his charges taking orders from him. But the fiery Selina has the audacity to defy him when he asks her to leave his lands. More infuriating, he cannot stop thinking about the seductive sway of her hips when she walks.

CAN HEAL HIS HEART ...

The sick tenants of Northrop Park depend on Selina, and she's not about to let a man tell her she must leave her village—even if he is a duke. And while Selina does not fear Colin's temper, she is afraid of the secrets she keeps from him and of the desire he sets off in her every time he is near.

He's under her spell...

BEWITCHING THE DUKE

CHRISTIE KELLEY

Enticing the Earl

ONLY HIS PASSION . . .

With his estate near bankruptcy, Simon Blakesworth, Earl of Harts-field, already has a perilous secret to keep. Still, when he finds Mia Featherstone badly beaten, he doesn't hesitate to shelter her in his home . . . and offer marriage to protect the lovely healer from her attacker. But Mia is concealing a danger this honorable earl never imagined—and can't resist . . .

CAN SAVE HER LOVE . . .

Mia's valuable discovery on Simon's land saved her patients' lives. Now the only way she can help the man she's always loved save his home is to secretly find the rest of a cache of hidden artifacts. But their passion is making it impossible for Mia to ever walk away— even from a love that may not survive the truth . . .

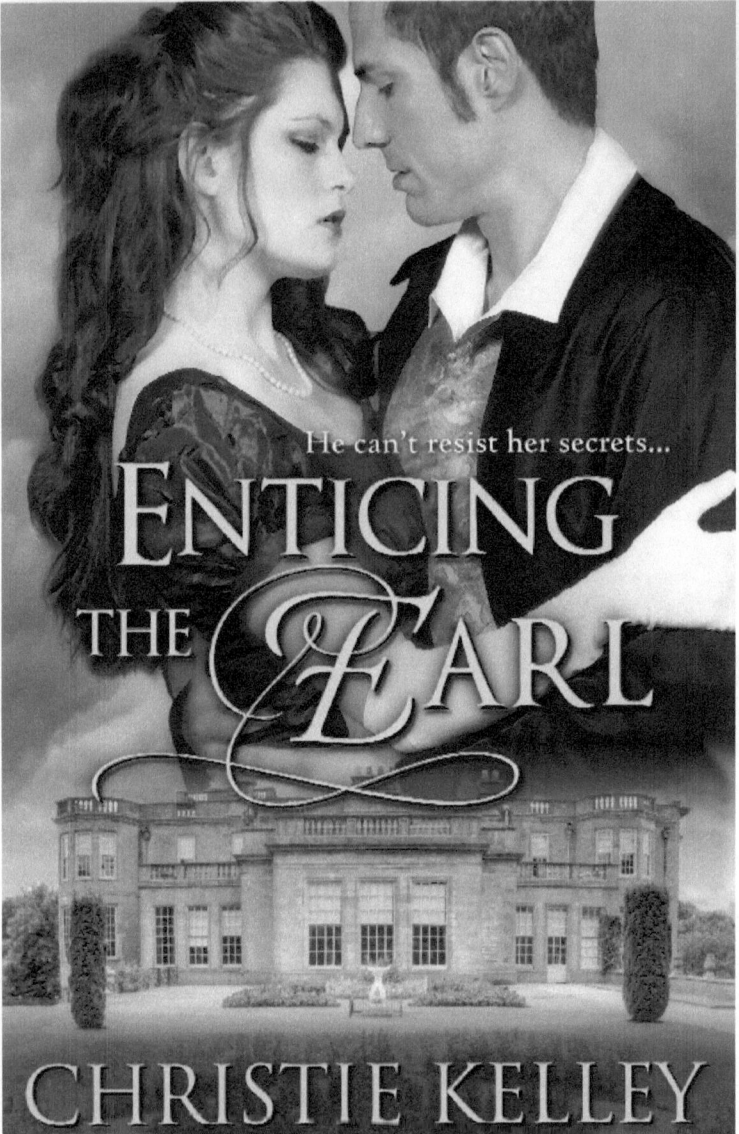

He can't resist her secrets...

ENTICING THE EARL

CHRISTIE KELLEY

And be sure to look for all of Christie Kelley's Spinster Club series!

Every Night I'm Yours

Every Time We Kiss

Something Scandalous

Scandal of the Season

One Night Scandal

Special Value $3.99 Canada $5.99

First Time in Print!

"Sometimes becoming a fallen woman
isn't as easy as it sounds. Oh! My!"
—Kasey Michaels,
New York Times bestselling author

One night is never enough...

EVERY NIGHT
I'M YOURS

CHRISTIE KELLEY

"Rollicking, sexy...
You'll enjoy this one!"
—Kat Martin

CHRISTIE
KELLEY

When desire's this sweet,
one taste will never do...

EVERY TIME
WE KISS

Something thrilling...Something secret...

SOMETHING
SCANDALOUS

CHRISTIE KELLEY

SCANDAL
OF THE
SEASON

CHRISTIE KELLEY

One
tempting gaze...
One
forbidden kiss...

One NIGHT
SCANDAL

CHRISTIE KELLEY

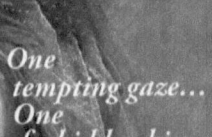

Award-winning author **Christie Kelley** was born and raised in up-state New York. After seventeen years working for financial institutions in software development, she started writing her first book. She currently writes regency historical romances for Kensington and now lives in Maryland with her two sons. Come visit her on the Web at www.christiekelley.com.